The Good Echo

To Anton,
who is #1,
in writing groups
and in so many
other ways —

The Good Echo

A Novel

With gratitude,

Shena McAuliffe

Black
Lawrence
Press

Black
Lawrence
Press

www.blacklawrence.com

Executive Editor: Diane Goettel
Cover Design: Zoe Norvell
Book Design: Amy Freels

Copyright © Shena McAuliffe 2018
ISBN: 978-1-62557-704-7

Published 2018 by Black Lawrence Press.
Printed in the United States.

For Jesse, with whom I wander

CONTENTS

PROLOGUE

First, Cleveland. City of my birth, city of my death. City of brick and ice and buzzing streetcars. Sausages and perch, tornadoes and rain. City of the winding Cuyahoga, the long gray shore of Lake Erie, steel bridges pivoting. Factories purling steam into a white sky.

I am—I was—Benjamin Donald Bell, child of Clifford and Frances Bell. I died of sepsis from an infected root canal. My father was my dentist. For now, I won't muddle through the logic of language arranged by a ghost. For now, simply this: death has made a storyteller of me.

Second, a lake named Mazinaw or Massanoga or Bon Echo, depending on who you ask. A few years before my birth, my parents built a lodge deep in the Ontario forest, looking north at The Narrows. Long before I was born in 1903, the Ojibwe and Algonkian had been corralled into reservations or dragged away to anywhere else. Their children were sent to schools near the cities, sent to be educated by Anglicans and Methodists, taught to believe in Jesus and English and arithmetic so they might forget their parents and grandparents, the ways of their people. But the lake remained a quiet place, inhabited by fishermen and vacationers and pilgrims who went to listen to the echo that bounces from the rock, a tremendous wall of granite that rises 100 meters from the surface of the water, marked with drawings in ochre and iron, its holes and divots stuffed with sap and scratched with stories. People have always gone to the lake to listen.

Lake Mazinaw: home to mosquitoes, blackflies, gnats, frogs, fish, muskrats, rabbits, deer, turtles, black bears, and wolves. It is still a wild place, and wildness is what my parents loved about it—what I loved about it. In summer, boys still jump from the rock—something I wasn't allowed to do. *When you're thirteen*, my mother said, but I was never thirteen. Girls, too, jump from the rock, in rubberized sandals and jeans cut short and fraying, their hair tangled with sun and lake water. They jump, and on the way down, they bellow to keep their fear at bay. Their bodies hit the water like joyful fists and they kick to the surface, gasping and alive. In winter, the water sleeps beneath thick ice. Cabins are boarded against snow. Stars spin slowly through long nights. A thread of smoke rises from a single chimney, and at daybreak, a solitary old woman ventures out, her breath steaming forth in the bright sun of January. She stomps her heavy boots, and the sound returns to her from the rock across the lake.

But we'll get to the lake soon enough.

Death has made a storyteller of me, and it is my parents' story I will tell. If things had gone otherwise—if I had not died a boy—perhaps it would be my own story I would tell, with my parents providing my genes and lessons in how to tie shoes, whittle sticks, do algebra. Or perhaps, had I lived, I would find no occasion for storytelling at all.

Does death make a storyteller of us all? Perhaps it makes musicians of some, carpenters of others. Perhaps nothing but sunlight and dust. I know only this story, these people—my mother and father, Clifford and Frances—and in life, they collected and invented stories. They told them to me, and they told them to each other. Perhaps they groomed me for this particular afterlife of listening and telling. And now I collect stories like a funnel, like a hole in a rock you put your mouth to and whisper. A hole in a rock you press your ear to. *Listen*.

In the history books, it is my father's story you will find. In the annals of dentistry, in journals and lab slides, in books he wrote. But you won't find me there, his son who died at the age of 12. A boy is nothing in the world. And you won't find my mother either, and so I listen especially for her voice.

I was a good-looking kid, if I say so myself. Curly hair. Bright eyes. Curious and smart. It's easy to believe in my lost potential. The viruses or cures I would have discovered. The music I would have composed. The woman I would have loved. The children I would have raised. But I might as well have led a humdrum life. I might have been average. Most of us are, after all. What if I wanted to compose music, but was not accepted to Berklee or Oberlin or Juilliard? Or what if I was accepted—labeled *brilliant*—but my father saw no value in it. He was tone deaf, after all. He didn't care a lick for music. Only for science. Maybe I would have died a soldier or a sailor.

I don't remember my death. What I remember is the way, in life, the lens of my magnifying glass swelled and distorted every blade of grass, every embroidery stitch, the warp and weft of a linen napkin, the whorls of my fingerprints, the fur of mold on a slice of bread. I remember the echo at the lake, and the lake itself, a bright mirror winking in the sun. I remember my lunchbox with its rusty hinge, my school books stacked and cinched with a belt, and learning to tie my shoes: rabbit around the tree, down the hole.

I remember singing at the top of my lungs in a fort I built of broken branches and a tablecloth stolen from the laundry line: wood and cotton, cotton and leaves. How my tent filled with wind and sun and I lay there for hours, dreaming over a book. And how my father tore it down in a rage. And I see now, in death—where I am free to listen and to speak— that his anger was not about me or my tent of sticks and tablecloths. It wasn't that I sang too loudly. It wasn't about my muddy shoes or that I sometimes forgot to take out the trash. It was always about him. His frustration, his ambition, his guilt. It was always about him.

But I am the wound at the center of my parents' story. I am the heart, burning like the one the Catholics paint within the chest of their Jesus. I am your tour guide: the recorder, the mythmaker. I am the funnel of an ear and the open mouth, singing. I am the quilter, the stitcher of squares. I am the storyteller.

So, where should I begin? A dark night. A hut on the banks of the Nile. Or a canoe on a lake in Ontario, way back when Clifford and Frances were newlyweds, before me, before they had even imagined me? They paddled a boat together for the first time, gliding across the smooth surface of the water. They hardly knew each other then, and they hardly knew themselves. They had not yet had a son. They had not yet lost him.

Or before they met, when their lives were still separate? When my father was a farm boy, and my mother was Frances Anthony, a tomboy in overalls who learned to sew so she could repair the tears in her clothing after her mother refused.

I know all the details. The trouble, sometimes, is choosing which to tell, which to stitch together. And beginnings? Beginnings are pliable tools for a storyteller. Let me build a threshold: shall I use paste or string? Thread or nails or staples? Of course: I will use words.

Clifford Bell and Frances Anthony were married on a Saturday in November, 1902, in the Methodist Church of Brampton, Ontario— Frances' hometown. The church was brick and sturdy and silent. Yellow light slanted through the high windows, touching the thinning hair on Cliff's head and lighting Frances' veil. They were both Methodist, but Clifford believed it all a little more than Frances, who felt no lasting presence after her father died, who watched fish decay on the shore, growing putrid, swarming with flies, eventually only delicate pale bones licked clean (and even those eventually disappeared, fish bones being so fine). But they called themselves Methodists when they married. As their story lengthened, they met trickster gods and gods that traveled in lightning bolts, gods that loved cattle or beer, dung beetle gods, and goddesses that birthed the moon. Tangled with these others, their God came out changed. Cliff or Frances might have said that all these gods were different faces of the one God with whom they began. But that comes much later, after they lose me. After they give up on everything they knew before. After Cleveland. After root canals. After the quiet brick house on Euclid Avenue. After the grief and the guilt and the grave beneath a pear tree. After they leave Ohio for Alaska and Switzerland and Egypt.

So where do we begin?

Close your eyes. Point to a place on the map—a game of the young and in love. It doesn't matter where they go, where they end up, how they get there. What matters is that they are together, walking the trail, or speeding down some gravel road, dust rising behind the tires of their car, the picnic in the basket, the camera loaded with film. What matters are the stories that pass between them. Go ahead: lay your finger down.

Switzerland, then! Switzerland it is!

June, 1931. A wet day, and rather dark. Here we find them, the dentist and his wife, Clifford and Frances Bell, my parents, years after my death, on a train, winding southwest through the belly of a mountain in the Alps. Soon enough, they'll board a bus to travel further into the hills, to higher villages built at the receding edges of glaciers. I will channel their voices for you. I will stitch the squares. It is my mother that speaks first, my mother that speaks most. So much of this story is hers.

Listen.

I.

SWITZERLAND

Frances, 1931

The train window is smeared with fingerprints and nose grease. Outside, silent houses and faded timber nestle against the flanks of the mountains. Our train moves swiftly, but outside is the slowness of soil creep, dirt pushing at itself like skin cells sloughing, always downward, always toward the river, always toward the sea. We slide past it all, each car pulling the next around this bend, around the next, higher and higher into the low-hanging sky.

In the aisle seat, Clifford examines a stack of photographs he has taken of grinning Scottish and Swiss children. He squints and compares, jots in his notebook, squints and compares, rarely looking up, not even to glance out the window. On my lap, I have a map of Switzerland and a small wooden box filled with teeth. Mostly, they are the teeth of animals, but a few come from human mouths, teeth that were pulled or fell out of their own accord—baby teeth and teeth tunneled with decay, teeth in various shades of white, yellow, and brown, with sharp edges and creases and cracks, rooted and rootless, each with its story.

This black shark's tooth: I turn it between my thumb and forefinger. It came from the Potomac, where, years ago, my sister Elizabeth retrieved it from the mucky banks and gave it to my son Benjamin, who was 8 or 9 then, and carried a small magnifying glass with him everywhere he went. "Pleistocene era," Elizabeth said, setting the tooth in his palm. Benjamin accepted it with a look of awe.

A porter delivers two tiny cups of coffee to the women in the seats in front of ours, whose voices bubble in Italian. I understand the melody of their language, but not the words, and on this journey, this is often the case. I exist within sounds, within music, but not in words. I understand so few languages. I have heard that Italian babies are sometimes born singing. That they slide from the womb slick with blood, or are yanked out gangly and blue, and when the doctor delivers a firm smack to open their lungs, they wail in the Dorian mode.

When Ben was born, he did not cry. Not at first. When, finally, his head emerged from my body, and the doctor pulled him out and cut the umbilical cord, there was a collective pause, an underwater silence. I thought he was stillborn. Only hours earlier I had felt him moving within me, but now, it seemed he was dead. The doctor held him up, a tiny thing with curled hands and grayish skin, smeared with blood and yellow, but he did not cry. The doctor and nurse huddled over him. I was so exhausted. My eyes closed. This baby that had grown within me was not me after all. He could die and I would go on living. My head was so heavy I could not lift it from the pillow.

But then the doctor held him up, and I saw his mouth, wide and red, and he cried loudly. His tiny hands grabbed at air, and I reached for him, and his wail was nothing Dorian, nothing operatic. It was complete disorder. It was all the scales in the world collapsing upon each other. It was a building burning in midwinter—that horrifying, glorious clatter as the roof caves and the windows burst and the girders crash: this was my child's voice. But I took him from the doctor, and I looked into his howling mouth. Every part of me hurt. I knew that screaming baby would be my only one, my only child. I held him against my skin and he stopped crying. He looked at me, quiet and blinking and perfect.

Benjamin would be grown now, twenty-four years old if he had not died a boy. He has been dead 12 years—as long as he was alive. Perhaps, if he had lived, I would not have grown so tired of Cleveland winters, of the neighbors' children rolling and stacking snowman after snowman. Wilting carrot noses and coal buttons fell into the snow and left black patches until spring. I grew to hate the dull sky of March, the endless rain of May, the houses facing square to the street, one after another, block after block, hunching their brick shoulders, exhausted and obedient.

After Benjamin died, Cliff began to proclaim the evils of root canals, but it wasn't something people wanted to hear. They preferred to keep their teeth in their mouths, even if they were drilled with holes and filled with gold and silver, molybdenum and mercury. They did not believe in the threat of the microscopic world. But if Benjamin had not died, Cliff might not have learned what he now knows—about root canals, first, and then about nutrition. He would have gone on as the president of the dental association, pulling teeth, attending conferences. We would not be here on this train through the Alps, and while I would give almost anything to have my child back, to have watched him grow into a man, to know him still, it is beautiful here, and strange.

In the months after Ben's death, I sometimes found myself clutching things I had no memory of picking up. A comb. An onion. Where had it come from? And why was it in my hand? Each time, each object, when I noticed it, was damp with sweat, or had left marks on my palm, as if I had gripped it too tightly. When I was a child in Brampton, I knew a part-Ojibwe woman, a seamstress, whose husband had died or left her. I never knew the whole story, but her daughter was taken away, sent to a school for Indian children, and while the child was there, she died. The mother, the seamstress, was silent after that, taking orders in her shop, completing her work, but for a long time she carried with her a doll made of birch bark and her child's hair. If it was not in her arms, it was tied into her dress. A mourning doll, my mother said. My mourning doll was a rotating cast of dishcloths and acorns, a toy truck, a butter knife.

My sister Elizabeth has always blamed Clifford for Ben's death. "Careless with his own son," she said then, when we still spoke of it, when the loss was fresh. "Negligent. With his own son." The first time she said it, we were walking home from the cemetery after placing flowers on Ben's grave. Every day for weeks after the funeral, I did so. I stopped going only because I knew I would never stop if I waited for the pain to fade. I would go to that cemetery every day for the rest of my life if I waited to stop missing him. And I stopped going because I thought of his body down there, his slender twelve-year-old body, already decaying. Were the worms and insects already gnawing through his clothing, through his skin? I stopped going.

It was 1919 and all across Europe men had died in the mud, shot and mortared and gassed. I was not alone in grieving. But grief is always private. And mine was for a child. A small death, but it was tremendous to me.

I stopped talking about him. It began to seem as if speaking his name was some sort of betrayal. No one, not even my sister, who was my closest friend, understood exactly, and their words of sympathy sometimes angered me.

Elizabeth wasn't there when Ben died. It was routine surgery that Cliff himself performed. A root canal is not particularly complicated. You dig the channel. You drain the decay. You fill the hole. But in Ben's mouth, the hole swarmed with spirochetes and staphylococci, microscopic swimmers that entered through his tooth into his gums, invisibly writhing daggers and corkscrews. From there, the path to his heart was short, and the heart is easily susceptible to such poisons.

Elizabeth wouldn't stand to be in the same room as Clifford. She came to the funeral, but wouldn't stay at our house. Grief quieted me, stealing my words, but Elizabeth was angry.

"It's a chain of events, Frances," she said. "Simple cause and effect."

But I wondered where the chain began, and to what it was anchored. I was the one who let Ben eat strawberry jam, root beer barrels, birthday cake. He ate them, and the sugar did its work. Or, as Clifford thought years later, maybe the trouble began before Ben was even born. Maybe it began when I was pregnant. Maybe I had eaten the wrong foods. Maybe it began when I was a girl, in those hazy years after my father's death, when my mother hardly cooked for us. Maybe it was *my* fault. Maybe I was the cause. I have never been able to blame Clifford. But Elizabeth still addresses her letters only to me.

Our wandering life is full of canoes and prop planes, trains and riverboats, igloos and thatched roofs and mountain ranges. We meet children with perfect dental arches and children with half their teeth rotted out. Everywhere we go, lines of children wait, ready to open their mouths for Clifford and his camera, and Clifford collects photographs of them, collects samples of their foods, measures their jaws and foreheads, the distance between nostrils, the width of their mouths, and we move on to the next place, the next people. We move on. We move on. There are always more teeth to see. More people to study. The feeble-minded boys at the school in Ohio, the Seminoles of Florida, the Incas of Peru, the Inuit in Alaska, the Hebrides Islanders, and now these children of the Alps. Clifford asks, and they open wide and let him look at their teeth. Or most of them do, while a few do not understand his request, or pretend not to, despite the interpreter standing by, despite the way Cliff stands behind his camera, waiting, the dark cloth draped loosely over his shoulders. He shows them examples, photographs of boys from Ohio, front- and side-views, displaying off-kilter jaws, gapped and over-lapping teeth. The children lean in and study the photos, curious about their counterparts from the other side of the world. They take the photos from Cliff's hands and turn them over, studying the writing on the backs where Cliff pencils names, dates, and locations. The children bend the corners and soften the edges. They leave fingerprints on the faces of the boys from Ohio. I look at the children and they look back. Sometimes we smile at each other. I never really know them.

As a general rule, people living far from cities have lovely teeth, solid and square. But in city mouths, we find teeth that butt against each other, shove each other aside, are twisted and withered and chipped. City mouths chew mostly white bread, sugary jam, polished rice, and soggy canned goods. City teeth gap. They are too long or too short, or half-transparent, with grooves, serrated edges and receded gums. Molars are decayed—rot runs through them like ore through rock. From city mouths comes the smell of the trash heap, the wet stink of the killing floor. And these mouths are malformed, the arches too narrow to fit their teeth.

Sometimes a child stares placidly at the camera, or bares his teeth fiercely. Sometimes, Cliff asks the child on the other side of his camera to laugh because he wants to see her dental arch. He demonstrates, tipping his head back and laughing a loud, false laugh, which often makes the child laugh, and he snaps the photo, but the sound of Cliff's braying always makes me cringe.

There is no photograph of me in the collection, but if there were, it would show that my teeth, too, are imperfect—one front tooth overlaps another. I have had three carious teeth, each filled by Clifford years ago, before Ben died. He no longer fills cavities—he simply pulls the rotten tooth—but since I am healthy, he has agreed I should keep my fillings. A photo of me would show a bland woman, a schoolteacher by training, graying brown hair, five-foot-two-inches tall, round but not fat, spine slightly concave. I would not laugh for Cliff to photograph my dental arch.

A photo of me would not show how, in this wandering life, I have walked for miles through grass as tall as I am. How I can sing so a child will sleep, and so a child will dance. How I can make myself invisible—it is not hard when one is a plain woman. How I can sometimes speak loudly—although this is still a challenge. "From the diaphragm," Clifford always says. He exhales, singing a long note, and I join him, and we sing a chord in perfect thirds, trained by years in a church choir. I hold my note longer and longer, until I have pushed every bit of air from my belly. Until I feel my abdomen pushing in on itself, pushing on my uterus, that withered old husk.

We have been travelling for much of three years, collecting photographs and samples of food, collecting teeth that have fallen out, or teeth that have been pulled, measuring jaws and skulls, counting carious teeth, measuring decay and nostril distance, but still Clifford wants the Torres Strait Islands, New Zealand, the Australian Outback, the Amazon. And there is nothing for me in Ohio anymore.

I spread the map of Switzerland across my lap. At its edges are parts of Germany, France, Austria, Italy, the curving blue of the Mediterranean Sea. We will spend a week in these Swiss villages, and then take a

train to Genoa. With my finger, I trace the coast. We will board a boat
and cross the sea to Egypt, to Port Said, where the land will be loose and
yellow and the people, I am told, live in houses of baked earth. From
there, we'll travel overland to Cairo, from Cairo to Luxor, and then
along the Nile to Aswan. We will spend some weeks in The Sudan and
Ethiopia and in the jungles of The Congo, about which I know almost
nothing, with only the word of the missionaries and the writings of the
anthropologists to prepare me.

If I lined up all the maps we've traveled across, hinging them
together like tiles, Cleveland would not even fit on this train, so many
panels of blue would stretch between us and the dot that would mark
New York City. Cleveland is 5,000 miles—a lifetime—away.

A FALSE START

Apologies are in order. I am, after all, only a boy ghost sorting stories. Switzerland seemed as good a place as any to begin. In Switzerland, cows wear charming bells around their necks and boys stand on mountaintops with alpenhorns bellowing. Plus, I've always been fascinated by trains— all that clack and whistle. The weight they carry on their wheels! As a boy, in Cleveland, I used to put a penny on the tracks and wait. After the train passed, the penny remained: bright copper smashed thin, the faint, stretched shape of Abraham Lincoln or the Indian head.

But we've already missed so much.

Let me begin again. So much happened before Switzerland, so much before me, before Clifford and Frances even knew each other. And so much happened after me. Switzerland is just a point on a line, a fly in a web.

Another fly: my funeral, which Frances recalls like a page in some sad photo album. My swollen face. My closed eyes. My pressed and starched collar. My fingernails, clean and trimmed as they never were in life. She missed the dirt beneath my nails. Without it, they were not my hands. Then came the foggy days, when she walked to and from the cemetery, before she decided not to go anymore. And my Aunt Elizabeth's long stay in Cleveland, during which she did not speak to Clifford, not even once, and the house was too silent, as if it were waiting for everyone to gasp and resume breathing.

Winter arrived, and the ground froze around my body, and my body froze within it, and the snow fell upon me. A crow plucked the fading ribbon from the dried bouquet that adorned my headstone and trailed it through the sky to its nest. Frances went to bed early and slept late, getting out of bed only when Elizabeth arrived at the house and bustled into the bedroom with tea. Clifford kept working every day, cleaning and pulling teeth. He worked harder than ever, scheduling appointments from breakfast to dinner, sometimes working straight through lunch.

And then, somehow, when the fog began to lift, and Elizabeth went back to Ontario, and the flowers opened on the pear tree beside my grave, and Frances stopped visiting the cemetery every day, the silence shifted. When Frances and Clifford sat in the living room in the evenings—he reading the paper, she reading a novel or doing embroidery—the silence began to feel something like a candle's flame, warm and moving and lively. And that was how Frances knew she'd live with the sadness, and so would Clifford. They held this new thing between them now. Their grief was a shared thing.

For my father, my death was the second major detour from his life plans. Typhoid fever had been the first. He nearly died at twenty-two, his first year in Grand Forks, North Dakota, where he had moved to start a dental practice of his own. When the fever broke, he awoke changed, blinking like a newborn in the sun. He returned to his family's farm in Ontario, and then went with his Uncle Donald to Mazinaw Lake, to pray and recover his strength. Donald had been a school teacher at an Ojibwe Reserve school and he taught Clifford his first lessons in nutrition, which he had learned from his students. At the lake, Cliff and Donald lived on berries and fish. They trapped rabbits and dried the meat. North Dakota was in his past: Clifford needed a new plan.

He moved to Cleveland and lived in a rooming house. He rode the streetcar to and from work, admiring the wasp-waists of women in long woolen dresses and the soft hair piled high on their heads, their pale, smooth cheeks and long fingers. Then he met and married Frances, who was not beautiful like the wasp-waisted women, but had bright eyes and a keen mind. She asked good questions and she listened when he spoke. She was, above all, a reasonable woman. She would be the mother of his children. Together, they built the Inn at the lake. Then they had me.

When I died, his plan shattered again. There would be no brood. There would not be two children. There would not even be one. It would be him and Frances until they died. Him and Frances and his patients, who wanted him to drill into their teeth and remove the rotting pulp, but he refused to do it anymore. Root canals were dangerous, he said. Unnecessary. Some of his patients left him for other dentists, men with broods and wasp-waisted wives and conventional notions about dentistry.

So there was my death, and there was everything that followed.

Frances and Clifford found themselves on a trail by a sparkling stream, walking between villages where houses were built from ice, or in a place where the houses were built from leaves or from mud, and they kept walking, and the trail branched again, and they found themselves eating berries they had gathered along the way, or they found themselves eating insects, and sending samples of insects back to the lab in Ohio to test their nutritional content. They had never expected to eat a mealworm in their lives, but here they were eating mealworms, and the mealworms crunched between their teeth like sunflower seeds or half-popped popcorn kernels. And days opened like flowers, surprising them both.

FROM THE NOTEBOOKS OF DR. CLIFFORD BELL: TOWARD A COMPENDIUM OF DENTAL INFECTION[1]

Crown: The top of the tooth, the part you see, the chewing surface and its flanks, white and strong like bone, although it isn't bone, but dense layers of tissue.

Root: The tooth's anchoring legs. Think of the tooth as a plant: the root anchors it to the soil, holds tight like a mandrake. Or, the root is like the leg or legs of the tooth, the crown is the torso and the head.

Abscess: an infection around the root, formed when bacteria gnaws its way in and then out of the tooth and into the surrounding tissue. Bacteria burrows a small space in the gums, and in this little cave, rot blooms.[2]

---

1. I, Dr. Clifford Bell, originally compiled these notes for my son, Benjamin Donald Bell, should he one day have chosen to follow in my professional footsteps. As of Oct. 2, 1919, the day of Benjamin's death, such a compendium is no longer necessary. However, I maintain these notes in hopes that they may prove useful for my current research into the causes and prevention of dental infection.

2. As a young dentist, I believed an abscess was evidence of larger vacancy— that it was the place where one's spiritual disease materialized, leaking from the tooth and gnawing outward, as if teeth were spirit chambers of good and

Dentures: A removable frame that holds synthetic teeth, worn to replace a partial or whole set of teeth. I have worn (whole) dentures since I was twenty-two years old, when typhoid fever destroyed my teeth. There are few advantages to dentures, but I am glad to be able to chew my food, and they give shape to my mouth which would otherwise be the collapsed mouth of a toothless old man. One advantage to dentures is that I am free from worrying about cavities. Prosthetic teeth cannot rot.

Vision:
   1. Physical (literal): our ability to see with our eyes.
   2. Scientific (metaphorical): a scientist's ability to imagine, based on research and evidence, what might be possible. Scientific vision allows a scientist to devise and develop research projects, to investigate questions, to see solutions to problems.
   3. Spiritual (metaphorical): God-given, spiritual vision includes such phenomena as Moses' burning bush or Mary's visit from the Angel Gabriel when he announced to her that she was pregnant with God's Son. These are not scientifically measurable, logical, research- based visions, but departures that rely entirely on faith. It is my belief that even spiritual visions, which seem like hallucinations, could be explained by science if we had God's perfect knowledge, but for the time being, they often seem illogical or insane.[3]

---

evil. This was a childish superstition, and I admit it here with no small degree of embarrassment.

When Benjamin was twelve, decay burrowed into his tooth and out again, and an abscess formed. He was still very much a child, more bone than flesh. He had not even lost all of his deciduous teeth. Of course, I know that all mouths foster microbes from the minute they leave the clean, salty ocean of the womb, but Benjamin's caries surprised me. Mouths are busy chewing and salivating and speaking and licking and kissing and sucking, but my child's teeth seemed too new to host such swarms. Perhaps my inability to recognize Benjamin's infection was a blind spot, and, like my foolish notion that spiritual decay manifested in teeth, due to naiveté.

3. **e.g.** One Sunday morning, years before my son grew ill, I slipped my dentures into place and raised the razor to my cheek. In a blink, I had a vision of my

Sugar: Short-chain, soluble carbohydrates often used to sweeten food and drink. Although we can remove sugar from the surface of teeth with careful brushing, consumption of it contributes to higher incidence of tooth decay. While there is sugar in almost everything we eat, in its refined crystal form, it offers little nutritional benefit and should therefore be avoided or consumed in scant quantities.[4]

---

future decay. I saw, or imagined I saw, straight through the flesh of my cheeks, into my mouth, and each tooth was surrounded by a squirming nest of germs. I saw my mouth as a network of teeming, rotted-out caverns. I blinked again and the vision evaporated. My face was again opaque, with smooth full cheeks and shallow creases around my blue eyes, the razor poised against my jaw.

My mouth was not rotten. If it were, I would taste the bitterness when I removed my dentures. Plus, dentures do not decay. There was no gnawing blackness in my jaw nor my heart.

But back then, I held that absurd belief that a rotten tooth was the dwelling place for spiritual decay—that an abscess was evidence of lust or rage or selfishness. I thought that an abscess grew in those moments when we doubted God (His goodness, His existence), or when we betrayed Him. I thought the abysmal soul materialized as an expanding blackness around the tooth.

I set my razor down and wiped the sweat from my upper lip. I am not a man subject to spiritual visions. While I have faith in God, I am, above all else, a man of science, a man of objective facts and empirical knowledge. But if God exists, then I must believe that He can inspire spiritual visions. Certainly, He can provoke questions or provide inspiration for scientific inquiry, but He can also indict us for lack of faith or spiritual vacancy. Was God challenging me to consider my vacancy?

Was my vision sent by God, or was it a run-of-the-mill flare of imagination, a dream prompted by nothing, signifying nothing? Was it a warning from God that my soul was rotten? Or was the vision sent to spark my deeper scientific inquiry into the grave dangers of tooth decay?

I had no way of knowing whether the vision was God-given. If it were divine, I reasoned, God would find a way to make Himself clear, and so I tried to forget what I had seen, but the horrible vision lingered. It lingers still. If I had paid attention to it in that moment, if I had earnestly sought its meaning, perhaps my son would be alive today.

4. At our lake house, Benjamin drank lemonade at the neighbors'. He snuck hard candies from the bowl Mrs. Olsen left on her table. She knew that he stole them and that he was not permitted to eat candy, but she pretended not to see. She restocked the bowl each time he came over, and she conveniently looked away. Sometimes, his mother fed him strawberry jam on toast. He ate birthday

BENJAMIN (Geography of): I did not know every inch of my child's body. I knew his knees and the dimples there that dissolved as he grew and his legs got lean. I knew the suntanned shade of his skin in summer. But I cannot remember his ears—were his lobes attached like his mother's? Or detached like mine? I cannot remember. Or rather, I never knew. I did not know the pattern of freckles on his shoulders. His eyes were blue, but I cannot remember the shade. His hands? Did he have his mother's brittle nails? His elbows were smooth: his mother rubbed them with butter when he was a baby. I knew his teeth, and that he had lost exactly half of his deciduous teeth when he died. I knew he would have had only two wisdom teeth, those on the top. The other two, like mine, would never grow in, but would remain submerged in the back of his lower jaw. He had my family's teeth. My brothers—nine of them— smile with identical, square-toothed smiles. I am the only brother that keeps his mouth closed when photographed. Although I am fitted with an excellent pair of dentures, I no longer recognize my smile as my own, but Benjamin had the grin of my youth.

---

cake and ice cream and Fourth of July blueberry pie. But I don't know what, exactly, caused the decay. After he died, I made a list of the foods he had eaten regularly. I checked the dates of his dental cleanings. But these records told me nothing. There is sugar in beets, in beef, in milk, in bread, in raisins, in snap peas, in lettuce. There is no avoiding it.

Benjamin hosted that lacy darkness in his tooth, that wormhole of decay, and he did not tell me about his pain. One night at dinner he ate four bites of peas, cut his steak with his fork and knife (as he'd been taught), set the knife down, switched the fork to his right hand, speared the steak on a tine, took one small taste, and set his fork down. "May I be excused?" he said. "I don't feel well." His mother pressed the back of her hand against his forehead.

"You don't seem feverish," she said. But he would.

In bed after dinner, Benjamin's pain was worse. His mother fixed him a ginger ale for the fizz. She stirred it slightly, but when he sipped from it, we saw him wince.

"It's your throat, darling?" asked Frances.

"My teeth," he said, finally. "My teeth hurt." He touched his jaw on the right side.

Root Canal:

> **1.** The anatomic space within the root of a tooth; hollows within the interior of the roots which are filled with pulp.

> **2.** A colloquial term for *endodontic therapy*, the surgical procedure in which infected pulp is removed from a tooth. The empty canal is then sterilized and the space is filled to prevent further decay.[5]

BENJAMIN (Leisure time of): I read the newspaper, and Benjamin brought me a handful of raspberries he had picked in the yard. He helped his mother roll out a pie crust. He sang in the bath, and all over the house we could hear his nonsense songs. *A giraffe on a bike is the keenest of sights. Its legs are too long to pedal!* He sang songs and put his face into the water to blow noisy bubbles. He was our only child. We could not have another. Even if we had seven children, even if we had ten, we would have loved Benjamin, but he was our only one.

Sometimes, on Sunday afternoons, I took him to fly a kite at Melrose Park. I held the string and backpedaled uphill, and he ran downhill, holding the kite above his head until it lifted and flew. I unfurled the

---

5. Benjamin's gums were swollen, one tooth raised slightly above its neighbors, and a dark spot marred the occlusal surface of the left premolar, a deciduous tooth. It was a tooth that would be pushed out within the next couple of years, replaced by an adult molar, hardly worth the trouble of filling it, but permanent teeth are more likely to grow in straight and solid if they follow the path of their deciduous predecessors. And back then, like all of us dentists, I thought it best to dig out the rotten pulp and seal the canal with silver or porcelain until the adult tooth took its rightful place.

I drilled into Benjamin's tooth. I snagged the pulp and watched one of my child's feet twitch against the chair, the way I have seen chickens kick in their last minutes, after their necks are broken and their legs are still busy following residual messages sent by their brains. He was in pain. I finished my work, and Frances came in. She smoothed Benjamin's hair off his forehead and pressed a cool, damp cloth against it. We watched his narrow chest rise and fall. I thought the tooth was hollow, nothing left to feed the hungry microbes.

string as quickly as I could, and Benjamin would shout. His hands were still raised above his head although the wind had taken the kite from him a full minute ago. Once, the kite string broke, and the kite blew away. As we walked home, Benjamin took my hand. "I wonder what adventures our kite is having," he said.

Un-/Ineffectively-Treated Abscess: Left untreated, or treated ineffectively, an abscess can perforate the jawbone and spread throughout the body either internally or externally. (It perforates the cheek.) The heart, blood, and bones are all at risk of severe bacterial infection.[6]

Fathers (Types of): I was a stern father. We all were, us fathers of Cleveland, of Rochester, of Detroit and Toronto and Montreal and Grand Forks. My own father was a wheat farmer who did everything with utmost efficiency: he spoke rarely, ate swiftly, opened and closed doors silently. He was fastidious about lubricating rusty hinges. Although I was not a farmer, he taught me that to be a man means to have doors with silent hinges.

Sepsis, Septicemia: derives from Greek for the decomposition of animal or vegetable organic matter. The verb *sepo* means "I rot." Homer used it in *The Illiad,* though he used it in the negative to say that Hektor's beloved body *did not rot* after Achilles killed him. Hektor's father begged for news of his son's body, which Achilles had been dragging from the back of a chariot, making circles in the dirt. The messenger

---

6. Why didn't he tell me? Was he afraid of me, his own father? Afraid I would be angry? Did he think the pain might go away on its own, drying up like the flu or the chicken pox? Was it sudden? Maybe he hadn't even noticed it until it grew overwhelming. Maybe my child had a uniquely high tolerance for pain.

reported that the body remained dewy-fresh; its resistance to rot was surely evidence of the gods' love for him.[7]

---

7. But worms began to gnaw at Benjamin even as he lived. On the morning of the second day after the root canal, he was out in the yard with a magnifying glass, his cheek swollen, but that was expected after a root canal. Just that once, he was allowed chocolate pudding for lunch and mashed potatoes for dinner. On the morning of the third day, he stayed in bed with a book, but it was raining, so his mother and I thought nothing of it. It was a good day for reading, and for letting one's mouth heal.

But then he was fever-wracked and dying, and I held his hand, and I watched his heart beat in his neck—too fast. In his pale wrist, I saw the blue-veined twitch of his pulse. His chest thudded, his blood circulating from his heart to his wrist to his fingers, and back around. He moaned and we called the doctor, who tried to drain the pus from his gums, to sterilize the infection in his mouth, but already his blood was rife with it. Already, he was gone from us.

His mother fussed, dipping the washcloth in a bowl of cold water, wringing it and pressing it to his head. I stood and paced the room. The sweat that coated his forehead dried. He was flushed and burning. His lips were ringed with salt. His cheek was swollen so that he looked like someone else's child. I held his hand. I knew so little of him. I knew so little.

The sun set on the fifth day. Benjamin never opened his eyes again.

TOOTH STORY:
WISHES & COINS

My tooth was loose, and I could not leave it alone. I worried it with my tongue until it hung by the thinnest strand of tissue. "Benjamin," my mother scolded. "For goodness sake. It will fall out on its own when it's ready." But I ran my tongue over the sharp edge of the dissolved root, and the nub of the new tooth under it, pushing its way through. I wiggled the tooth with my finger—back and forth, back and forth—and finally, without so much as a pop or a tear, it let go. I spit it into my palm, a bloody pearl, the edge sharp and thin as filigree.

For each tooth I lost, I earned a penny under my pillow, and so I tucked the tooth into the little gingham pocket my mother had sewn just for that purpose, and placed it under my pillow for *La Bonne Petite Souris.* I tried my hardest to stay awake in hopes of catching a glimpse of the Good Little Mouse, about whom no one could tell me anything of importance. When I asked my mother what *La Souris* did with all the teeth it collected, she said it gave them to toddlers who were just getting their teeth, but somehow this struck me as wrong. "Well," she said, when I expressed doubt. "The truth is, no one really knows. What do *you* think the mouse does with them?"

I imagined the mouse using the teeth herself, or sharing them with geese or squirrels, but squirrels and mice have better teeth than people, at least for the purpose of cracking the black walnuts that fall from the trees, against which a child's tooth would be useless. I had no idea what a little mouse would want with hundreds upon hundreds of children's teeth. Perhaps she decorated her den with them, the way people hang paintings, or lined them up like crown molding along the ceiling.

I proposed we set a trap for the mouse, and use my tooth as bait, but my mother pointed out that there was no way I'd get my penny that way, not to mention that mousetraps were designed to break a mouse's neck. I had no interest in killing *La Souris*, thereby ruining a moneymaking opportunity for children worldwide, so I gave up the trap immediately.

That night, after my mom tucked me in and kissed me goodnight, I slipped out of bed and spread a few toys on the rug. I strung fishing line across the doorway at mouse level and hung from it a jingle bell, although I wondered if the mouse would use the doorway to enter my room. Despite my efforts to stay awake, I fell asleep quickly.

I was woken by a clatter of toys followed by an angry *"Drat!"*

I kept my face pressed against the pillow, but I opened one eye and watched the giant, father-shaped mouse pick his way to my bed, lean over, and pilfer beneath my pillow for the tooth pocket. For a moment, I thought my father was robbing the mouse of her rightful spoils, but then I saw he was digging in his pocket for a coin. I gave a small snort as if I were deeply sleeping. He tucked the coin into the gingham pocket, and tiptoed out, somehow avoiding both the toys and the fishing line.

It was an uncharacteristically whimsical role for my father, but I never said a word about it. I did, however, begin asking more questions about *La Souris*: where she came from, what she looked like, where she lived. He never admitted that the mouse didn't exist, but told me that children in other countries did different things with their teeth. Our mouse was French, he said, but there was another mouse named *El Raton de Los Dientes* that gathered teeth in Mexico, and in Spain there was one named *Ratoncito Perez*. Japanese children, he said, threw their teeth onto the roof if they came from the bottom jaw, and down to the floor if they fell from the top jaw. In Egypt, children threw their teeth straight into the sun. If your tooth didn't return to earth, it had burned in a holy fire.

I drew a picture of *La Bonne Petite Souris* with giant ears and shining black eyes. In her paws, she clutched a large tooth. As a final touch, I gave her round spectacles like my father's.

After I died, my mother transferred the teeth *La Souris* had collected from the little envelope labeled "Extra Buttons" to a glass jar that sat on the kitchen windowsill above the sink. Then, one day, she took the jar from its sunny perch. She unscrewed the lid, spilled the teeth into her palm, and took them to the garden. Sixteen of them she buried like seeds next to the tomatoes. She kept only one, a central incisor, one of the first I had lost. She pressed the tooth between two layers of waxed paper and taped the edges shut. In her tooth collection, it was the only tooth individually wrapped.

When I died, three of my primary molars were still in my mouth, teeth I would have lost in the next year or so. One of them was the tooth that killed me, its pulp removed and replaced with silver.

FROM THE NOTEBOOKS OF DR. CLIFFORD BELL: TOWARD A COMPENDIUM OF DENTAL INFECTION

Tooth Decay (Process of): Natural exposure to acid and bacteria can damage a tooth, eventually leading to holes through the tissue. Each day our teeth bathe in jam and apple juice, broccoli, potatoes, rib eye steak, etc. How does that one little particle, minute and nearly invisible, take hold, fester and bloom? It destroys the host tooth, spreads to other teeth, burrows toward the gums, the root, the jaw. A little sugar gone awry; it builds itself an elegant cave, ruffled and brown. It is both admirable and terrifying, the power of such decay. It cannot be underestimated.

Chemoparasitic Caries Theory (W.D. Miller, 1898): *In the presence of fermentable carbohydrates, bacteria produce acid that causes tooth enamel to decay!!!*

Focal Infection Theory (W.D. Miller, 1898): *Bacteria lingers in and around a tooth even after the canal has been drilled. These lurking bacteria can cause continuing pain and infection that begins in the tooth but spreads throughout the body.*

NOTE: Remarkably, even though Miller shared my findings about the danger of tooth decay to the entire body, he recommends root canals and fillings, not the removal of the tooth.

CASE STUDY (Introduction and Hypothesis): A woman (Patient X) came to my office in a wheelchair. For years, she had been disabled by severe arthritis, but she said this had nothing to do with her visit. She was there because she thought she might have a cavity. A mild ache. She said I might as well go ahead and clean her teeth, too. It had been a while. Patient X reported that in 1918 (18 months prior), she had undergone root canal surgery for a carious tooth and the resulting abscess. No problems since. Visual inspection revealed a healthy-looking mouth: pink gums, mild staining on teeth, no gum recession. However, I have recently been considering how Ben's mouth grew infected immediately after the root canal, before his mouth had even healed. Based on Focal Infection Theory, the question arises that maybe infection lingers even after the pulp is mined from the tooth, and that such lingering infections possibly go undetected for years. The tooth is the center of operations, the home base of the infection, but the bacteria might slip into the bloodstream, penetrate the bones, prowl the tissues, wreak quiet havoc throughout the body. Thus, I told Patient X that I would need to pull her tooth. Of course, she demanded to know why, and I told her it was infected. (In truth, I could see no signs of infection. No pus, no redness, no swelling.) I pulled the tooth, rinsed the hole with sterilizing chemicals, and sent her on her way. I kept the tooth and washed off the blood and saliva, but I did not sterilize it.

Procedure: The infected tooth was implanted beneath the skin of a rabbit in order to observe whether the bacteria would spread beyond the local infection point.[1] I chose a calm brown creature, lifting it by the

---

1. I had nine rabbits in three hutches in the yard. It began with a single pair that Frances and I thought we'd raise for company or stew, but soon there were nine. Since then, I have tried to keep the animals separated by sex to halt their incessant breeding.

neck, supporting its soft weight with my other hand. Frances stroked its ears, then held it down on the table so that it couldn't kick.[2] I made a tiny incision at its shoulder, between jaw and scapula. I cut through the fur and the dermis. I separated the skin from the muscle, made a little pocket between them, and, with the tip of my scalpel, inserted the tooth. I sewed the pocket closed with red thread and snipped the strand. Frances dipped the creature's ear in pink dye and returned it to the hutch.[3] It hopped to the back corner. The other rabbits ignored it as if it had betrayed them.[4]

Procedure (T+3 Days): In three days, the rabbit has aged a lifetime. With the tooth beneath its skin, it is stiff and slow in its movements. It does not run from me when I open the hutch. It burns with fever, beats an erratic pulse, and refuses to hop.

---

2. Rabbits look squat and round, but they have long spines. Laid bare of muscle and fat and skin and fur, you can see the different types of vertebrae—at the top, thin and bladelike; along the arc of the back, chunky. A live rabbit, however, with skin and flesh and ears and cottontail, is the softest thing. Its heart beats quickly—much faster than a human heart. And rabbits are so easily scared. We watched its whiskers shiver. "Its heart is racing," Frances said. Her voice was higher than usual, revealing that she was uncomfortable. She tended to think of the rabbits as pets. Perhaps she even named them.

3. "Sweet thing," she murmured. "Noble beast."

4. Frances tells me that the Japanese look at the moon and see a rabbit where we see a man. She pointed it out to me once—the long, curved torso tips back and its ears are upright. They say the moon is populated with rabbits busy making sweet rice cakes. At Bon Echo, where Frances and I built the Inn, back when we were young, before we had Benjamin, there was a rock wall that the Ojibwe people painted with streaks of red iron. They drew portraits of Nanabush, the long-eared trickster who named the things of the world the way Adam named the things of Eden. They say Nanabush visits in the shape of a rabbit. But rather than tricksters, I find that rabbits are simple creatures, dumb and tender, driven by procreative and survival urges. Think of a rabbit in a field: when you spot it, it freezes, only its nose twitching, as if it can make itself invisible. It only runs if you make a sudden move. But then, I do not know how many times I have *missed* seeing a rabbit in a field because it did just that—sat still and waited. Perhaps they are smarter than they seem. There is really no way to test this question.

Procedure (T+4 Days): The rabbit has died.

Conclusion (hypothesis for further testing): A tooth carries infection to the blood even after decay is drilled and filled.

Evidence (Exhibit A): Patient X has resumed walking! She came to my office and shook my hand. She reports that she pushed herself right up out of her wheelchair, took a few slow steps across her kitchen, and prepared herself a cup of tea! It was the first time she had walked in seven years. Of course, I wasn't there for the miracle moment, but I have seen her walking.

"To think," she said. "All these years, it was that rotten tooth. All these years."[5]

Procedure (Expanding the Sample): The skin of a rabbit is somewhat loose, easily sliced with a paring knife or scalpel. Again and again, I have pulled the skin away from the bone and inserted the tip of the blade, jerked it upward just a bit, made an inch-long incision, and tucked a tooth beneath the top layer of flesh (like a pat of butter beneath the skin of a turkey).

Evidence (Exhibits B-G): I have harvested teeth from a man with heart disease, another woman with rheumatoid arthritis, two men blinded by eye lesions, a man who suffered a stroke, a man with kidney failure. I placed a tooth beneath the skin of 6 different rabbits. In the course of 14 days, each rabbit has sickened and died, of heart disease or rheumatism or kidney failure. *Each rabbit died from the disease carried on the tooth it was given.*

---

5. Her eyes brimmed with tears. "Thank you, Doctor," she said. She gripped my hand in both of hers and held my gaze until I felt embarrassed by her gratitude.

Animals (Wisdom of): Animals are not wise in the ways that human beings are wise—capable of reason, of conjecture and hypothesis, of testing hypotheses—but they are wise in the ways of nutrition. While we eat the tender muscles of our prey—haunches, shoulders, rumps—and we eat them because the muscles (with some fat) are delicious and nutritious, animals eat what they *need*. It has been observed, for example, that lions will tear open the abdomen of a fallen zebra and devour the liver, leaving the rest of the beast for the jackals. The assumption, which has been widely applied in zoos, is that lions need extra iron if they are to reproduce adequately.

Last week, some common rats dug through the mesh of one of my rabbit hutches and killed four of my animals, draining them pale and bloodless. They dug out the eyes and ate them. They gnawed a hole in each rabbit skull and sucked out the brains. The plump rabbit bodies were sunken and dry, but they were still covered with fur, untorn and unshredded, the fat and flesh untouched.[6] And this is how I learned that the eyes of a rabbit are rich in vitamin A—something a winter rat lacks. Rats cannot name what their bodies crave, but they know intuitively where to get it.

Rabbits (Breeding of): Newborn kittens are hairless, gray and pink, tiny. Two or three of them can rest in my palm at once, like bald, quivering, mice. They are blind, naked little things—quite revolting. But when they yawn, it doesn't matter that they are hairless and strange. They look, then, like sleepy human babies. And in only a few days, their fur grows in like velvet. Sometimes they fight viciously, biting at each other's ears and kicking their sturdy legs. They eat their own droppings. But at two weeks old, a rabbit is one of the most perfect creatures I have seen.

---

6. Frankly, it was a hideous sight. I did not tell Frances the details of their murder. I am so grateful she was not the one to find them. Fortunately, it was a warmish day, and the frozen soil had thawed enough that I was able to bury them quickly in the garden.

Hypothesis (Development and Support of Focal Infection Theory): *A tooth pulled from a person with heart disease and implanted beneath the skin of a rabbit will create a heart involvement in a rabbit. A tooth pulled from a person with rheumatoid arthritis will provoke arthritis in its rabbit host.* (I need a control group.)

Control Group: I have pulled healthy teeth—backmost molars and wisdom teeth.[7] I also went to the morgue and got teeth from the dead, which I thoroughly sterilized. The rabbits with clean teeth embedded beneath their skin live on happily. They eat and sleep and hop and breed. These rabbits live. The evidence is staggering: ***Teeth carry dangerous bacteria and fatal disease, even after endodontic therapy! Perhaps root canal procedures even exacerbate such infections.***

---

7. I may have lied a little. I told my patients that the teeth I pulled were rotten. I wish there were a better way, but I needed those pure teeth. May God and Science smile upon me.

TOOTH STORY:
RABBIT INCISORS

When one of the lab rabbits died, cutting the tooth out from beneath the skin was a standard part of autopsy. Cliff sliced the tooth out and swabbed it for bacteria, which he planted in a Petri dish and daubed onto glass slides for examination. When he was done with a tooth, he wired it to a piece of wood and labeled it in neat black letters with the date, bacteria content, and cause of the rabbit's death. None of these teeth made it into Frances' collection. They were lab specimens.

But once, after a batch cremation, my mother discovered a pair of rabbit incisors in the ashes. They were long, upper incisors, the two top teeth, which grow from way back in the rabbit's jaw, only revealing a small part of their total length in the rabbit's mouth. Like human fingernails, the teeth of a rabbit grow continuously, and when a rabbit eats, its teeth grind together and wear each other down. The teeth Frances found were from a rabbit that suffered what my father would label *malocclusion*—its teeth didn't meet, so they couldn't wear each other down. Instead, the teeth kept growing and growing until they began to curl back on themselves like the fingernails of a vampire. Frances hadn't noticed malocclusion in any of the recently deceased rabbits, but the two long, sickle-shaped teeth were evidence of her negligence. Their biting edge was sharp and pointed, almost unusable for mashing grass and leaves. The animal would soon have starved to death if it hadn't died from whatever infection Cliff had implanted in the poor beast's shoulder. But then, Frances wondered if maybe it *had* starved to death—maybe it hadn't died from rheumatism or heart involvement or whatever Cliff had noted in his files. She showed the teeth to Cliff, but he dismissed her concerns.

"Many of the rabbits are underweight at death," he said. "But none have been skeletal. Anyway, at this point, I have no way of tracking the animal from which those teeth came. There were thirteen in the batch."

It seemed to Frances that a dental exam should be part of the autopsy process, but she let it go, like she let so much go. She added the teeth to her collection: two long, curved scythes that reminded her that she was sometimes inattentive. She sometimes missed details. She was sometimes careless. She could never be careful enough.

FROM THE NOTEBOOKS OF DR. CLIFFORD BELL: TOWARD A COMPENDIUM OF DENTAL INFECTION

Purpose (God-given, Recognition of): As a child, I prayed with fervor. Each night, I knelt beside my brothers, all of us with our heads bent. We did not pray aloud, did not recite the Lord's Prayer in unison, but each held his own conversation with the Heavenly Father. I prayed that I would be a great man, although I did not know what it meant to be great, or what kind of greatness I wanted. It wasn't wealth, and it wasn't acres of wheat or cattle or hops. I didn't want to be a farmer like my father. For a time, I thought I'd be a pastor, so I asked for great knowledge, great faith. But at the end of each prayer, I asked the Lord to do what He thought best. To use me in the way I could be most useful. *I am your servant,* I said. *Make me great for you.*

The Lord took my son. And in this way, He taught me that root canals are a deadly practice. The Lord has taken rabbit after rabbit, providing evidence for my hypothesis that a decayed tooth teems with dangerous bacteria, and it is extremely difficult to eliminate the infection in the wider system of the body. Even if we drill into the tooth and remove the pulp, the disease remains and can spread, can cause terrible suffering, and eventually kill the host. But few of my fellow dentists believe me. I have published a book about my findings, but they have stopped their ears to me. They write falsehoods that contradict what I know to be true, what I have proven. They call me a quack. Thus, many people will suffer. Many people will die unnecessarily.

I no longer pray for greatness. Instead, I pray that they will hear me. I ask God to lift the veil that covers their eyes, to unstop their ears.

Evidence (Exhibit T): At a convention in Michigan, I dined with a group of colleagues. One of my companions assured me that he could fill 95 percent of molar roots entirely to the apices. The root of a tooth is a narrow chamber, and no matter how skilled the practitioner, it is nearly impossible to fill a tooth to its very apex. Instead, we dentists leave a tiny, unintended gap, and in this space, the bacteria continue to fester, further decaying the gums and jaw, or even worse, involving the lungs or the heart or the joints. This little pit of bacteria destroys the body. It is best to pull the entire tooth.

An improperly filled root canal is a matter of life and death.

I challenged my friend, but not because I thought he was incompetent. In fact, he is an excellent dentist. Truly, I believe his work is above average. Being a man that takes great pride in his work, he held his ground, declaring that he could fill a tooth perfectly. We agreed that I would cast a set of teeth for him, using plaster of Paris, and he would demonstrate his expertise by filling them. We undertook this little experiment, and suffice it to say, I was right. He is an excellent dentist, but even so, he was unable to fill the teeth to the root in over 5 percent of the samples, and in some 25% of the successful fillings—those teeth he had filled completely—*his filling penetrated out of the tooth*. Had they been real teeth, the lingering bacteria and molybdenum alloy would have leaked into the mouth, slowly poisoning the patient.

We must discontinue the deadly practice of root canals. We must pull all infected teeth.

Edwin Logan (National Dental Association): In the past two months, attendance at NDA meetings has drastically dwindled. I know that the others would like me to resign, but my term as president is nearly over. I will not quit, but they will not have to oust me, either. Last night I ran into my friend Edwin Logan at the library. He was one of the only members to attend the February meeting. I was in the reading room, my books spread out around me, and Edwin pulled out the chair opposite mine and sat down. He apologized that he could not invite me out for a whiskey due to the new laws. I laughed, but only to be polite. I have never been a drinking man. I don't miss the dark, crowded bars or the noisy laughter of the drunks, although the word is you can find plenty of places for a whiskey if you want one, and I suspect Edwin knows the places. He leaned close to me, his elbows on the table. He told me I had better lay off the root canal crusade. He said everyone thinks it's about Benjamin. I had to agree. I told him it *is* about Benjamin. Why wouldn't it be? I'm an excellent dentist. If root canals were safe, Benjamin wouldn't have died. I told him it's about all of our sons. And our wives and our daughters and all of our patients. *Root canals don't work, and it's clear that they're unnecessarily dangerous.*

He put a finger to his lips. Apparently, I was speaking too loudly, and the others in the reading room—there were only one or two—were glaring at us. Edwin whispered, but I could tell he was angry. He reiterated that root canals are *standard practice*—that even if I am on to something, the benefits of root canals far outweigh the costs. He said I don't have to perform them, but that it's no use trying to convince others to give them up. But the benefits do not outweigh the loss of lives, and I said so. And what is the use of *standard practice* if it is wrong? It was standard practice to burn witches in Salem, standard practice to believe that the earth was the center of the universe.

Edwin said nothing. He pushed his glasses higher on his nose, embarrassed for me, not even angry anymore. He wouldn't argue. He threw his head back and looked at the ceiling. He pushed his chair back and stood up. He shook my hand roughly and pulled on his leather gloves and was gone.

I will make it easy for them. On the day of elections, the last day of my term as president of the NDA, I will tender a letter of resignation that will also serve as a manifesto. If they won't listen to reason, if they can't adapt to scientific developments, or at the very least respond to serious scientific inquiry into an outdated and deadly practice, I want no part of their organization anyway.

Procedure (continued): I injected rabbit ears with the bacteria that live around a tooth, the very ones that multiply in an abscess. The animals developed arthritis and spinal lesions. Like Benjamin, they died of heart involvements. They suffered lung involvements or tuberculosis. Again and again, I have seen how the bacteria of an abscess poison the entire body.

Abscess (revised): The cluster of bacteria fights for survival, multiplies, devours the gums, the jaw, the cheek, burrows outward toward the light. It happens to some that the bacteria chew outward, gnawing their way entirely through the cheek. The soft flesh feeds them. And it happens to others that the infection settles in the joints, or—as in Benjamin's case—it hitchhikes through the blood to the heart. Infection can also scatter like spores in the lungs.[8]

Edwin Logan (continued): Upon receiving my letter of resignation from the presidency of the NDA, Edwin Logan wrote me back. In a way, I am grateful for his note. I know he was a friend. He wrote that he cared about my future, about Frances' future. He at least acknowledged my decision. *You will not be able to practice effective dentistry outside the NDA. Your patients will leave you. It is not too late to rescind your resignation.* I have not written back. I do not plan to.

BENJAMIN (Death of): I should have pulled that tooth.

---

8. But I know now that an abscess is an infection of the flesh, of the blood, of the pulp of the tooth. *It is not—as I thought when I was a young dentist—an infection of the soul.* There was no vacancy in my son. Had Benjamin lived, he would have been a man full of wisdom.

Tornado (update on the rabbits): I had 40 rabbits in 4 hutches when the tornado struck. It was a muggy, quiet Sunday in June. Frances was weeding the garden, and I was reading on the back porch with a cup of tea, and the sky filled with puffy clouds. Darker and darker they swirled, and when the gray turned green we knew to head to the cellar. We took a kerosene lantern, some crackers and apples, cold chicken, a jug of water. I was pulling the cellar door closed when Frances said *The rabbits, Cliff.* She is rarely so insistent.

She pushed past me, heaved the doors open, and ran across the yard to the hutches. Because I knew I could not stop her, I followed. We made three trips, back and forth, each holding three rabbits per dash. On one trip I managed four, two hanging from each hand, their bodies stretched and dangling from their scruffs. They didn't even kick, the terrified creatures, but hung silent and dumb. Frances wanted to go again, but the twister was coming—a low, fierce roar—and the sky to the west was nearly black. I pulled the cellar door shut and slid the wooden plank through the handles.

The ten rescued rabbits nestled in a corner, piled together and sniffing at each other as if meeting for the first time. A single fat beast hopped away from the group, and Frances reached for it. She held it on her lap and stroked its ears.

We heard a rapid clattering against the outside of the house, and banging, like doors slamming. A crack like a baseball against a bat, like the bat splitting. The twister was close, tearing tarpaper and planks from our house. Hurling nails and garbage and untied shoes. Spitting rocks and shingles like the teeth of a boxer.

And then it was gone. The rabbits had not left their corner. In the silence, Frances hugged her rabbit to her chest.

Tornado (Aftermath of): When we went back out to the yard, the sky was pale yellow and gleaming and scoured. Broken tree limbs were scattered in a line and electrical wires swung low from poles that tipped at a strange, parallel angle all along the street. In one of the hutches, three rabbits were dead. The others in that hutch were huddled as far from the dead animals as they could get, as if death was catching. But worse was one of the hutches laying on its side, the door torn from its hinges and the rabbits gone, their straw bedding gone, their food pellets and bits of lettuce and droppings and water dish gone. I pictured the animals in the eye of the twister, ten brown rabbits, swirling in the sky like water in a drain, eyeing each other across the storm, whirling with straw and tree branches and flowers and chairs and spoons and tricycles.

I imagine them perfectly calm, but it would not have been like that. The wind would have torn the fur from their backs, from their throats and from their bellies, where it was thickest, and spit them out naked, loose fur scattering with shingles and nails. It would have hurtled their clumsy little bodies perpendicular to the earth. For a moment, they might have flown, but then they would have been broken. Stunned and broken and dead as the funnel whirled on.

Proposition: Is it possible the cyclone could have held the rabbits close, and when it lifted, set them gently down? You hear about it sometimes—a person who survives a twister. Maybe the tornado freed the rabbits to find each other again, to sniff at each other, damp and blinking in a wide grassy field, while the funnel dissipated in the sky as if it had never been. But even if it had somehow happened like that, and the cyclone set the beasts down physically unscathed, how could they go on as if it hadn't happened? How could they again be soft, dumb animals? How could they, in that newly opened world, with the mesh of their hutch gone, their yard gone, Frances' hands, my hands—everything they had known—gone? How could they, having seen the whirling interior of a cyclone, ever be simple rabbits again? Somewhere, if they lived—however unlikely, miraculous survivors—they are changed creatures, beginning anew, taking their first bites of grass and discovering that it is bittersweet.[9]

---

9. In the yard, I bent to set the overturned hutch upright, but then I thought better of it. The rabbits deserved a gesture of memorial at the very least. I left the broken hutch in the yard for weeks, overturned and empty, evidence that they had once lived, evidence that they faced that dark howling.

II.

ONCE UPON A TIME

My father was a farm boy and my mother was a tomboy.

My father had eight brothers and my mother had one sister.

My father was a dentist and my mother was a teacher.

My father was ambitious and my mother was bored.

My father was stricken with typhoid fever, and my mother crawled through tunnels of grass, staining her knees green.

My father had a dog and my mother talked to a crow she saw every morning sitting atop a fencepost, and the crow talked back to her. (*They're very smart,* she told me, years later. *They have a life and a world of their own that we don't understand.* She made up stories about the crows and we left bits of ribbon and tin on the porch for them. We watched from the window as they hopped up the steps and took the treasures in their beaks.)

There were not many cameras back in once upon a time, but there were a couple of photographs of my parents from their life before me. I liked to take the small, leather-bound album to the rug and flip through it. There was one photograph of my mother as a girl with her mother and my aunt Elizabeth, all of them in dresses and hats with flowers on the brim. But even when looking at that photograph, I couldn't really imagine what my mother had been like. Even faced with evidence, it was hard to believe she had once been as young as me. It was strange that my parents had not always been married, not always known each other. But, of course, they hadn't. Their lives began before me, and continued after me. I changed them. I was a beginning, a middle, and an end. But the strands of my story are so tightly woven with my parents', and their strands braid every which way, like a river, still flowing.

THE HORSE LATITUDES
Frances

Ontario, 1901-1903

As a schoolteacher, I often bent to tie the shoes of the youngest children. I tousled their hair at recess. I was restless, smoldering, quietly devouring roots, acorns, midden, mice. Chalk in hand, I learned to teach and scold, but the children looked past me, out the window, watching clouds or waving grasses. I learned to speak more loudly. Each day, on my walk to school, I practiced my lectures in my head.

Winds blow their way around the world in circular cells, colliding with each other and turning back, spiraling in on themselves. Crash and circle, crash and return, a parade of wind cells aligned like boxcars, chugging across the surface of the earth.

On the chalkboard, I drew the winds as boxcars along the lines of latitude. Over and over, the same diagrams, the same lectures.

Divide the earth into bands. Circumscribe her latitudes with invisible lines. Number these lines, name them with their angle from the center of the earth.

In the schoolyard, the children shrieked and stumbled. They were not my children. I had no children. I wondered: does giving birth make a girl into a woman? Until then, until I had a child of my own, would I remain a girl?

After lunch, all in a line, the students chanted their multiplication tables, their voices like a train accelerating downhill, but they did not understand what it meant to multiply.

Between the lines named 30° and 35°, both north and south of the Equator, there is a gap between wind cells. Here, above the flat yellow-brown of the Sahara, or the green-blue-gray-black of the ocean, winds whirl away from each other. These are glossy bands, where ships lose speed, stall, and drift. Their sails luff and flap while the crew lounges topside. Lips crack.

I pretended I did not have favorites, but I loved the dreamers, the ones who made strange drawings of people with heads shaped like lumpy hearts, the ones who called purple "amethyst" or "lavender," and forgot to comb their hair. I thought a child that watched birds was far more interesting than one that could breathlessly recite her multiplication tables. They came to school with mud on their faces, or they smelled like dandelions and bore yellow streaks on their arms. They carried weeds like bridal bouquets, like royalty, and the flowers drooped and browned on their desks, but still they refused to throw them out.

If you sailed from the North Pole to the South, you'd go through three such dead zones: The Calms of Cancer, the Doldrums, and the Calms of Capricorn. The Calms are also dubbed the "Subtropical Highs" (referring to atmospheric pressure) and "The Horse Latitudes."

Each night: chamomile, cross-stitch, and the branch against the window (*crit-scritch*). In winter, I let the fire burn, and the room glowed like quiet hell. Saturdays, I walked the four blocks to the store for the same groceries every week. In summer, maybe a little basket of berries.

Trade ships bogged in the subtropical zone quickly ran low on food. If only the ship were lighter, the captain may have reasoned. If the ship were not so heavy, this stale breath, this sorry excuse for wind, might be enough to push the boat along, to fill one sail to billowing, to stretch it taut.

I met Clifford at a picnic. I was standing in the churchyard, spitting watermelon seeds into a wadded napkin. I noticed his smooth skin, and then the way he looked steadily at me when he spoke. He wasn't afraid of people, like so many others. I looked away. Flying birds, running children, a storm cloud moving in from the north. His eyes were the palest shade of blue. Not like water, but maybe like ice. Like thin, cool glass. His spectacles were round with silver frames. They were not scratched nor smeared with fingerprints. He was an immaculate man. He pulled a square of chamois from the breast pocket of his vest and polished the spotless lenses. He was wearing a bowtie.

Horses are heavy. They eat and drink so much. So the sailors pushed them overboard.

"Pleasure to meet you, Frances," he said. He didn't look like a dreamer, but there was something about him. He glanced at the wadded napkin in my hand, the watermelon rind gnawed to the white. He took a slice of watermelon from the table beside us and bit into it, the juice running down his hand, so he had to lean forward to avoid dripping on his shirt. No, not a dreamer. A practical man, but at least he wasn't afraid to get a little messy.

Sailors ran up debts in port, but by the time they reached the subtropical zone they had worked their way back to zero. In celebration, they burned a straw effigy of a horse, the burden of debt drifting away, sparks and smoke in the darkness.

I told him I was there with my cousin. She went to the church. "Do you know her?" I asked. "Emily Anthony? She's in the choir."

One of his younger brothers had been in her class at school. "There are ten of us," he said. "A big family means you know a lot of the town."

I straightened my hat. Tipped the brim back a little so he could see my eyes. When I was young, they were greenish and I considered them one of my best features.

You've been there so long. You've screamed and screamed. Your screams do not suffice to propel you into the choppy water, but your voice is raw. Who hasn't been there? Waiting for the next wind. Hungry and bored. The job was supposed to be temporary. The brain was supposed to be resting. The illness was supposed to go away. You were supposed to grow up. You were supposed to find an answer. Why do people look at you that way, now squinting, now soft-eyed? Compassionately. Sympathetically. Or impatiently, raising an eyebrow, waiting for you to bring them tea, coffee, a slice of pie. Or maybe they do not look at you at all.

We walked across the grass together, stopping to watch a game of horseshoes. One of his brothers was playing, and so our conversation was punctuated with outbursts. "Atta boy, Andrew! That's a ringer!" But then he'd turn back to me, give a little nod, and resume our conversation.

He was a dentist. A good, solid set of teeth, he said, resembled a well-tuned Steinway, felt hammers striking in chorus, ivory keys aligned. A superb dental arch was like a stone bridge—each stone in its place, mortared by pale pink gums. A tongue should rest like a lily pad on a pond. He demonstrated this by patting the back of one hand with the palm of the other. The owner of such a mouth breathes through her nose without effort: her nostrils are wide-open corridors from the world to her lungs.

"And a poet, too," I said. I did not point out that his metaphors were mixed, or that it all seemed rather hyperbolic. I thought he was lucky—that such people are lucky, those who find something they love so deeply, something to which they commit their lives, from which they never look away. I did not love teaching, and so I envied commitment in others. I envied passion.

Dust bunnies congregating in the corner. Dead flies in the light fixture. The tiniest gust might get you going. Might push you out of it.

Clifford was the ninth boy in his family. A week later, he brought me home for supper, to meet his parents, and I paused in a half-lit hallway to study a photograph hanging on the wall. Mr. and Mrs. Bell stood at one end, hands flat at their sides, shoulders squared to the camera. Their ten sons were arranged from tallest to shortest beside them: ten perfect sets of teeth.

Clifford's smile was slow and easy, but his lips were not generous. His top lip fell like a curtain over his teeth, flat and fleshless. When, finally, he kissed me, after we had been courting for two weeks, I felt his teeth press hard against my own. He did not tell me then that he wore dentures, that he had lost his perfect teeth to typhoid fever at the age of twenty-two.

But even on a windless day, the ship is moving, however slowly. Scattered ashes drift and flutter, but they find their weight. They sink and disappear beneath the glassy surface. And the boat moves.

It was eight months later, on our wedding night, that I went into the washroom, and there they were: a pair of dentures in a glass at the edge of the sink. I was startled. Dentures, when they're not in their owner's mouth, are awful things. Too pink. Too slick and shining. Too jeering.

Shaking a little, I accused him of lying to me, but he said he hadn't thought it important. It wasn't a secret, he said. He pointed out that I had not seen him without his clothes before, either, but I didn't seem to think it a lie when I discovered that he had a line of hair running downward from his belly button. *Incomplete knowledge,* he said. *Dentures are like underclothes, like hidden scars.* And anyway, he said, his teeth were genetically excellent. It was the fever that had ruined them. An outside force. Our children would have the teeth of rhinoceroses.

All of this he said without his dentures in his mouth while I held the glass with the dentures leering within. Without his teeth, he looked ancient. His lips puckered in on themselves as if his mouth would swallow his face. He took the glass from me and fished out the teeth. He slipped them into place and he was again himself.

Waiting for a favorable wind—a stir, a squall, a thunderstorm. The sailors leaping to the sheets and winches. The boy in the crow's nest climbing down fast, dropping to the deck on his bare feet. The swinging hammocks, the heavy keel. The ship heaves and is free.

How incomplete our knowledge was! We did not yet know that we would have only one child, and that his teeth would be his demise. But had we known how things would go, had we seen our hidden future, would we have done things differently? Would I have stayed a schoolteacher, alone and restless, tying the shoes of other peoples' children, drawing lines of latitude on the chalkboard, while Clifford, in Cleveland, drilled into his patients' teeth, drained the pulp and filled the roots with silver and molybdenum, a single man doing imperfect work, making his quiet soup for dinner each night. Each of us living a safe and lonely life.

It is impossible to know what we begin and where, impossible to recognize the middle or the slow movement of the boat. *Incomplete knowledge*, he said. Like underclothes and hidden scars. The scars we hadn't earned yet. The wounds that would never heal. But how we drifted once, for days—for years—on a bright and glassy sea.

TOOTH STORY:
TYPHOID FEVER, 1900

Less than a year, but already he knew this town—their names, their cavities, the geometries of their jaws. He knew their family overbites and apnea. Their poultice recipes, chipped incisors, and missing molars. Headaches and Sunday dresses, limps and whispers.

Today the street was a little busy. His hat was in his hand more often than on his head. They all knew him. *Doc,* they said. And *Doctor Bell* and *Sir.* And he grinned at them, and walked a little straighter and said their names: Earl, Mr. Johnson, Naomi, Mr. Hendrick. Good to see you. Fine afternoon. How is your mother? How is your son? Hello. Hello.

Grand Forks sat in the middle of hundreds of miles of wheat fields, which confused Clifford's sense of scale. From a distance, the hills looked like the back of a beast, its yellow pelt rippling in the breeze. If this were true, Clifford reasoned, then he and all the good citizens of Grand Forks were nothing but fleas on the back of the beast. And what was the use of a flea? Insipid, non-sentient little survivors, producing nothing but offspring and misery. Could a flea contribute anything to society? Wood-ticks, mites, microbes, viruses, writhing corkscrew spirochetes—gorging themselves, reproducing, then dying. He imagined a giant flea comb made from the straight trunks of lodgepole pines. The comb was a thresher, collecting him and his pesky human-flea companions, relieving the beast from the relentless pounding of their feet on its back, from the plows and seeds and crops, from the relentless digging and burying of the dead.

But here Clifford's imagination failed. He could picture the comb but not the hand that moved it. For Clifford, God had never been a giant man, a white-haired father-in-the-sky with humongous hands and clouds trailing from his beard. God did not comb wheat field beasts unless it was with wind and lightning, unless it was with fire.

Despite his mother's pleas that he not move to "that other planet"—North Dakota! So far away!—Grand Forks was not all that different from Ontario. But Clifford felt different. Here he was a dentist, an outsider, and a gentleman. Here he was Dr. Bell. No longer just one of his father's many sons, nearly the last in a line of many brothers.

He pushed open the door of the hardware store and the bells jangled overhead. At the end of the plumbing aisle, he saw Dirk Krueger, a wheat farmer, and his boy Will, a teenager with perfect skin and lank, red hair. Will had a length of rope looped from shoulder to hip like a sash, and he held a section of pipe in one hand. Clifford stopped his smile—too broad, too quick. He coughed, felt the heat at the back of his neck.

Six weeks ago, Will had visited Clifford in his office to have a tooth pulled, and when Clifford stepped into the exam room, he found Will already reclined in the chair, legs crossed at the ankles, hands resting on his stomach, fingers interlocked. They were a man's hands, too big for him, long-fingered and strong, sunburned and freckled and covered with soft red hair. They were hands that could tie bales and string fence. Hands that could right a calf twisted in the cow's womb and slide the creature effortlessly into the world, help it stand, then soothe its mother. His voice cracked a little when he greeted Clifford, still snagging on boyhood. When Clifford wrangled the rotten tooth from Will's mouth, the boy's hands remained folded. The only sign of the pain he must have been experiencing was the crease in his forehead and the way he uncrossed his legs and pressed his feet hard against the footrest. Clifford liked Will. He had often hoped to see the boy in town, had even looked for him.

"Afternoon, Dr. Bell," said Dirk.

"Hello, Sir," said Will.

"Dirk. Will. Good to see you. How's the tooth? Or rather, how's the hole?"

The boy grinned, showing off his gap. It had been one of the lower incisors.

"No more trouble then?" Cliff said.

"Almost good as new, Doc." He winked and stuck his hand out to shake Clifford's.

His voice cracked on "Doc," proof he was still a boy for the day, or at least the afternoon. Clifford shook Will's hand, then grasped it with his other hand and, squeezing a little, looked Will in the eye. The boy held his gaze.

What was it, Clifford wondered as he walked back to his office, that finally pushed a boy over the edge and into manhood? Will Krueger was toeing that line. Cliff pictured manhood as a crevasse a boy tumbled through on his way to the grave, a fall so exhilarating, uncharted and undefined.

A teenager, a boy like Will, had hard angles and muscles, but he also had soft skin. Will had a scar on one cheek—a pale, vertical gouge. Maybe from barbed wire. Maybe from fighting. His fingernails were dirty and splintered.

What was it that pushed a boy out of that last bit of girlish softness? Clifford didn't remember leaving the edge himself. Maybe he was still standing there, his hair grown thin, but his toes still jutting over that edge, waiting for the proper gust of wind.

In his office, he found Mrs. McMahon waiting in the chair, skirts adjusted over her fat thighs, the scuffed toes of her boots tipping away from each other. All his life Cliff had been around farm women. He was used to the traces of dirt in the creases of their foreheads and their callused hands, but his mother had always been clean. She smelled of castile soap even on the hottest days of the summer, even during the harvest, when everyone was ragged and windblown and sour. His mother was an exceptionally clean farm wife, and Mrs. McMahon was her exceptionally filthy counterpart. Every fold of skin was lined with grime. Cliff imagined lifting those folds of flesh to wash the creases, the way a mother must wash a chubby baby, wiping mashed carrots from between tiers of double chin.

He was half the way across the room, halfway to his stool, and the smell of her was already overwhelming. Acidic and sour as water in the mop bucket. She smelled like the mop itself, tipped on end against the porch railing, gray and soggy with vinegar water.

And then he felt a streak of pain in his belly. He stumbled, but found his way to his stool and hunched there for a moment.

"You okay, Doc?" Mrs. McMahon asked. Her fingers, when she clasped his hand, were greasy and cold. He was fine. Just a little light-headed for a moment. He straightened up.

She said she had a toothache. The culprit would have to come out, she was quite sure.

He nodded. "Let's have a look."

She opened her mouth. He smelled the poultice before he saw it: overripe pollen and the sweet rot of leaves in the gutter. It was wedged between her cheek and her lower molars, a soggy gray mass of cheese-cloth. Why hadn't she removed it before sitting in his chair? He took the tweezers from the tray and plucked it from her mouth, watched her wince. He dropped it on a silver tray. The room was full of the stench of it. She blinked her pale eyes and he let her close her mouth and swallow.

"The best poultice recipe," she said. "Licorice, honey, mint. A little witch-hazel—" She coughed.

"Go easy on the honey," he said. He breathed through his mouth. "Terrible on the teeth. Now, let me have another look." She opened her mouth. Again, he felt the pain in his abdomen. His vision swam. He steadied himself, held a breath behind his paper mask, closed his eyes a moment and steadied his hands. Was he coming down with something? Or was it just the stink getting to him? He reminded himself to drink more water.

She was right: the culprit would have to come out.

Afterward, Mrs. McMahon asked to keep the tooth he had pulled from her mouth.

"On the Judgment Day," she explained, "if you're missing any teeth, you have to hunt for them. You can't go to heaven without all your teeth."

He had heard it before, and he thought it stupid that time, too, but he gave her the tooth in a white paper sack and, humoring her, asked what she would do with it, how she'd keep track of it until the Judgment?

She shook her head as if he were the fool. "That's the thing. If I account for it in the here and now, I won't be held accountable for it at the Judgment." She said she'd take it home and say the special prayer and then throw it into the fire. It seemed such a pagan ritual, despite being linked to the Christian Judgment. She went on. "You have to say a little prayer when you throw the tooth into the flames. Good tooth, bad tooth. Pray God, send me a good tooth."

Clifford didn't bother to tell her that a tooth wouldn't burn. The tooth would remain whole, just a resilient chunk of calcium lingering like the soul after the body had been destroyed by time.

At home, the pain in his belly returned. He was so short of breath. He was so tired, falling asleep at the table, then dragging himself to bed, leaving the dishes unwashed and a lantern flickering, the flame devouring the wick, shadows blooming on the walls. He woke late the next morning, flushed and feverish, and lurched to the bathroom. Rose colored spots mottled his chest. Back in the bedroom he pulled the curtains tight and fell into bed. Waited for someone to wonder where he was.

Someone was Mrs. Able, who helped him at the office. She stopped by at lunchtime when he hadn't shown up. She found him sleeping and shook his shoulder hard. He woke only to groan at her. "Take a bath," he mumbled. "Use soap." She pressed a damp cloth to his head, put a glass of water on the table beside him, wrote a note that she'd return.

Typhoid fever is something you eat. *S. Typhi*: a type of salmonella. Pink on the laboratory slide, with waving longlegs, like those of the spider, scattered across the Petri dish like the rosy rash that spread across his chest and back.

Perhaps he caught it from the hands that made the biscuit he ate last week at the café. Or the hands he shook in the street before buying that bag of roasted peanuts, the hands of the peanut vendor. Or the feet of the housefly that landed on the countertop and tiptoed over his potatoes and baked whitefish, tiptoed across his tongue and down his gullet. Or the water ladle at Olsen's farm on shearing day, the one everyone passed around, everyone drank from. Half the town would be sick.

The heavy curtains were drawn, but a slice of light showed between them. Not even a fly circling. He was alone. The sky between the curtains was white. The sun, that white dot, burned his retinas. The bubbles were gone from the ginger ale. There were crumbs in the bedclothes.

He dreamed of burning horses, of masks and sparks, of faces in the flames. *Throw it overboard*, he mumbled. *All of it*—the straw effigy, the empty suitcase, the baby with tiny teeth, the peacoat and the dictionary. The soggy saltines and the pillows and the mourning dove. Watch them waterlog and drift. Watch them go nowhere. Let a little blood, if only to color the water.

He kicked at the blankets. The dog, sleeping halfway under the bed, bit and licked his dangling hand, and for a minute, he knew he was awake. The room smelled of seaweed and sweat and peat smoke. What he would do for a glass of whiskey! The dance and the gleam and the clink of the ice! A single cube melting on his hot tongue!

Maybe he was being punished. For leaving his mother. For leaving his brothers. For missing the harvest. For seeing in his mind, over and over, the broad hands of Will Krueger. Those broad hands covered with copper hairs. For thinking about the boy. For wanting him. For the disgust he felt at the vinegar scent of Mrs. McMahon. For wanting to rest his head on her pillowy shoulder.

But he had never done those things. He had only thought them. Except for moving to godforsaken North Dakota, he had never done much of anything. If he was going to be punished, if he was going to burn, he wanted to lick the boy's earlobe first, he wanted to smell the very top of the boy's head, and run his own hands—so much more refined than the boy's, so much smoother—over the boy's firm thigh. He wanted to press his fingers deep into Mrs. McMahon's flesh, to knead it, to leave a mark. He wanted to return to his brothers, return to the farm, wearing a new suit with a silk scarf pressed and folded in the pocket. He wanted juleps! A horse race, a big bet. A porcelain belle sailing by in hat and gloves, all sugar and mint. He wanted a whore from the street. He would feed her sugarplums, and take a bath with her, and when they were warm and clean, he would touch every inch of her. He would have her: his whore, his feast, his bottle of wine. He would curse God, just once, *goddammit.* He would slam a door, *goddammit.* Just once he would have that terrible caress.

To reach manhood through fever seemed like cheating. To burn his way to it. The sheets twisted around him. The heat—the Refiner's fire—was in him. On him. He was malleable.

Hammer me smooth.

And then, through the red of his eyelids, he heard his brother's voice.

"My God, little brother." It was Albert. "Just where do you think you're going?" A hand on his chest that was not his own. "Get on back here, Cliff. Get on back."

He lost his teeth.

A neat pair of dentures and he blended back into the family, back in Ontario, shaking hands with guests at Richard's wedding, six months later. "Welcome back," the people said. They squinted at him. "Dr. Milligan's getting up there, you know. We need our dentists here, too." Beneath his pants his knees were knobby, his legs wasted by fever. And in his mouth, only slick empty gums and false teeth. The holes into which he could push his tongue when his dentures were out.

His teeth hadn't fallen out completely, but had withered to brownish stumps. Clutching his pliers, he leaned close to the mirror, twisted and yanked. He dropped them, one after another, onto a saucer. There was less blood than he expected, and less pain. They were no longer firmly rooted in his mouth. He didn't throw them into the fire, but tipped the saucer toward the waste bin and let them slide in. When the dentures were new, there were days of drooling, his mouth mistaking the false teeth for food, salivating, working to digest the plastic and porcelain. He was twenty-two years old.

Clifford Bell stood with his brothers, the prodigal returned, shaking hands with aunts and uncles, with the minister and the schoolmaster, with his old schoolmates. He stood in line beside his brothers, each of them smiling his milkfed smile.

A SELKIE STORY

Frances

Brampton, Ontario, 1891

If our mother was a selkie, her skin had to be around somewhere—stuffed beneath a rock at the shore, locked in a trunk, or draped like a regular old coat on a hanger. Elizabeth and I looked for it in the attic, in the hanging garment bags. We found a few faded dresses, a fur stole, and a suit that belonged to our father, slimmer than we ever imagined him and much in need of mending. Our mother's wedding dress was there, too. She had sewn it herself, of pale gray cotton with lace trim and a blue satin ribbon around the waist. Elizabeth tried it on, dragging 8 inches of it across the floor when she twirled for me. Our mother was tall. Elizabeth curtsied, holding the skirt out. "Princess Elizabeta," she said, offering me her hand.

"*Enchanté*," I said, and kissed the hand.

"This thing smells awful," she said. "Like pee." But she waltzed with me for a minute before letting it fall into a heap at her ankles and giving it a kick.

"Maybe that's because it's been stored next to a nasty old seal skin," I suggested, turning back to the garment bags, where we found nothing but regular clothing. The floor was littered with dead bees and glinting flies and mouse droppings.

In stories, selkies were seal-people, swimming between islands, and when they swam to shore, they took off their skins and walked about like humans. The stories might come from reports of travelers in sealskin kayaks. A woman in a sealskin boat might look half-woman/half-seal, her boat riding low in the waves. She would be a strong paddler, gliding onto the beach and peeling herself free of her boat, stretching her human legs. And seals don't help the confusion, the way they splash around the fishing boats like pets or children, shouting with their almost-human voices and blinking their sentient eyes.

To gain a selkie wife, a human man must steal the selkie's seal skin. On the beach, hiding behind a rock, he watches the seals strip themselves of their skins and dance with human limbs, feeling with pleasure the sand and stones beneath their bare feet. Bonfire, gleaming moon, waves lapping the shore. He sneaks closer and steals a single skin, hides it away, and *bingo!* He's got himself a wife. Loyal, too, the selkie wife, raising the kids, baking the pies, savory and sweet. But she'll always pine for the sea, her fins and her seal children, who are out there somewhere, frolicking motherless in the waves. But as long as the man keeps her skin, he keeps her bound to the soil, the dry land, her legs.

"Show me your sharp teeth," our mother would say to Elizabeth and me. She wanted fierce daughters, daughters like bears, like wolves. She wanted bonfires, oil slicks. We sneered and growled, held our hands up like claws. Our father shook his head, went off to sit in his armchair with the newspaper, wearing his slippers.

Before she met our father, she was Agnes Clery. Black hair, black eyes, pale skin. A raspy voice she blamed on an illness she had as a child. Scarred vocal cords, she said. Her students were the best behaved in the school, every one of them afraid of her, even the older boys. She became Mrs. Anthony by marrying our father. She was known to wield a mean ruler. A swift swing. Seeing those big Ontario farm boys cower, I learned that there are different types of fear, or at least different types of power. A slap of my mother's ruler could not have hurt as much as losing a finger to the thresher. Not as much as frostbitten ears. Her power was in her voice, in her scorn. Those boys were fireflies in a jar that she was not afraid to shake. *Yes, ma'am. Certainly, Mrs. Anthony.*

Elizabeth and I searched the garage for her seal skin, sure it would be in our father's tool chest, which he kept locked, but Elizabeth had long ago discovered the key. He kept it under the whiskey bottle, on the shelf with coffee cans full of pencils and nails and measuring tapes. The level of the whiskey got lower and lower until it was gone, and then a new bottle would appear, always Canadian Club. The key was always under the bottle. (He also had three guns, but those he never locked up. They hung over the fireplace. He took them down a couple of times a year, for target practice, deer hunting, and the annual cleaning and polishing. He handled them like infants.) We were sure the skin would be in the locked chest, maybe hidden beneath the wood planes and saws, but there was nothing there but a heap of tools, a couple of old ropes, and some half-decayed fishing buoys.

In the stories, male selkies are never tricked into human marriage. Instead, they're the swarthy lovers of bored or lonely human women. Male selkies walk as men for just long enough to woo some poor lady, to make her sweat and tremble, and then they walk out to sea, duck beneath a wave, and disappear, quickly as they came.

Human men can be so brutish and dull, smoking their pipes and drinking their whiskey, grabbing at you like they do. To gain a selkie lover, a human woman must cry into the ocean. A lonely woman, the stories say, need only cry seven tears, and a handsome selkie will find her. He'll swim right up to her ankles. No need to mend his pelt or rub his sore shoulders or wash his socks. He'll love you, but he'll be gone in a flash, long before romance or passion gives way to tedium or servitude.

It was our mother who taught us to swim. She waded into the lake with us before we could walk, holding us as we rested on our backs, close to her body. She murmured to us, and then, on a count of three, ducked beneath the surface, taking us along, blowing noisy bubbles to show us how. She always laughed when she told this story. "You were so surprised when I dunked you!" she said. "You just stared!" Our cheeks puffed full of air, our eyes wide and terrified—and then she brought us back up, and we screamed. "It was good for your lungs," she said. "And anyway, you were barely out of the womb. Barely used to having lungs at all. That's the best time to learn to swim, before you forget how."

I don't remember those early swimming lessons. I don't remember learning to swim. It is as if I have always known how to move myself through the water, how to turn my head for a breath, or pause and kick my legs like an eggbeater, looking around, effortlessly afloat. (And though in my mother's stories, it seemed a cruel method, when Ben was born, I taught him just the same. I suppose because I have forgotten the cruelty of it, or the fear, and have instead my skill in the water, and the water has given me so many pleasures. Ben loved it, too.)

Our father never swam with us. He was a big man, sheepish and milk-mild, and that's what our mother called him: Milky. A pet name, but it was something she hated about him. She was always trying to get him riled. Teasing him. She wanted to see him stutter and flush. If he had ever, out of rage, thrown a dish, a hammer—even a pillow, for Pete's sake—she would have kissed him for it. "Have a spine," she would say, fed up with his passivity. She wanted heat and hunger, but doubted he had a carnivorous bone in his body.

He was always out on the water, pulling up fish. Sometimes he took me along. He knew his bait: night crawlers, flashing lures, bobbers, cut bait, alewives, herring, dough balls, spawn sacs. Silver scales, blue scales, gray and black. We spent forever waiting for a bite, and even then, we often lost the fish. And if we got it, we had to gut it, and cut off its head. The fish flopped across the bottom of the boat or on the ice, a writhing muscle. But soon the flops became feeble and the black eye clouded over. Scraping the scales seemed entirely unfair, like removing a sequined gown, chipping at mica, sweeping away the glitter. I liked eating fish, but I didn't enjoy catching them or watching them die. I definitely didn't want to kill them myself. I had no interest in slitting the belly and spilling their lunch, their eggs, their excrement into the bottom of the boat.

But how I loved the ice shanty! Built of scrap wood, it smelled of sawdust and cedar and paint. I loved sitting next to it with a little fire burning in a can raised up off the ice on a couple of bricks. Rubbing my hands together, quick and hot. Tart cider from the thermos. Exhaling the steam, I pretended I was a dragon. I watched the hole my father had drilled through the ice, the dark water, watching for the shape of a fish, the darting shadow. I imagined the fish down deep in the water looking up at the light fracturing the water above it. The hush of their water world, the muffled scuffing of boots on the ice overhead, the squeak of the augur, the occasional groan of the ice shifting. I studied the gray horizon where the pale ice met the darker gray sky, the shanties with their dashes of color like wounds or celebrations: red door, tin chimney, green ski-planks for dragging them from the shore. My father wore a wool cap the color of autumn leaves.

I've never understood why, in the stories, men hide their wives' skins instead of burning them. If you want to keep the woman you love, why would you keep that smelly old skin around? She's bound to find it. And when she does—and in every story, she does, packed away in the boathouse or the tackle box or picnic basket—you can be sure she'll be angry. She'll squeeze her way back into that old thing and be off. Why not burn it and be sure she'll never find it? Would she feel her skin burning? Is the skin always a part of her even when she isn't wearing it? Does she feel the flames like an amputee feels twinges in his missing arm? But then, maybe there are a bunch of selkies that never find their skins, that never become seals again. Maybe they've forgotten that they used to be sleek swimmers, blinking their wet eyes. Maybe we just don't hear those stories. Their husbands would tell them. Maybe, in her long years as a human, such a woman spends Saturday afternoons in the bath, then wraps herself tightly in towels or sheets, aching to feel the compression of her form, the containment of her messy human limbs, but never quite knows what's wrong, what's missing.

Their final spat was over ice skates. Mom wanted Dad to take her to a skating party in town. Every winter, our town flooded a section of the park next to City Hall and all season it was full of hockey games and children scooting along and sweethearts holding hands, skating in predictable circles. But our father didn't have skates. Nor did he want to go to the party. My mother brought him a pair of skates anyway. She brought them to the table, tied together and swinging, before she served us chocolate pudding. "Look what I found in town today. Just your size." All sing-song sweetness.

Elizabeth served the pudding in the cut-glass bowls. Our father ate with too much deliberation, too much silence. Finally, a quiet "Thank you, dear," and the spoon in the empty dish. He took it to the sink himself.

No ice skates hit the wall that night. Not even a plate or a spoon. I don't think he even raised his voice over it. He probably never tried the skates on. The party ticked closer: Thursday. Friday. On Saturday, he died.

Seals smell of fish, salt, seaweed, the dense muck of the lakeshore. I've never lived near the sea, but I know its smell. The terrible smell of babies being born, of blood and piss and feces. And babies are like seals anyway, like selkies swimming free, just barely human, blinking their new eyes in the light, leaving their fins behind, learning to breathe through their mouth and nose, kicking and barking and crying their saltwater tears. In some way, we are all related to the seals. Or at least to the sea. But Elizabeth and I had it wrong. If we had selkie blood, it came from our father. It was our father who wanted to leave his human form behind.

It was my father that taught me that four inches is the thinnest ice safe for fishing. He had lived in Tonch Lake all his life. He knew the ice, the lake, the fickleness of winter. People blamed it on the fog. They said he must have gotten disoriented. They said it was an accident. But the ice he went through that day was no more than two-and-a-half inches at its thickest. *Rotten ice*, he would have called it. Honeycombed. Only an inch thick some places.

The rescuers were local men, neighbors, who found the place where my father had broken the ice and fallen through, not far from shore. It was early on Sunday by then, and the lake had refrozen during the night, but the recent break was evident. Chunks of ice were scattered across the surface around the scar. *He fought,* they said, nodding, so certain. Elizabeth and I stood beside our mother, holding hands, while the men hacked through the ice. There was no dragging of hooks through the muck, no dynamiting the ice as they had for Fred Huggins only a month earlier. No hauling up boots and tin cans and rusted wheels.

He was on his back, not five feet from the place he had gone through, still wearing his fur-lined parka. They pulled him out with a set of slender metal jaws. His skin was gray. When I think of him, his face is always pressed against the underside of the ice while the air runs out of him, like a child, or a dog, with his nose against a window.

Our mother did not cry, but she dropped my hand and pulled her coat tight around her throat. When Elizabeth tried to hug her, she shrugged it off and walked away. The rescue crew loaded his body onto a sled and wrapped him in woolen blankets as if he still had use for warmth. After they had taken him away, one last man asked us if were okay, if he could help. No, we said. There was nothing. "Don't stay out here too long," he said. "Take care of each other. Take care of your mother." He put his hand out to shake ours, such a formal gesture, but we shook, and then he turned and left us there.

I have tried to understand how easily water takes a life. Intellectually, I know that even if I could force all the air from my lungs and keep swimming, my trachea would collapse from the pressure. If the water was cold enough, I'd shiver until I felt I was burning. My mouth would open, and my throat would open, and my lungs, a vacuum, would accept all the water rushing in. But it never feels true. I wonder if that was how it was for my father—if he couldn't quite believe that the water would kill him, or if he couldn't imagine that drowning would hurt, that water could enact violence. All that silence and drift, a little sunlight shining through the blue, and your body so wonderfully weightless, or nearly so, and your limbs rising, your hair a halo of tendrils lifting like seaweed, the bubbles sparkling from your mouth to the ice above. I know, *I know*, that the noise would come—the surging blood, the collapsing lungs, the sounds of the body destroyed. And then, when I could no longer hear it, the real silence would begin.

My mother, sister, and I moved into town where we lived above a dry goods store. My mother never remarried. She was twice proposed to by local widowers, and she turned them both down—outrageous, according to the local gossip. A single woman, a widow with two daughters? Where did she get the nerve? Mr. Abernathy was a *decent, hardworking man*, and Mr. Krause was even handsome. Who was she to turn them down? But she said they offered security, not love. And she was secure enough. She liked teaching and planned to keep at it until she died. And Elizabeth and I had everything we needed, didn't we?

The truth is, Mr. Abernathy and Mr. Krause were too timid for her. My mother was an unusual combination of romance and pragmatism. The man had to be bold, earn a decent living, and offer her something she hadn't already experienced with my father. She always said a man who really knew what he wanted would make her weak in the knees.

"Your father had the most delicate ears," she said once, sighing a little, maybe a year after his death. It was the most tender thing she ever said about my father, and somehow, I understood that she had loved him after all. But I have long since given up any claim that I understand how love works between other people—the magic of each story, the measure of its thickness, the mystery of its melting point, the pallor and silence with which it thins.

HONEYMOON
Frances
Lake Mazinaw, 1902

For two days, I have been Frances Bell, a more solid name than Frances Anthony, although I always liked Frances Anthony for its lilt and assonance. I am a little sorry to part with it. The lake where we are honeymooning—a few days of camping—also has multiple names. Some call it Mazinaw or Massanoga, its older and more sacred name, the one given by its first people. Cliff simply calls it "the lake." But when it first came into view, cold and glistening among trees, I shouted across the water, and my voice returned to me from the rock, and so I called it *Bon Echo*. Naming is a way of claiming a thing, a way of knowing it, and so I have made it—just a little—mine.

Cliff says God had a plan for us to find each other, but I do not believe in true love, nor in fate, nor singularity, nor soulmates. I don't think Clifford and I were born for each other. We are not two halves of a whole. God did not plan for us to find each other, out of all the people in the world, but I am happy that we did. I love him nevertheless.

In fact, I think love that is built and deliberate is superior to that mythical, fated love. Fate is easy. Nothing can break or thwart it. If love is fated, it will continue no matter how one bumbles. If it breaks or disintegrates, it must not have been fated after all. Fated lovers are easily excused, but they are also helpless.

As I see it, we are sculptors chiseling a block of marble, finding the natural contours and helping a form emerge. And if we break the rock— say we chisel at the wrong angle—we will make the best of what remains. We will make a new form. We'll sand and polish until we find the heart of this rock.

Through the trees, the face of the granite cliff glows in the setting sun. It is this escarpment that has drawn people to the lake for hundreds of years. The narrow waterway opens onto the stillest lake I have ever seen, and there it is: the rock wall that rises 100 meters from the surface, face bright as a coin, and looking twice as tall because of its perfect reflection. Cliff stops paddling, and I feel the canoe drift off-course. I lay my paddle across the gunnels.

"Hellooo!" Clifford shouts, and his voice bounces off the rock face and returns to us. "I'm pretty sure God made this place to teach us humans humility," he says.

I nod, but the rock and the echo do not make me feel humble. They make me feel grateful and awed. Cliff and I are the only people here now, but so many have been here, on this quiet lake before me. They, too, shouted, and listened to their voices echoing back. It is as if, in the echo of my voice, I hear theirs, too.

Clifford has been coming to the lake for a few years. Three summers ago, when he was recovering from typhoid fever, he spent a season camping with his uncle, eating wild berries and game, fishing and praying. He says he couldn't have recovered without it. It is a holy place for him. But despite how small I feel beside the rock wall, it makes me feel powerful. I want to touch it, to run my hands across it.

We paddle for a while, crossing the lake, and as we near it, I can see that it is scraped and smeared with pictographs and pitted with holes.

"The holes are plugged with sap," Clifford explains. "It's an offering. Usually to Nanabush, the Ojibwe trickster. But this place is sacred to many people."

"Hello!" I call, tentatively. Then, louder. "Hellooo! I am Frances! Bell!" My voice is everywhere—in the cedars and the water and the clouds and the sap. It vibrates through the paddle in my hand. I laugh, and that comes back to us, too. There is laughter everywhere. I am laughing with all the people who have ever been here. We will never know each other, but we are laughing together anyway.

But when the echo fades, Clifford seems far away, as if the sound of my voice has stretched our canoe like chewing gum, as if the vibrations have pulled us apart.

When we were girls, Elizabeth and I would sing a song while we spun the jump rope:

> *Thistle, pickle, butter brickle*
> *Life is short and love is fickle*
> *Marry not for swoons nor honey*
> *Wait for one with bread and money!*

But the thing was, the song worked just fine if we reversed it, too:

> *Marry not for bread nor money*
> *Wait for kisses, swoons, and honey!*

Supposing one takes her love advice from jump rope songs, it was all rather confusing. I think that I have married in part for children, and in part for adventure. I was restless. I was sick of teaching other peoples' children.

While Clifford pitches the tent, I begin building a campfire. It has been years since I have built one, but my father taught Elizabeth and me when we were young and allowed us to build campfires on the shore near our house. We'd stand around the flames, poking them with long sticks and watching the sparks spiral up into the night. I build a tipi of sticks, leaning them carefully together. Cliff sets an armload of wood beside me and stands there, head cocked to the side, lips pursed.

"What is it?" I say, looking up. He takes off his glasses and polishes them on the handkerchief he always keeps in his breast pocket. "What's the matter?"

"It's too narrow," he says. "It won't burn well."

I strike a match and hold it to the structure to prove him wrong, but the flames won't catch or keep. A cloud of white smoke rises, as if the wood is wet. No flames.

"It needs more oxygen," Cliff says. The sticks smolder and die. I get up from the ground and kick the structure over. I leave him to the build the fire, stomping into the woods, presumably to gather wood, but really because I am angry.

He can be so arrogant. And all my life I will have to put up with his smugness. He will take over everything, anything I try to do.

Back at the campsite, I drop an armload of wood from standing height. I am sweaty and scratched. Cliff looks up at me with surprise. He has a little fire burning and is feeding twigs slowly into the flame. I stand with my hands on my hips.

He gets up and walks to the edge of the lake, where he dips his bandana in the water. When he returns, he raises the wet fabric to my face, and I let him wipe away a beaded line of blood that is crusted across my cheek where a stick scratched me in my anger. He presses the cold cloth to my forehead, my closed eyes. He pulls me close, but I stand stiffly, my hands at my sides, still angry. The lake laps at the shore and the fire crackles.

I give in, put my arms around him, my cheek against his warm shoulder. I imagine my anger drifting off like the smoke. It feels good to surrender.

I would be glad to stop thinking so much of love, to stop waiting to find out what it is and how it will go. I want it to run under everything silently, like a thawed creek flowing beneath snow. It could be the base of everything, but unseen and unheard.

The campfire almost dead, we lay side by side, looking at the moon. Cliff says it will be full tomorrow night. The stars are barely visible in its glow.

"A full moon is the saddest moon," I say. "At its fullest, there's nothing left for it to do but wane."

"But it grows again," Cliff says. "It's just a cycle. And a full moon is gorgeous."

"I don't know." I sigh. "It is beautiful, but that's part of why it's so sad. I feel the same way about the summer solstice. Finally, such long, perfect days. But I wake up so early. And all that light makes me a little crazy. Restless. And the corn is growing, and the kids are all running around barefoot and wild. It's the best part of the year, but it just means winter is coming. That we've reached it—the day we've been waiting for. And once you reach it, it's gone."

He takes my hand and pulls it to his heart and holds it there. "My darling pessimist!" he says. "We aren't there yet! We're only just on our way. The pinnacle is still such a long way off."

I close my eyes and find that the moonlight is bright enough to make my eyelids glow a little red. A breeze moves the leaves against each other, a constant rustling. A few frogs sing at the edge of the lake.

When my father died, I thought I would be sad forever. And then, when I found that the sadness had lifted, I thought that I would never feel such sadness again. That I had triumphed over despair. I thought that I would be joyful forever, just to be free of that deep sadness. But we have no idea what pain will strike us. And how it will fade again. There will always be new grief, and each time it will be the worst thing. But for now, we are here, Clifford and I, together, in love.

What will it be—this marriage, this life? A honeymoon is the fullest moon, oozing and sweet as an August pear, ready for harvest or sugary rot.

The night is too warm and bright for sleep. Clifford rubs the skin between my thumb and forefinger, the place my mother always said to rub if I had a headache, though she never offered to rub it for me. He tells me an Ojibwe story about a great flood and a muskrat that dives down to the bottom of the endless water just to get a little mud. The world was built again on that gob of mud, he says. The mosquitoes continue to buzz around us despite the smoke from our fire.

We paddle slowly to the middle of the lake, following the path of light laid across the water by the moon. In the middle, we stop paddling and drift across the dark water, saying nothing, listening to the water lap at the boat, the sound of frogs and crickets faded this far from the shore. I can't imagine loving Cliff less than I do now. I can't imagine loving him more.

My parents bit at each other like gnats. Elizabeth, who has been married some years now—loves quietly. She takes her husband for granted. They're busy running their farm, and it seems that love is irrelevant to them. Maybe this is the goal of marriage: to love without thinking about it. If one has to think about it too much, the work is too hard?

We have been naked together only once—last night—and it was very dark in our hotel bed. Will I someday know Cliff's body almost as well as I know my own?

Let the bees buzz around the oozing pear, taking its sugar for their honey. Does it work that way? Or do bees only take pollen from flowers, miraculously transforming powder into liquid sugar? I don't know, but the bees always hover around the watermelon and lemonade at picnics. I was once stung on the lip while drinking lemonade. So the bees must love something about a ripe pear.

I slide my paddle beneath my seat in the canoe and kneel on the bottom of the boat. I put my hands out to steady myself, but when I stand, I do a clumsy half-dive, half-somersault into the water.

Cliff shouts and scrambles to get his paddle into the water to rescue me.

"Just a little swim!" I say, rolling onto my back. "I'm fine. I'm completely fine."

I tread water while I unbutton my canvas shirt, which is suddenly so stiff and cumbersome. I fling it over the edge of the boat and peel off my trousers and socks. I float on my back for a while, looking down at my white brassiere that floats like blossoms on the surface of the lake. I flex my pale feet so my toes stick out of the water. I kick a little, frothing the water, feeling the bubbles fizz against my skin. I take a breath and then force myself under, letting the air leak from my lungs, a stream of bubbles rising as I sink.

I am a stone.

I open my eyes, and even in the dark, I can see the bubbles sparkling upwards toward the pale bottom of the canoe.

I am the muskrat, diving for mud to rebuild the world.

But my lungs begin to burn, and I kick to the surface with a gasp.

"I was about to go in after you," Clifford says. He helps me climb back into the boat—no small feat. The canoe tips wildly and water spills into it. I drag myself the rest of the way into the boat, panting and exhilarated and freezing. Cliff unbuttons his shirt so I can wear it. I run my hand over his chest at the V-neck of his undershirt, feeling the coarse hair.

"It's wonderful down there," I say. "You should try it. No bugs. I promise I won't paddle off and leave you."

He shakes his head and adjusts his shirt over my shoulders, pulling it around me like a blanket.

"Not tonight," he says. He shakes his head and laughs. He runs his hands quickly over my skin, rubbing it to warm me.

Let the bees harvest this pear and transform it into other sweetness, transpose it into a sweetness that does not rot, but fuels other bees, a sweetness that feeds the hive.

But I also want to taste the pear while I can.

TOOTH STORY:
FRANCES' RENEGADE

In the first years after their marriage, Frances and Clifford returned to the Bell family farm every July for the first hay mowing of the season. More than the haying, though, it was the annual Bell family reunion. The hay was mowed and dried and baled, and then there was a weekend of croquet and sack races, roast corn and pig and marshmallows. My cousins, I've been told, loved my Dad, who was the reigning watermelon eating champion for seven years running. It's strange for me to imagine my father gorging himself on slice after slice of watermelon, the juice running down his forearms, dripping from his chin. The man I knew as my father was fastidious. He would never be so undignified as to gorge himself, to let his hands and face get sticky. His oldest nephew beat him two years before I was born, when the nephew was 13, but my uncles remembered the days when Clifford, my father, their second-youngest brother, had been a different man, a messy, hungry one.

All of Clifford's brothers had children. Even the youngest had two before I came along, and so summer visits meant questions from the aunts, and from Clifford's mother: *When are you two going to add to the family line? Isn't it time for a Clifford Junior? A little Francie? Are you ever going to give me another grandchild?* Frances dreaded it. Already after the second year, she had begun to think that she and Clifford might not have a child after all, that they might not be able to. Had typhoid damaged him beyond repair? But then, maybe the problem was hers? Perhaps she was not meant to be a mother. Perhaps God had something else in mind for them. She loved the nieces and nephews, but the children's voices had begun to seem shrill, and she let their shrieks linger in her ears. She noted their fights and temper tantrums. She remembered how she had not liked teaching, and wondered if maybe she disliked children in general. And finally, after four years, the questions stopped. She would be Aunt Frances, it seemed, but never Mama, never a mother.

And then, one September afternoon, when she was pulling weeds from the garden, she was laid low by intense stomach pain. Cliff came home to find the garden half-weeded, the tools scattered. The sun was still high, but he found her in bed sweating. He called Dr. Ellis, who arrived at the house promptly.

"Probably nothing serious," the doctor said, pressing his fingers gently into her belly. "But I'll have to take a closer look." He spoke of tubal pregnancy, of cysts, fibroids, tumors. He made an appointment for her at the hospital for the next day.

She felt unclean, broken. All her life she had been so healthy, so strong. Only a month-and-a-half ago she had baled hay alongside the men. Let the other women serve the lemonade. But this—her inability to have a child, and now the thought that her insides were riddled with bumps, curdled with growths—she felt like a monster. Plus, she was scared. But Doc Ellis held her hand and counted backward with her: *Ten. Nine. Eight. Seven. Six. Five*... the anesthesia did its job by four. The world faded to shadows: bean pickers bending in a field, leaves fluttering across the sun.

It was a cyst, Doc Ellis explained afterward. A sort of tumor after all, but lucky for her, it was a harmless one. Painful, yes, but nothing was wrong with her. Nothing at all. Nothing serious. He had removed one of her ovaries, but she could still have a child, he explained. In fact, perhaps getting rid of the one would help the other to do its job.

A *teratoma*, he said, from the Greek, meaning "monstrous tumor." A bit unsettling, he said. He held up a small jar. Inside it, she saw a few hairs wrapped around something white, like a bit of chicken cartilage.

"Ugh," she said. "What is it?"

He turned the jar around for her, held it closer to her face.

"A tooth!" he said. He laughed. "Quite a little miracle! A tooth inside the dentist's wife! It was inside your tumor. I'd say it's confirmation that the two of you were meant to be."

It was disgusting, but she took the jar from him and looked closer.

"Teratoma can contain other things as well," the doctor went on. "Fluid, bone, liver or lung tissue, and on rare occasion, even an eye or a little hand. They can be found anywhere in the body, but usually they're in the ovaries—like yours—or in the testes, or even the brain. Most people never even know they have one. They're often found by accident because of some other problem, some other surgery. Or even after death. But the good thing is that they're usually benign. There's nothing wrong with you, Mrs. Bell. You'll be healed up in no time and ready to go."

My God, it was revolting. As if a child had tried to grow there, and gone completely wrong.

"Was it a baby?" she asked. "Before?"

He assured her it was not and had never been a fetus. She had probably housed that bit of tissue and tooth her entire life, since she was an infant herself. "Just some confused cells," he said. "Cells in the wrong place. Although we don't know much about them, to be honest. A medical oddity. But quite harmless. Some people like to keep them. Would you?"

She surprised herself by saying yes.

She called it her renegade. Her wild tooth. A tooth like a beansprout. A tooth like an idea getting ready to grow.

"A terrible idea," Cliff said. He would hardly look at the thing, and while she found it fascinating, she couldn't blame him. It was what she imagined would happen if a person squashed down her deepest, darkest desires or her worst sins: they would grow like this, into a tooth of loathing. Her envy of other people's children, for example. Her anger or rage or lust. She was lucky, then, that hers had been removed. The seed of her bitterness was gone. She had a clean start. She never kept the teratoma with the rest of the collection, but stored the little jar in the back of a drawer, where the glass grew yellow over the years.

THE LEOPARD FROG

Frances

Lake Mazinaw, Ontario

Amphibian is a word from the Greek *amphibios:* both kinds of life, double life. Living both in water and on land, a frog is equal parts swimmer and hopper. It breathes in air and in water. It has nostrils and lungs strikingly similar to those of a human, but it also breathes through its skin, osmotically exchanging carbon dioxide for oxygen.

At the lake, frogs sang every night. In the afternoon, they were quiet because they were submerged or swimming, keeping cool in water or mud. But at night their voices were our chorus, the slow creaks overlapping like ripples on water. A single bass voice would emerge from the masses and then submerge again, emerge and submerge. I walked with Ben to the edge of the lake, his small hand clammy in mine. We sat on the pier and listened to the rusty hinges of frogs' songs.

A child that dies young is a perfect child, uncompromised by his inevitable mistakes. He hasn't hurt anyone yet. Not seriously. Not wittingly. The wounds inflicted by a child are forgivable accidents of judgment. He doesn't know better. Time bleaches his selfishness. His failures fade to quiet bones. Memory sculpts his recessed chin to perfection, muffles his tantrums to sleepy kicks and tangled hair, polishes his flushed cheeks to a July-ripe, sun-warmed peach. Woken from a nap, Ben always smelled like hot sugar.

A frog's eyes are situated on the sides of its head. They have excellent peripheral vision. To catch a frog, you must grab it firmly from behind. Close your hand over its bulging lungs, its folded legs. Feel its slick, cool skin, coated in mucus. Let its nose and eyes stick out the front of your fist, between your index finger and your thumb, so it can breathe, so it can see. Hold tight. Feel its lungs strain, its heart beat faster.

When Ben was angry, he narrowed his eyes, and I would laugh at him. "I'm serious," he would say. "It's not funny." His father never laughed, but I couldn't help it. When he was studying something, peering through his magnifying glass or reading a book, his eyes were placid and wide, almost vacant. When he slept, I watched his eyelids twitch. I imagined the world of fish and flora through which he was wandering. An exhibit of chicken eggs, arranged from smallest to largest, speckled and plain, white and gray and brown and green. A treehouse full of books and animals, praying mantises and squirrels and the dog we had refused him.

If you open your hand and let the frog sit on your flat palm, it will jump. You can hold it by the legs, by the ankles, like the tiger toe in eeny-meeny-miny-moe, and it will stretch from your hand and swim through air. Inspect its circular brown spots, green belly, pale throat. Four toes on its forelimbs and five on its hindlimbs. Let it go. Watch it swim deeper through the water until it disappears.

There was a girl at the lake his last summer. Eleven years old, the same age as Ben. Emily taught him the difference between deciduous and coniferous trees. *Deciduous* was the word Clifford used to describe Ben's baby teeth, what others call "milk teeth," the little pearls a child trades with the tooth mouse for a penny. Ben wanted to know if leaves were like teeth, if they were replaced by bigger, stronger leaves the next year.

We looked the word up—it means "fall." And so he thought of teeth as leaves, molting and drifting. And I thought of children's teeth as more delicate than I had before, something like fish scales.

On the porch, Ben and Emily ate sandwiches I made for them. They argued about which was the more beautiful flower, trillium or lady slipper.

"Mom, what do you think?" Ben asked, looking for a tie-breaker. I agreed with Emily: the three drooping white petals of the trillium are the loveliest of that forest. They are humble flowers. The puffy yellow lady slipper has always looked carnivorous to me, as do all orchids, with their thick petals and heavy heads, their stamens extruding like sickly fangs. The lady slipper droops like a blister, like the distended throat of a bullfrog. It looks swollen and poisonous, like a goiter.

Clifford always said that it was a boy's job to learn the lessons of the natural world. If he is lucky enough to have both the time and the mind for studying, he had best be serious about it. Ben made it his business to study echoes every time he stepped onto the porch. He cupped his hands around his mouth and shouted across the lake to the cliff. "Yooooo-hoo! Bonjour, Echo! Bonjour, Mama! Bonjour, Emileeee!" The echo never failed, a playful ghost sending his words back to him.

You will need:

- One medium- to large-sized frog (A small frog will make your cutting and parsing tasks more difficult. Viscera are more easily discerned in a larger specimen, and there is more room to navigate your scalpel. *Rana Pipiens*, the Leopard Frog, is a fairly large species [5-7-inch torso], and they are plentiful in the northern U.S. and southern Canada.)
- 15-20 pins
- A scalpel or small, delicate scissors
- A probe or fine-tipped awl
- Tweezers

- A dissection tray (A true dissection tray is coated with a bed of wax so that you can insert the pins. A corkboard will also work, but it will not be as easily washed clean after the dissection.)

Ben had a science book full of diagrams and instructions for experiments. He and Emily smeared their fingertips with petroleum jelly and pressed them to the side of a jar, then dusted them with flour to study their prints. I helped them make pink dye from beet juice, and they dyed old white pillowcases. Ben cut his into two heart-shaped pieces and sewed them clumsily together. I showed him how to turn the heart inside out, stuff it with cotton, and close the final seam.

Chloroform is the best way to kill a frog for dissection because it leaves the body soft, the skin, skeleton, and skull intact. The frog dies painlessly, as if falling into a deep and gentle sleep. It is, however, difficult to measure a dose of chloroform; the gas is dangerously imprecise.

That day, we killed the frog, instead of watching it swim. That day, Ben dampened a cotton ball with chloroform and dropped it into the jar. Screwed the lid tight. I didn't watch, but Ben and Emily did, on either side of the jar, eyes wide.

When captured, the leopard frog sometimes lets out a shrill, scream-like sound.

A few feeble kicks. A half-hearted attempt to scale the steep sides of the jar, toes spread wide, it slides back to the bottom. Like a small rock, it sleeps.

Is the frog male or female? A frog's sex organs, either testes or ovaries, are bean shaped and situated near the kidneys, deep within the frog's torso, nestled under loops of intestines. While a frog's body shares many anatomical traits with a human body, the sex organs are distinctly different. Frog eggs travel a winding, threadlike tube through the female's body, and she releases them into the water. A pond becomes the womb, the site of fertilization and growth, keeping the eggs wet and floating. An egg morphs into a tadpole. First, the egg grows a tail, then tiny legs and eyes and organs. The creature begins its double life, breathing both on land and in water, living between worlds.

Dorsal side: spotted. Brown on dark green.
Ventral side: smooth. Very pale green. Solid colored.
Length: 9.5 cm from nostrils to cloaca.
(*Cloaca*: a small slit opening in the anterior of the frog through which waste, sperm, or eggs leave the body.)

The diagram showed the places he should cut: a long slice from throat to crotch, and two perpendicular cuts, armpit-to-armpit and hip-to-hip. Ben teased the skin from the muscle, pulled the skin flaps open, and Emily pinned them to the corkboard. He pulled back the muscle (again, Emily pinned) so they could view the organs: stomach, lungs, three-chambered heart.

Ben peered into the body of the frog, splayed open on the corkboard. "Have a look, Mom?" He offered the magnifying glass, polished clean. He kept it in a box, wrapped in chamois. "You can see the liver here." He nudged it with the tip of his scalpel. "These triangular things. And the stomach is this tube. I'll cut it open. Maybe there's a fly in there or something." He consulted his book. "This is the small intestine." He prodded a tangle of small coils. "I'm going to remove the digestive system so we can see the lungs and the heart." He picked at the frog with his scalpel. "I wish that I could breathe through my skin. That's why a frog only needs three chambers in its heart, you know. Because it processes gasses through its skin. Oxygen in. Carbon dioxide out."

In salt water and waste Ben had breathed within me, floated in me, breathed through what would one day be his skin. But he led no double life. Like a tadpole, not a frog. He couldn't have lived outside me then, couldn't have breathed air, barely had lungs, a nose or mouth.

"What do you think our skin does, besides protect our muscles and organs?" I asked.

(What does our skin do besides contain us? Besides define the borders of our bodies?)

"That's a lot," Ben said. "What if we didn't have skin? We'd be gooey and bloody. We'd be raw meat."

Emily read aloud. "The skin is the body's largest organ. Among other things, it senses pain, which communicates to the brain that the body is vulnerable to danger. The skin can serve as a warning system. Skin also regulates temperature," she added. "It produces sweat to cool us, or shivers to warm us."

But human skin doesn't breathe. What is it like—what does it mean—to breathe through skin? Skin cells swell when they're well hydrated, but human skin is waterproof, too. Such a strange coat we wear.

Ben unpinned one hind leg so he could move it and watch the knee joint. Emily unpinned the other. Together, giggling, they worked the legs as if the frog were swimming a lazy backstroke.

A frog's ear has no external structure. Two ridges on the sides of its head. Two holes. Two tympanic membranes. A higher voice vibrates the tympanum more rapidly.

In the woods, Ben and Emily compared the fascicles of pine needles. Bundles of two. Bundles of five. White pine. Norway pine. Red pine. Jack pine.

I did not watch them all the time. It was safe there, at the lake. There were artists and writers working in their nooks, their cabins, at the water's edge. The lake itself was the greatest danger, but they were both strong swimmers.

It was an experiment. Ben said. When he came running, and when he told me about it later. *An experiment.*

Emily took the pins out. Ben closed the flaps of skin and muscle. He lifted the frog from the corkboard.

Using your scissors or scalpel, slice the jawbone at the corners on both sides of the mouth. This will require some pressure: you're cutting through bone. Now you can open the frog's mouth wide. You should be able to examine the nostrils on the roof of the mouth, the throat, and esophagus.

They were not very scientific about it—the experiment. They took a scarf from the hook in my bathroom—pale blue silk. The chloroform was in a brown glass bottle. Clifford had given it to them so they could collect insects and small animals for dissection.

Lift the tongue with the tip of your blade. Note how it is attached at the front of the mouth instead of at the throat. The tongue of a frog is magical—a long, flickery tool for snatching insects from the air midflight.

Pine needles. Midden. Loose scales of last season's pinecones. Ben tied Emily's hands loosely in her lap, with a double wrap of rope borrowed from the boathouse. He tied the damp scarf over her mouth and nose. *Breathe deeply.*

A whisper vibrates the tympanum so slightly. The tiny hairs of the inner ear shiver.

I have imagined them, two children in the woods, alone. The blue scarf, the chloroform. They were young, but not that young. Over and over, I have imagined it: Emily closes her eyes. *You are getting sleepy.* Ben strokes her hair. *So sleepy.*

Cut into the skin of the frog's inner thigh. With tweezers, pull the skin back, peeling it down to the knee so that you can explore the muscles of the frog's leg.

Ben unties the blue scarf, slides it away and touches her face. Her mouth
is open. Her breath against his cheek. He unbuttons a vertical line of
buttons, touches the perpendicular wave of her collarbone. Peels back
the flaps of her dress—not muscle, not skin—dissecting the smooth,
washed-soft cotton. Her skin is dry and powdery. Three moles in line
on her sternum, like spots on dice. Two small pink nipples, not so different from his own. His fingers are the scalpel, the tips of the tweezers.
He draws a line from hip to hip along the elastic band of her underwear.
Runs the palm of his hand across her stomach. Counts her ribs.

When Ben was four, I found him in a closet with the neighbor boy, also
four. I reached for a tablecloth on a high shelf and heard them laughing. They were naked and crouching behind a row of winter coats. The
neighbor boy clutched a toy truck. I pulled them out by their wrists,
one at a time, smacked their bottoms. My palm stung. *Where are your
clothes?* The neighbor boy bubbled with high-pitched giggles. He zig-
zagged through the kitchen, a wild animal, so small and pink and laughing. But Ben sat on the floor at my feet. Ben cried.

Her breath against his cheek. *Emily,* he said, insistently, but she didn't wake.
A line of sweat on her forehead. Ben held her hand, rubbed at it anxiously.

Unpin the frog and turn it dorsal side up. Cut a small rectangle in the
skin on top of its head, beginning near the nose, between the eyes.

A child lives a double life. An adult body still houses a child.
    Two children, a boy and a girl, each with bony shoulders, and nearly
identical flat chests. They measure themselves against each other, back
to back. Each to the other, they press their matching spines. They play
each other's like piano keys.
    In the forest, they find a hoof and a deer spine, picked clean, the
vertebrae in a line like a puzzle, a row of dominoes set to clatter. So like
their own knuckled spines.

They open their mouths. Press each other's tongue with a depressor stolen from Clifford's leather bag. *Say ahhh.* They inspect the blooming garden of tastebuds, the dark tunnel of the other's throat. *Ahhh.*

The leopard frog will eat anything it can swallow: ants, bottle flies, spiders, beetles. The tongue unfurls, catches its prey, then flings the morsel into the throat.

Her shallow breath against his cheek. *Emily,* he says. More loudly: *Emily.*

Remove a patch of skin from the skull to make a portal through which you can remove the brain, but don't press too hard or cut too deep. Avoid slicing into the brain so that you can examine it whole.

There was to be a talk that evening at the lodge. A watercolor artist would discuss his techniques and show his work. I wanted Ben and Emily to help move chairs around in the living room so there would be room for more people to sit. I called to them from the back porch.

Possible Effects of Chloroform on Human Beings (when used as an anesthetic or to induce deep sleep)
1. Nausea and vomiting
2. Unconsciousness
3. Skin rash or lesions where skin has made contact with the liquid
4. Brain damage
5. Kidney and/or liver failure
6. Death

He came running from the woods, flushed and panicked. *It's Emily,* he said. *Please come.* Explaining something and pulling my hand, but I couldn't understand what it was. *An experiment. An experiment. Breathing too fast.*

When we got to her, she was awake and sweating. Her eyelids were heavy, but she sat up and smiled at us, a slow smile. She said she saw perfect things. *Tied to a clothes line. A cork jacket and a paddle. An upside-down bouquet. They danced with each other.* She sighed. *I have such an awful headache.* She lay back down.

Ben and I helped her back to the lodge. I gave her a glass of water with mint. She sat on the sofa and pressed a cold compress to her forehead. Her buttons were mismatched with their holes. *Let me help you.* One of her shoes was untied. I unbraided and re-braided her smooth hair.

We wanted to know what it was like. Ben said. *I was going to try it next, after she woke up.* He fluttered his hands as if there were something sticky on them.

Ben. Bring me the chloroform. A brown glass bottle. I poured it down the kitchen sink and rinsed it.

The frog was on the back porch, still pinned to the corkboard, drying. One forelimb was folded over the torso as if the frog was covering its own heart. It was brown now, the skin flaps brittle leaves. Nothing about it looked as if it had ever been alive.

I sent Emily home to her mother, who never came by, never said a word.

The next winter, Ben died from an infected root canal. Clifford and I returned to the lake only once. Emily was there, a few inches taller, her hair longer, but still stick straight, a gangly girl, only twelve. I watched her standing at the shoreline, skipping stones or sitting on the pier, but more often she was on the porch of her family cabin reading books.

Did it happen as I imagined? The unbuttoning. The finger as scalpel. Even if I asked her, she wouldn't know. She had not been conscious. Two children, alone in the woods. Each the other's specimen. Hers was the only female body he would know, lost in a chloroform dream. Her straight sternum, two pink nipples, twelve pairs of ribs, pale skin, her lungs inflating, deflating.

I paddled with her one afternoon, across the lake to the rock. We did not speak much, but she said that she missed Ben. That no one tested the echo anymore. We paddled close enough to the rock to inspect the pictographs. The gray rock is streaked red with iron that bleeds like an error, but some of the marks are animal shapes with backs like combs, with teeth, the hollow forms of beasts. And between them are small pocks of darkness, holes plugged with offerings of sap.

Emily leaned out of the canoe and pressed her mouth to a hole. She whispered something I could not hear, then turned to press her hands and her ear to the rock, as if to hear an answer whispered back. Maybe there were other voices caught there—ancient ricochets and murmurs that only she could hear.

Do I remember him inaccurately? Do I exaggerate his wit, his tenderness? He was incomplete. In remembering, I also create him; I fix him in my mind. A boy who lives refuses to be pinned down. He is not fixed in the silver of a photograph. But a boy who dies is unchanging.

In my memory, he is like a charcoal drawing—a few swift strokes, some color, the implication of volume, of moving fingers, each with a trimmed nail. Blond curls. One dimple. Small white teeth. The fine hairs upon his arms shine. On his knee is a faint scar, a kidney-shaped patch of nubbled skin—evidence that he learned to ride a bike, and that it was not easy. He ripped off the bandage and the surgical tape left an outline of gray gum. He picked at the scab. For days, he watched its perimeter shrink inward as it healed, like a lake evaporating in the desert. He inspected the visible pores with his magnifying glass, the stippled topography of the scar, one inch wide, curved below the inside of the right knee cap, two and a half inches long.

III.

DIFFERENT TYPES OF LIGHTNING

Frances
Cleveland, 1928

St. Stanislaus School for Backward Boys is home to 189 students, ages 7-21. Of these, 156 demonstrate marked abnormalities, including evidence of prenatal injury and/or prevalent Mongolism. 32 have been referred to St. Stan's for previous delinquency. The aim of our study is to illuminate the relationships between nutrition and backwardness, delinquency, physiology, physiognomy, dental health, etc.

"Monsters," says Father Reilly, the headmaster. He guides us through the kitchen where boys are peeling potatoes and washing dishes, into the sewing room where they are busy mending trousers and darning socks. He opens the door to a classroom so we can see the boys bent over their desks. He points them out, names them. The boys do not look up.

Henrik's chin is deeply recessed. John's juts out too far. Liam is handsome, with a wide, square jaw, but his eyes are squinty and he has the wildest, thickest eyebrows I have ever seen, making him look as if he is plotting something mischievous, or worse. Albert, one of the youngest, is only 7 years old, a Negro child with tiny ears too low on his head, and teeth like cypress knees.

"They were born this way," Father Reilly says. "Empty-headed. Or nearly. They lack sufficient brain tissue."

But Father Reilly loves the boys. At least the quiet ones, the ones that came to St. Stan's as babies or toddlers. "That one there," he says, pointing to a boy in the front row of desks, a little fat, with reddish hair and freckles, his head bent to his work. "James." The boy does not look up, though the room is quiet but for Father Reilly's voice. "His mother fed him what scraps she could find, but it was never enough. She was forced into prostitution, the only thing she had to sell. Left James at home with only his brother and sister, barely older than he was. It was his sister that brought him here. She was maybe thirteen herself. About a year ago now. He's a lucky one."

"All these boys are lucky now," says Cliff.

I suppose it's true, in a way, though "lucky" isn't a word I'd ever think to use to describe these children. They have food and clothing and beds and books and teachers. A warm, dry place to sleep each night. But most of them started out unlucky, fed on liquor and fried potatoes even before they were born. They didn't grow right. Not their feet from their ankles, not their brains in their skulls. It's hard to make up for such unluckiness at birth. James clutches his pencil as if he means to stab someone with it, his hand making its fierce and awkward way across the page.

Father Reilly tells us that a few of the boys are from wealthy families, but when they arrive at St. Stan's, they are dressed like everyone else, in white shirts with ties that arrive as donations in paper sacks and boxes. The sisters are excellent menders, and some of the boys also sew. The boys do the laundry and the pressing. Everyone wears black shoes, knickers with high socks, white button-down shirts. Often, the wealthy boys are forgotten by their families, although occasionally the school gets a large donation. "Guilt money," says Father Reilly. "Might as well call it indulgences." Parents rarely visit. Boys don't go home for Sunday suppers or Thanksgiving. Few even leave for Christmas. For most of them, St. Stanislaus will be home until they turn 19 or 20, when they finish their schooling. Then some will find jobs. Some will find another home. Some will move on to another institution, some other cubby for storing the feeble-minded or insane. Others will find their way to prison as soon as they get a chance.

Saint Stanislaus School for Backward Boys is all straight lines: windows, gables, floorboards, desks. Everything in rows and columns and grids. Even the winter sunlight is segmented by windowpanes, washing the place in rectangles that move slowly across the floorboards and walls. In the dining hall, Father Reilly explains how the boys sweep daily and wash the floors once a week. They polish them until they gleam. The scent of the polish makes me dizzy, but Henrik (club foot, severely recessed chin, imbecilic, busy polishing the floor) loves it. He mops vigorously, with his entire body, but pauses every few minutes to pull a damp rag from his back pocket, which he holds to his nose and inhales.

Nutrition shapes us even before we are born. With each generation and each so-called advance in food (canning, preservatives, uniformity of white bread) we degrade ourselves further, degrade our genes, our children, and our grandchildren.

Cliff tells me that much of the trouble for these boys began in their babyhood, or even earlier, with the poor nutrition of their mothers, or with the consumption of highly processed baby foods. He thinks poor nutrition could explain—at least partly—the rise in delinquency and criminal types. And so we will measure the boys' jaws, foreheads, and skulls. Cliff will photograph each boy straight-on and in profile. We'll make imprints of their dental arches. (We expect, as a rule, they'll be terribly crowded.)

To study the boys' diet, we take our meals with them. Cliff asks the school cook to write down the menus and recipes. "Every detail. If you butter the broccoli, I want to know about it." Meals are served on segmented plates. Fried beef (webbed with fat, sliced thinly but sufficient), peas from a can, potatoes (peeled and boiled, with salt and pepper, no butter), white bread. For dessert: strangely pale chocolate pudding. The boys adore gravy. Waiting in line, James whines for more of it until the cook threatens him with no lunch at all.

At the table next to ours, a boy finishes his meal and begins rolling his plate like a wheel across the surface of the table. Gravy and peas run onto the gleaming wood, and he plows the plate right through the mess, making engine noises. *Vroom!* One of the nuns gets up from her seat and takes the plate out of his hands, sets it firmly in front of the child. "Edmund," she addresses him. "We've been over this. A plate is not a toy." The boy studies the plate, wipes the back of his hand across his cheek. He nods solemnly. When the nun leaves him, he does not touch the plate, but begins pushing his fork across it, his quiet *vrooms* followed by *putt-putt-putts,* the fork moving in accord with the sounds. He is a small boy, certainly no more than seven years old.

The faces of these boys are notably narrower than their healthier, non-back-wards, non-delinquent counterparts. Likewise, dental arches and oral cavi-ties are smaller and shallower. (Note: Consult studies by Hooten, Petersen, etc.: facial structures offer evidence of personality type, delinquency, crimi-nality. How do these boys' facial structures align with Petersen's compilation on mental defectives, epileptics, etc.?)

After lunch, Father Reilly leads us to a drawing room, and one of the sisters brings tea with dark rye, butter, and marmalade. We ignore the marmalade. The crumbs from Clifford's toast collect on the napkin he has tucked into his collar. A bit of butter is smeared at the corner of his mouth.

He looks up from his notebook. "What would you say makes us distinct from animals? What makes us *human?* . . . It isn't manners. Not really. There are plenty of people without them, and they're certainly still *homo sapiens,* certainly human beings."

I propose that it is our thumbs. "Darwin says, quite rightly, that it is our thumbs that separate us from apes."

"But there are some primates have opposable thumbs," Cliff says.

But it's too simple anyway. Thumbs or not. That's not what makes us unique beings. I know that's not all of it. Cliff will want notes, so I push my tea aside, open a notebook, and begin to write.

What makes a human? I underline the question. Beneath it: *Neither manners nor opposable thumbs.*

"Our nesting instinct?" I propose, jotting it down. Cliff nods and purses his lips. His thinking look. I try again. "Our highly-developed sense of home?"

"Home?" he says.

"Mere shelter is not enough for humans. While a bear is happy with a cave, or a pig with a pen, maybe some soft straw to sleep in, people are always busy sweeping and bleaching and hammering and sanding. We hang curtains and paint our walls. We eat off porcelain plates…"

Nesting instinct. Sense of home.

"Some say it's writing," Cliff says. "Our ability to transmit knowledge across generations without even being there. Our ability to communicate using symbols."

Writing. Communication via symbols.

"Are there animals that use symbols?" I ask. It seems likely. "Perhaps, it is our belief in God. Or not *God,* exactly, but a higher power? Our insistence on a soul. Our *possession* of a soul."

"Yes," Clifford nods vigorously. "That's it! Our *beliefs*. Our *ability* to believe. Our souls. Our minds make us human. Our ability to conceive of God." He stands, scattering crumbs from his lap to the carpet, beginning to pace. "Everything circles through the mind."

"Like the earth around the sun," I say. He nods again.

In man, the predominate feature is mind. I underline it twice.

"And the mind," he continues. "The mind is shaped by what we eat. The *body* is shaped by what we eat. So, while the mind makes us human, *food* shapes our minds. Which means food is still the root of everything."

Food is the root. Food shapes our minds and bodies.

He sits again and spreads photographs across the table, forming a grid of faces. Front views, profile views, jaws that slope in or jut out. Dark skin. Pale skin. A boy with his hat pulled low. The same boy, bareheaded, hairline receding although he is only a child. Teeth that overlap. Mouths with missing teeth. Lips in sneers, in smiles. Bow lips and thin lips and furrowed lips. Hair slicked back or cropped close or falling over a brow. Each photo is small enough to pocket. I watch him study the faces, my pen poised for dictation, but for a long time, he says nothing.

Finally, he plucks a photo from the table. "This one," he says, holding it out to me. It's James, the boy with the mother who is a prostitute. "Breathes through his mouth. Very noisy. Sister Thomas tells me they have to position his head at a particular angle before he falls asleep, or he will wake himself choking. His right nostril is entirely occluded by tissue or bone structure."

I take the photo from the table and study it. James is wearing a dark woolen suit. His hair is cut too short, too severe. In the front view, his mouth hangs open.

"I want to stretch his maxillary arch," Clifford says. "To move the bones apart in order to open his nostrils. The proper amount of oxygen might encourage mental and physical development."

"How?" I ask.

"I'll put in an expandable brace. I don't know if it will work, but the boy's got little to lose."

He pushes his chair back again. "Let's find Father Reilly. I'd like to get started with the boy tomorrow," he says, standing. His shirt is untucked in the back, but I let it be and follow him out of the room.

Subject: James S.
- *Sixteen years old. Typical Mongoloid. Lethargic. Mouth-breather. Mentality of a 5-year-old. Genital development of an 8-year-old. Typical dental crowding. Mother was 48 at the time of his birth.*
- *Previous medical treatment has included use of cocaine and adrenaline to shrink the tissue occluding his nostrils (unsuccessful).*
- *Exhibits oral cavity features typical of Mongoloids. (Tongue too large for mouth in 70% of subjects examined.)*
- *Exhibits typical Mongoloid personality: docile, happy, tractable.*

Sister Thomas asks James to give us a tour of the garden. He holds my hand as we walk, towing me along the brick pathway, but he has no interest in Clifford, who must seem to him just another man with a notebook.

"Roses," James says. He points to a cluster of them, still tightly closed. "Lavender. See?" A spray of pale purple flowers. "Hullo, bees!" He shouts and waves at the hovering insects. I try to shoo them off, but James puts his hands out to them, extending his fingers like branches. "Bees are our friends, see?" His pose reminds me of St. Francis, calling to the birds, and I watch a bee buzz around his outstretched hands as if they're flowers.

"What's over there, James?" I ask, pointing to the other side of the garden.

"Hopscotch!" He pulls me along. The hopscotch squares are painted with thick yellow lines. His mouth is always open, like a door on a faulty hinge, making him look as if he is puzzled or awed. He throws the stone for me and waits for me to jump. Never mind my age, my creaky knees and curved spine. There is no arguing with him. I complete my turn and drop the stone into his hand. I click my heels together and salute him. "Aye-aye, sir!"

His laugh is clumsy and soft. All around us, bees kiss the flowers and sing like zippers. While I've never quite thought of bees as my friends, it is miraculous how they make honey from pollen.

Words used to describe the boys: morons, idiots, criminals, drunkards, racketeers, degenerates, imbeciles, abnormal, deformed, defective, backward, retarded, disturbed, disorganized, unsocial, insane, aggravated, injured, underdeveloped, vacantly staring, unfortunate, feeble-minded, infantile.

In the St. Stanislaus chapel, the walls are built from wide, vertical boards that seem to dampen sound. The chapel is blurry with light, and hushed, completely unlike our Methodist church on the other side of the city, which is dark and echoing, made entirely of stone. In St. Stan's, sun slants through yellow and red stained glass windows that depict the Passion of Christ. Sun shapes move slowly across the shoulders and hair of the boys in the pews in front of us, like blessing hands laid gently on their heads. Even the oldest boy, who is nineteen with a concave chest, is only a sickly bird of a boy. His shoulders are narrower than my own, and sharper. Here, in the chapel, the boys look vulnerable and delicate.

James sits in the front row but keeps turning to look at the boys behind him. The choir begins to sing. First, there are only the reedy voices of the youngest boys, but soon the older boys join in, their voices deeper and more resonant. A chord spreads like the whistle of a train, and the room is filled with thrumming song. I close my eyes and listen, the yellow sun glowing through my eyelids.

Procedure: Lateral movement of maxillary bones (1.5 inches in 30 days). Two false teeth (porcelain) added on a bridge appliance between subject's canines.

The procedure takes place at our house, upstairs, in one of Clifford's exam rooms. Cliff says it will take about two hours. He holds up a plaster mold of James' mouth, explaining the procedure to Sister Thomas, who brought James to us on the streetcar. The boy sits in the exam chair, feet not quite reaching the footrest. I bend to adjust it and he pats my hair. "Hello, Mrs. Frances."

Cliff's tools are lined up on the table beside the chair: paper surgical masks, bone saw, scalpels, sterilizing liquid, stretching apparatus. The plan is to cut into the roof of James' mouth and insert the apparatus, which will hold open a new space in his mouth. With increased flow of oxygen and blood, Cliff suspects James' circulation will improve, along with his hormone levels, but no one has ever tried anything like this before. During the surgery, James will be sedated. Blood and saliva will be suctioned out through a tube. Oxygen will reach his lungs through another tube that will be inserted down his throat after he is anesthetized. I will not stay to watch.

"To be sure, success isn't guaranteed here," Cliff says.

"Of course not," says Sister Thomas. "But it's only his mouth." She gathers herself, preparing to leave with me. "I don't know that you could make things worse for the boy."

I take James' hand and squeeze it.

"Everything will be fine, Mrs. Frances," he says. "Fine, fine, fine."

Downstairs, I put the kettle on for tea. Sister Thomas sits at the table, her Bible open before her, but she is not reading it.

"Dr. Bell isn't the first doctor to treat him, you know," she says.

"No?"

"Last year there was a doctor that used to visit St. Stan's once a week. He was concerned about James' breathing, too. He treated him with some sort of stimulant, something to clear his nasal passages. James was always full of energy after the treatments. But his nose became... I don't know... too sore and raw to continue. He got a lot of nosebleeds and headaches. He was so angry. Can you imagine? James? Angry?"

I shake my head.

"We finally asked the doctor to stop the treatments. But James didn't seem any different after that. The same wheezy breathing. He stopped being angry, though. That was a relief. And eventually the headaches and nosebleeds stopped."

I set a cup of tea on the table next to her Bible.

"I used to pray for his mother's forgiveness," the nun says. "But it was God that planted the boy within her. *Fearfully and wonderfully made.* She's not the one who needs to be forgiven."

"Who, then?" I ask, sitting down across from her. She takes the teacup between her hands. The tea's too hot to drink, but she holds the cup anyway, blowing on it, the steam rising into her face and clouding her glasses.

She shrugs. "He's only a boy," she says. "I think he'll always be a boy. Even if he outlives all of us, though Lord knows, that's doubtful. Maybe this is just how he's supposed to be. Or maybe he's meant to contribute some great knowledge to science. Something that will help others like him. Maybe that's what God intends for him."

I nod. James is sixteen, but he seems like a much younger child, too soft, too silly. Unable to control all of his muscles. When our Ben was only a couple of months old, he could already hold his head up on his own, and soon enough he could sit up and watch us working. There were rolls of fat beneath his chin and around his knees. But as he grew, he became lean.

James seems like he has never outgrown that softness and baby fat, like he is still learning to hold his head up. His face is pliable and uncontrolled, quick to smile, but often uncomposed, the jaw hanging open, the muscles slack.

I leave Sister Thomas with her bible and go into the yard to hang the wash. White clouds scoot across the sky. I take deep breaths, holding each one deliberately in my lungs, feeling grateful that I am able to breathe. Such a simple thing—it's so easy to take it for granted. I listen for doors opening and closing inside the house. I wait for voices, for signs that the procedure is over.

With movement of the maxillary bones comes new blood. New heat. New bone has filled the new space in James' mouth. There is new downward pressure on the pituitary gland—the captain of the ship, the pea in the prince. Thus, the circuit between gland and brain is finally complete. We are forcing open the central cavern of his mouth. His tongue now rests and spreads like a fat man, exhausted. It's as if we're winding his glandular clock. Perhaps the brain is like an electrical circuit, and by repositioning the wires within his head, the circuit will be complete, the wires will meet; the bulb that has remained dark so long will finally glow with light.

Sister Thomas brings James to us each Thursday afternoon. The two of them ride the streetcar from St. Stanislaus to our house. When they arrive, the nun is always laden with bags and boxes to complete her various errands—the post office, the market. She always seems harried, tiny gray curls sneaking out the edges of her wimple. She pushes James through the door ahead of her. James, on the other hand, is always placid and a little clumsy, like a kid goat, just tripping along.

"He seems more alert since the surgery," she says. "More confident. At least since his mouth healed up. Isn't that right, James?" The boy nods emphatically.

"My mouth doesn't hurt anymore. See." He opens his mouth for my inspection, then snaps it shut and marches across the room. He settles himself on a chair and begins unlacing his boots.

"No need to remove your shoes, dear," I say. He sits very straight on the chair, tracking the conversation between Sister Thomas and me as if it is a tennis match.

"I think you'll agree," she says. "He's like a new boy." She tucks her hair into her habit, smoothing the black cloth and adjusting her glasses.

I lead James to the exam room, where he hides behind the door to wait for Cliff. He places his finger on his lips. "Shhhh…" he hisses. "Don't tell that I'm here." I sit down and pretend to read a book, while James tries to stop giggling. When Cliff enters the room, James leaps from behind the door.

"Boo!" he shouts. He dissolves into giggles, doubling over and squealing. "Didn't I scare you!" He gasps. "Didn't I scare you, Dr. Bell!"

"You certainly did," Cliff says. "You'll have to be careful, or you'll give this old man a heart attack."

Cliff takes James' hand and presses it to his chest. "Can you feel my heart beating?" James' eyes are wide. "Would you like to listen to it?" Cliff asks, and James nods enthusiastically. Cliff takes the stethoscope from its hook on the wall and fits the earpieces into James' ears. He positions the bell over his own chest. "Do you hear it?" Cliff says quietly.

"I hear it!" James shouts. "I hear your heart!" Spit collects at the corners of his mouth. Cliff taps the rhythm of his heart on James' shoulder. For a minute, I imagine them as father and son.

Ben loved the stethoscope, too. I had forgotten, like I have forgotten so many things. He tried to hear the pulse of everything. He listened to my wrist. He pressed the stethoscope to the wall of Cliff's office and listened to him type. He listened to his own heart. He took it outside to listen for worms crawling through the soil. He was convinced that maybe worms had voices, that maybe he would overhear them talking to each other. That was probably when Cliff took the stethoscope away.

James has grown nearly two inches in eight weeks. Mustache and whiskers have sprouted. Notable genital growth. New body odor. Seems to be growing into quite a prankster.

James sits looking out the window, waiting for Sister Thomas to return. I pull a chair near to his and sit down.

"Lightning," he says, without looking at me. The sky is flat and overcast, but it isn't raining. No rain, no sun, no individual clouds, and certainly no lightning. Just flat gray.

"There's more lightning in summer, see," he says. "Sister Thomas says we can't go outside when there is lightning." He holds up his hand and begins listing types of lightning, folding one finger down for each type. "Sheet lightning. Cloud-to-ground lightning. Water lightning." When he runs out of fingers on one hand, he keeps listing, unfolding one finger at a time. There seem to be infinite varieties. "Finger lightning. Imaginary lightning. Eyelash lightning. Tree branch lightning. Old-lady-hair lightning…"

He is parroting someone, perhaps a lesson at school, or Sister Thomas, although she seems an unlikely source of information about lightning.

Types of lightning:
  (1) Intra-cloud-electricity: moves from one part of a cloud to another part of the same cloud.
  (2) Cloud-to-ground: a strike. Electricity moves out of the cloud, downward, to the ground, or to some object on the ground. (Tree, telephone pole, person out in the open.)
  (3) Cloud-to-cloud: Electricity stays high, but connects from one cloud to another.

Within these basic types, there is a variety of different appearances, including "bead," "ribboned," "sheet," "forked," "staccato," and "sympathetic." Most are self-explanatory by name.

I check a book out of the library, and on his next visit, he flips through it, moving his lips, pointing at pictures and words. His list had begun accurately enough, but I wonder where the invented types came from—if they were linked to lightning he has seen, or simply the words that came to mind.

I imagine James as a small cloud sending a bolt of electricity my way, and myself as another cloud, or maybe an object on the ground. I imagine us all as clouds, storing electricity, and when the charge within us is too great, we send it out, connecting to another cloud, or a tree, or to the ground, sometimes transferring our charge to someone or something else, sometimes neutralizing our charge with another's, sometimes setting the other afire, sometimes destroying them entirely.

Note: James has exceeded the average life expectancy for Mongolism by five years.

Research questions: What influences the severity level of Mongolism? How old was the oldest surviving Mongoloid? If we reshape James' Mongoloid features, can we reverse the Mongolism, or only the appearance of it? (This is a question of symptoms vs. condition, chicken or egg.)

James is not interested in the wax crayons I spread on the table beside him. Instead, he gathers pins from the corkboard and positions them on Cliff's chair. "Shhhh…" He says, finger at his lips.

"Hello, young man!" Cliff booms, entering the room. James hugs him around the waist. Cliff pretends not to see the pins on his chair, pretends to sit on them, pretends he's been stuck, and James dissolves into hysterical laughter, tears running down his cheeks. Cliff pretends to pull a tack out of his behind, squinting as if in pain, and holds the pin out to James.

"How did this pin get on my chair?" he asks. "James? Do you know how this pin could possibly have gotten on my chair?" James giggles.

Ben was not allowed such pranks, not even when he was five or six years old, but with James, Cliff is different, far more permissive. James is too old for such games, but he requires different measures, different standards, and then, he's not our child. He goes back to St. Stan's every night.

I wonder, sometimes, if we were too stern with Ben. I remember hearing him laugh when he was with other children, wild out-of-control laughter, similar to James', but Ben never laughed like that around us.

He called Elizabeth the Tickle Monster, and she never even had to tickle him to get him laughing like that—she simply held up her hands and wiggled her fingers, threatening him, and the laugh would overwhelm him. But with Cliff and I, he was always serious.

When James leaves, he hugs me, enveloping me in the tangy odor of his sweat—horses, hay, cumin. "Goodbye, Mrs. Frances. I will miss you," he says, utterly serious for the first time all afternoon. He takes one of Sister Thomas' shopping bags from her hand, and with his free hand, he takes her hand and leads her down the walkway, tugging at her hand, pulling her toward the street.

It seems to me that James has never really belonged to anyone. He doesn't even belong to himself. He offers himself openly to everyone, his smile completely unguarded, but most people don't want his clumsy laughter, his squeals, his perpetually open mouth, his sour sweat and doughy flesh, his strange little lectures on bees and lightning. But he belongs, for now, to my husband, and to science. He belongs, at least a little bit, to me. Or rather, we have borrowed him, Cliff and I. And if Cliff's work is successful—if James grows into a man, a man who breathes normally—it is possible his mind will grow, too. Will he learn to control his laugh, his ridiculous smile? Will he understand that he belongs to no one? Will he belong to himself?

Viewed from a distance, sympathetic lightning appears to be traveling from one cloud to the next, as a sort of call and response, a game of electrical telephone, the shapes distorting as they copy each other.

The following week, when Sister Thomas is supposed to arrive with James, the phone rings instead.

"We won't be able to make it today," she says. "I'm sorry, I know you need to see him to track his progress, but right now I'm ready to knock that apparatus right out of his mouth."

I hear James in the background, talking too loudly, though not loudly enough for me to understand what he's saying. Sister Thomas scolds him, her voice briefly muffled by a sleeve or hand.

"I know the observations are important," she says, her attention returning to me. "And I'll gladly give you an update. He's been busy." She begins to list James' recent crimes. I have the phone wedged between my ear and my jaw so I can take notes, but I can barely keep up, and have to fill in the list after we hang up.

- *Sticks his foot into the aisle between desks to trip his classmates when they walk past. He did it once in the dining room, and his victim spilled a plateful of food. (James thought this was hilarious.)*
- *Dumped a cup of water out an upstairs window and onto the headmaster who was walking in the courtyard below.*
- *Pulled a chair out from under Sister Catherine, just as she was sitting down. (Lucky she didn't break her tailbone.)*
- *Unscrewed the top of a salt shaker, so when another boy tried to sprinkle salt on his potatoes, the top fell off, and the salt heaped onto his food.*
- *Continually tries to answer the phone when it rings.*
- *Laughs hysterically at all reprimands.*
- *Steals things and hides them in his room. Two quarters, a pair of glasses, a slide rule, a stuffed bear that belonged to another child. (They had been looking for it since bedtime the night before when its rightful owner missed it.)*

"I don't know where he's learning these things, but we hardly know what to do with him," she says. "I'd take the old sleepy, slow James over this devil any day."

I read the list to Cliff, but he deems the behavior a phase. "He's growing up," he says. "Just like any child. He's simply doing it more quickly. His body's playing catch-up. At this rate, he'll be a new boy once again by this time next week. He'll be a man in no time."

I wonder if more oxygen and pressure on the pituitary gland could really cause such a change in personality and energy level. He was so sweet and docile before. And how can we separate hormone levels and efficiency of breath from the attention we've been giving him? We have separated him from the other boys, taken him from the school where he is one of nearly two hundred children. And we certainly aren't disciplining him—not that I want to. Most of his pranks are harmless, and none of them seem deliberately hurtful, but it's a strange development. I don't know that *pranksterism* is a typical phase of adolescence.

Subject exhibits developing romantic/erotic behavior.

James scoots along the perimeter of the room, keeping his back pressed to the wall.

"What are you hiding, James?" I ask.

He giggles, and presses closer to the wall.

"What do you have behind your back, dear?"

A dramatic pause and he thrusts a loose bouquet of flowers at me. "For you, Mrs. Frances." Orange spotted lilies and gangly hostas—not your typical bouquet. With one hand, he rubs his crotch distractedly, and I see that he has an erection. It seems unlikely it has anything to do with me, and either way, I ignore it. I take the flowers from his outstretched hand, playing along.

"They're beautiful, James. Where did you get them?"

"A gentleman never reveals his secrets," he says, beaming.

I take the flowers to the counter and begin sorting them so I will not have to look at him. I'll have to apologize to the neighbor from whose yard James probably picked the flowers. James comes up beside me and puts an arm around my shoulder in a protective gesture. We are about the same height, and he pulls me tight to his armpit. I pull away, and I'm grateful to hear Cliff arrive.

"Hey now, James," he says, entering the room. "That's my wife you've got there. I guess I'm going to have to keep an eye out to make sure you don't run off with her."

"I'm going to run off with your wife!" James says. "I'm going to run off with your wife!"

Cliff begins to sing. "Hey diddle-diddle, the cat and the fiddle. The cow jumped over the moon. The little dog laughed to see such sport, and the dish ran away with the spoon!" He goes to the basin to wash his hands. "What do you think, James? Are you the dish?"

James takes his hand from my shoulder and begins to rub his crotch obscenely, but Cliff has his back to the boy and doesn't see. "I'm just going to go put these flowers in some water," I say, leaving the room, my face burning.

Sometimes, in a cloud-to-ground strike, an object on the ground also reaches out with its own limb of electricity, the two bolts meeting in the middle, fusing somewhere in the sky between ground and cloud.

Sister Thomas calls to tell us there was an accident on the streetcar. A man fell into James and the fall dislodged the apparatus from his mouth, but no one noticed. "James was scared," she says. "I was so concerned about getting him off the streetcar and getting him home, I didn't even notice the thing was gone."

"Is he okay?" I ask.

"Mostly, yes. But he was very upset," she says. "It seemed like an accident. Like the man just fell into him. But James was…well, he was rubbing himself. Like he's been doing lately?" She tells me that an argument had broken out between the man and another passenger who accused the man of picking on a poor unfortunate, although she hadn't noticed anything developing before the fall. The whole time the men were fighting, James refused to get up from the floor of the streetcar, tucking his head between his knees, hiding his face, terrified. No matter how Sister Thomas pleaded with him, stroking his back, trying to comfort him, he wouldn't even look at her.

I can't really imagine Sister Thomas soothing anyone, but of course I say nothing of the sort.

"He was so scared," she says. "He was making this cooing noise. He wouldn't even look up until I told him it was our stop, that we were home. Even then, I had to pull him along quite forcefully. Some of the other passengers shoved him along, which got him off the trolley, but probably didn't help his state of mind, poor thing."

No one noticed that James' front teeth were missing—the false ones that were attached to the apparatus, the ones that closed the gap formed by the stretcher.

"It's just awful," she says. "He smiles and there's nothing there. Just this big gap. It's just awful. He didn't even eat breakfast. He won't take part in croquet. You know that's usually his favorite activity, but he just sits on the bench and talks to the bees. Can you have Dr. Bell come see him? I don't think I'll be able to bring him to you anymore. At least not for a while, and I'm not sure what shape his mouth is in now."

I assure her that we will come see the boy as soon as possible.

Subject's maxillary bones have collapsed inward. Subject maintains physical growth but resumes former sluggishness and mouth-breathing. Maintains sexual behavior and public masturbation, although he does not seem aware of his actions or that they are inappropriate.

In the dormitory, James shows me how to make the beds, his assigned daily chore. His voice seems different, with weaker annunciation. "First, we tuck the corners," he says. "No. Wait. Let me start over. First, we move the bed against the wall because sometimes it *budges*. See. It *budges* because it is a magic carpet when we are sleeping." He shoves the cot against the wall, rubs his crotch. "It must be like this." He presses his palms flat together, as if in prayer. "Bed and wall. Then we tuck the corners. See." He tucks the sheets tight beneath the mattress. "Tuesday we take the sheets off the bed. Tuesday morning the sheets are soft like hair. Tuesday night the sheets are crunchy like scrub brushes."

"We do laundry on Tuesdays," Sister Thomas says.

"My hands are like an iron. See." He smooths the sheets. "And we can punch the pillow because it is bad to punch people. Gerald put Henrik's head in the toilet and spit on my shoe. But I did not punch him because it's bad to punch people. It's okay to punch the pillow. You have to make your fingers flat like bricks. See. And you make your thumb like a boy hiding around the corner of the bricks, because if the boy stands in front of the bricks he will get smashed."

He makes two perfect fists, thumbs tucked low, hands squared to the pillow, which is leaned against the wall at the head of the bed, as if the wall is a proper headboard. He hits the pillow and dust rises, catches the sunlight and drifts downward. He keeps punching. *Right-left. Right-left. Right-left.* James stops punching, plumps the pillow up again, and smooths the pillowcase. "Then we fold the sheet back. See."

"James is a big help to us," Sister Thomas says. James sits on the bed and swings his feet. He scratches at his ear, then his crotch. Sister Thomas looks away. "He's hardly a bother. And he's very good at his chores." She turns back to him. "Isn't that right, James?"

James doesn't answer.

"We'll keep you here with us. How does that sound, James?"

He hunches forward and smooths the sheets compulsively, each hand flat on the bed beside him. He seems like a child again, vulnerable and small, the mischievous prankster subdued.

Three weeks since the dislodging of the apparatus: subject remains unchanged. Clifford has determined not to install a new apparatus as progress was mixed. The gap in his teeth remains, although it will likely narrow as the maxillary bones continue to heal. Despite the inconclusive results of this operation, the apparatus did improve the subject's breathing. After his mouth heals once again, it may be worth consulting with a surgeon to determine if his airway can be further and more permanently improved.

This experiment has provided additional research questions for the future: Does opening the airway, and/or increasing pressure on the pituitary gland, provoke the rapid onset of previously delayed or prolonged puberty? (Or did the subject arrive at puberty naturally and coincidentally when his airway was opened, his gland pressured?)

Out the window of Cliff's study, the sun is bright and setting, the first glimpse of it we've had all day now that it is sinking below the cloud cover. On the desk are four human skulls shipped from South America, lined up like apples for a teacher's favor. They are porous gray bones, like old pine next to the plastic model skull, white and shining and flawless.

"Why not try again?" I ask. "It was working, wasn't it?"

"It depends what you mean by working, I suppose." He picks up the plastic skull and rolls it against his palm.

"He was growing up." My voice is too high, too strained. "He was changing."

"But what if it wasn't for the better?" Cliff said. "I don't want to turn him into a criminal or a pervert. And anyway, we don't know that he didn't just enter puberty on his own. Maybe it had nothing to do with the apparatus. There's really no way to test it."

"What if he just needed more time?"

"What if more time just made things worse? We'd have to try the operation on a number of other Mongoloid boys to even have a control group. It's just not feasible.... And I think it's too late for him, anyway. For boys like James. I think he might be better off without my messing around."

"But what if he just needed more time?" I repeat. "What if you could help him? It seems unfair to give up so quickly."

Cliff is silent, looking out the window. "There was never any saving him," he says, finally. "Never any saving any of those boys. Not really. Their parents were dimwitted, too. Before they were even born, they had already gone wrong."

"That seems unfair. I mean, we can help them. We can at least improve things for them."

He rolls the plastic skull back to its place on the desk and picks up one of the others, a real skull. He knocks on it, a dull sound.

"I don't know," he says. "I wasn't sure before. I'm not sure now. I wanted to help him."

"But now you don't?"

He puts the skull back on the desk and walks to the window. For a minute, I think he might just ignore my question altogether.

"I still want to help him, but I think I underestimated the risk. The cost to him. I don't know…" He turns to me. "I want to travel," he says. "To do serious research. *Fieldwork.* We could collect samples of food. In every place we go, we could get samples for lab analysis. We'll study the diets that people have thrived on for centuries."

"But what about our work here? The school? The boys? We've barely started…"

Cliff shakes his head. "We'll continue the work, but elsewhere. We'll build on what we've learned here. On a broad scale. A global scale. You can think of James as the starting point. We'll tell him so. That he has been the starting point."

For a moment, I think that we could take James with us. Continue the work. But we can't. Of course we can't. Even if we could manage traveling with a child—and a child like James—I know it wouldn't be good for him. It wouldn't help a thing. He has a home at St. Stanislaus. He needs his routine. Making beds. Playing croquet. Speaking with the bees. James was never ours, I remind myself. He belongs to no one.

Cliff claps his hands together. "We could go to Egypt!" He says, walking back to me and taking my hand. "I've always wanted to see the pyramids."

"What do they eat in Egypt?" My voice sounds flat and tired, strange even to me. I think of Ben's grave, quiet under the pear tree. The snow that will fall on it, and melt again. "How long will we be gone?"

"I have no idea," Cliff says. "But we'll find out. Even if we never see another Ohio winter, we'll see *something*." He picks up the plastic skull once again. "What do you say, Pfeff? You'll be my research assistant…Egypt. South America. Mexico. Italy…"

Instead of Ohio, jungles. Instead of bricks, moss-covered stones. To swim in the deep blue water I have only seen in paintings. To watch the fishermen hauling nets heavy with fish. It seems impossible.

"I don't know," I say. I close my eyes, shutting out Ben's grave, James, this house we have lived in for so many years now, this office, the sunset, and imagine us somewhere else, somewhere new. Eating corn or fish or lentils. Collecting them for study. Traveling by airplane and canoe. By foot. By camel, perhaps, like the explorers in the National Geographic Society magazine. "Maybe," I say, nodding. "Maybe."

Cliff's eyes flash. He begins to pace. I haven't seen him excited like this in a long time, if ever. Still, I wonder if it is a passing notion. Like the rabbits. Like James. So much research begun and left unfinished.

"I have to think," he says. "I have to plan."

I know he will need my help in the planning, but that right now, this is my cue to leave. There is dinner to make, dishes to wash.

In the darkening kitchen. I don't turn on the light, but stand, for a minute by the window, watching the blue darken in the sky.

Which type of lightning were we, James? Cloud-to-cloud, sympathetically responding? Cloud-to-ground, meeting in the sky? Both of us striking, both of us struck? Or cloud-to-ground—a one-way bolt? Which of us was the cloud? Which the ground?

His tired head resting in my lap. *Mrs. Frances, would you touch my hair? Mrs. Frances, would you tell me a story?* He pointed at the pictures. He laughed so coarsely. *Mrs. Frances, I love you.*

When I had Ben, who was so smart, I wondered how people could love a child who was not intelligent, who was not beautiful. But James has showed me how foolish that was. Too large for himself. Clumsy and overgrown and always breathing through his open mouth, spittle collecting at the corners. Unlovely. But I love him still. The way he pulls me across the garden, talking to the bees, completely unafraid.

Every type of lightning changes something, whether it strikes a tree or meets another bolt on its way across the sky. However briefly it flashes, it sends a charge through the roots and soil. It lights the sky for an instant. It wakes children from sleep. There is no electrical discharge that does not result in change. But afterward, the cloud dissipates. The storm blows through. The tree, if it hasn't caught fire, sometimes goes on living for years, split down the middle, blackened and scarred, silently growing around the damage.

FROM THE NOTEBOOKS OF
DR. CLIFFORD BELL
MAY, 1929

Hypothesis: Primitive, local diets, untouched by modern processes, are healthier than modernized diets (such as those we consume in American cities). Healthier diets mean healthier teeth and better physical architecture.[1]

Background: After several years of studying modern American diets and oral health in Cleveland[2], I have begun to wonder if the increase

---

1. Modern foods such as white bread, polished rice, canned vegetables, potted meats are killing us. In the space of a single generation, there is evidence of increased tooth decay and physical degeneration. Old timers—grandparents and great-grandparents, those who grew their food and hunted and drank milk from cows they raised themselves—dwell within solid bodies even as they age. They've got good bones. They're like the *Notre Dame* cathedral: ingenious architecture. God's design. But now we consume milk packaged in jugs, pasteurized and homogenized, and we eat meat by the spoonful from awful little tins. I see mothers buying bread in a plastic bags, bread that is made to last for months—*months!*—without molding. This generation, *our* generation, is increasingly fragile. Our teeth are full of decay. We sicken too easily. You can see it in our children's faces. We are raising a sickly generation.

2. I have examined and photographed over a hundred children and adults to-date. The evidence of genetic degeneration is everywhere in their broken, rotted teeth and the deformed structures of their facial features: pinched nostrils, underbites, sloping foreheads, etc.

in incidence of tooth decay (and other broader physical ailments such as tuberculosis) may not be due to what we *are* consuming, but rather, what we *are not* consuming. Industrial food processing, such as refining flours and sugars and canning and preserving vegetables and fruits, may also deplete our foods of nutrients, stripping them of essential vitamins and minerals. In order to test this idea, it is essential to study the diets of primitives—those isolated tribes and cultures that are still eating the foods of their ancestors and have (ideally) never tasted our processed modern foods.

I will embark on a major nutritional study in which I will compare the diets and health (both oral and general physical health[3]) of people existing on modern diets with those of people who continue to eat primitive diets. This second group lives in remote locations (such as the mountains of Peru, the Alaskan and Canadian bush, distant islands, and deep jungle villages). When possible, I will study people and nutrition in cities that overlap with or are not too terribly distant from primitive tribes. (For example, diets and health of people in Cairo will be compared with nomadic tribes who live in the surrounding desert and still consume mostly traditional diets. The diets and health of people living in Alaskan cities will be compared with those of people living in the bush.)

In addition to analyzing oral and systemic health, I will analyze the nutritional content of the foods people eat, seeking a correlation *and causation* between them.

Expectations: To find a higher incidence of dental caries in cities and in the mouths of people who consume modern, industrialized diets. I expect to find healthier mouths and bodies in those people who continue to eat traditional diets rich in unprocessed foods.

3. *The body and mind are one.* This is not a new idea, but we tend to forget. What we feed the stomach, we also feed the brain.

Research questions: How does the nutritional content of modern, industrialized foods compare with the nutritional content of isolated, primitive foods? Is there a higher incidence of tooth decay in one or the other group (modern vs. primitive, urban vs. rural)? Are there other notable trends in the oral or systemic health of either group?

THE ROOF OF HIS MOUTH

Wires, sensors, gauges, ticks, whirls: there is no scientific method with which to measure love. No precise way to test it.

Before Frances and Clifford became my mother and father, way back when they first kissed, Clifford pressed his hands against the back of Frances' head and their teeth knocked together and her heart beat quickly at the pressure of his mouth on hers. Back then, she didn't yet know his scent. But by this point in their story—we'll call it the middle, though we haven't yet made it back to that train through Switzerland—Frances knows that he smells like baking bread, and sometimes like onions. When they're traveling, he takes on the sour odor of the boathouse, of ropes and cork jackets left too long in the bilge water. Sometimes he smells like paint.

Yesterday, Frances watched while Cliff had blood drawn from his arm. They would test their blood before and after their travels, and periodically throughout, to see how it might change depending on diet. The needle pierced his skin, and the syringe filled with blood, and she winced in sympathetic response. His blood, she noted, was darker than her own. She had seen it before, of course, when he slapped a mosquito mid-bite or sliced his fingertip on the edge of a page. He always squeezes a papercut. Best to let a wound bleed, he says. But she wouldn't be able to pick a drop of his blood out of a smattering of assorted drops. She couldn't recognize his blood outside his particular network of veins, bluish and braided on the backs of his hands, veins that swell on especially hot days, those days when his wedding ring grows too snug and he fiddles with it, trying to force it to budge from the groove in his flesh.

She doesn't know the taste or scent of his blood. She has no idea how his intestines coil—differently in every person!—or how large his lungs are, or what color they are. But then, she doesn't even know the coils of her own intestines, nor the size or color of her own lungs. Bodies are such mysteries—so much hidden. She has no idea what the skin on the back of Cliff's heels is like.

But these days it is Cliff's business to document the features of the people he meets, and to make meaning from those features. To recognize patterns and links. To trace causes and effects. To read underbites and overbites. He measures the distance between nostrils, the size of foreheads. In each feature, he sees a code waiting to be cracked.

He isn't unique. None of us are, influenced as we are by the newspapers we read, by the conversations that surround us, the radio broadcasts, the chatter of our friends. He's rarely invited to dinner these days, nor even to coffee or tea, but all around him, others are reading bodies, too. Charles Darwin has been dead for 49 years, and his cousin, Francis Galton, wasted no time applying Darwin's ideas about the fitness and survival of beasts to the fitness and survival of human beings. In Europe, in New York, in Cleveland, there are hospitals and asylums for those deemed less fit: the *mad*, the *feeble-minded*. People are classified by race, by sexual deviancy, by disability, religion, genetic legacy. Had I lived, perhaps I would have studied eugenics at University—it's 1930, and it's a thriving field. How do genes lead to the right—or wrong—blood, skin, skulls, eyes, hair? And what Clifford wants to know is how food shapes our bones and blood, our faces, our brains, our morality.

But in 1930, we are in the middle of our story. We have not yet reached the mass exterminations, the murder of Jews and Poles and homosexuals and the disabled and the mentally ill and the artists and intellectuals who wrote the wrong words or thought the wrong thoughts or had the wrong hearts, the wrong imaginations, the wrong words, the wrong language, the wrong God, the wrong genes.

We are not there yet.

Clifford doesn't know where we're headed. How all this measuring and classifying—along with fear and hate and hunger—will lead to mass murder. The word *genocide* won't exist for another 13 years. Words! They help us sort and categorize and tell our stories. But they also fail us! They are never precise enough—always splintering and shimmering with other implications, other interpretations. And then, they're also too precise, trapping us, limiting our possibilities. No, the word genocide does not yet exist, but genocide exists, has existed.

But I am getting ahead of myself.

It is 1930. We are in the middle of the story.

Once upon a time there was a dentist whose son died from an infected root canal.

Here is the dentist, years later, reading the newspaper, taking a break from packing—tomorrow he and his wife leave for Alaska, and then they're off to Europe—to Scotland, and Italy, and Switzerland. He's sitting in his chair with his feet up, and Frances is washing dishes in the kitchen, thinking about how the plates and bowls will collect dust while she's gone—and how long will they be gone? They don't know. They'll follow the facts, the map, the teeth. And here she is, hands growing soggy in the sink, thinking about how little she knows her husband, my father, her Clifford. She doesn't even know what the inside of his mouth looks like, although he knows everything about hers. He has cleaned her teeth many times. He's drilled and filled three cavities. And teeth are so distinctive! The police even use them to identify dead bodies or remains after a fire. But if their house burned, and Cliff within it, or if their plane crashed, and somehow Frances survived, but Cliff burned, and she was asked to identify his dental remains, she would have no idea.

Except that Cliff has no teeth. She would know his dentures—she has seen them plenty of times since their wedding night, when she was first startled to see them soaking in a glass by the sink. How he had flushed with embarrassment. How old he had looked, even then, without the dentures in his mouth. But she does not know the roof of his mouth. Not his tonsils. Not the color of the flesh.

Frances leaves the dishes in the sink, sits down next to Cliff, drying her hands on her apron.

"Darling," she says. "Would you open your mouth for me?" He looks up, then back at the paper. "Cliff, dear." He scowls and ignores her. "Please, dear. Just for a second."

He lowers the paper. "You want to see my mouth?" She nods. "What for?"

"I'd just like to see what it looks like. I don't know."

He shakes his head. Lowers his eyebrows. Annoyed.

"Oh, would you just do it? Just for a minute? You look in other peoples' mouths all day, and you won't just let me have one little peek?"

"You're being strange, Pfeff."

"So I'm being strange. Indulge me. Opening your mouth would take far less time than arguing about it."

He opens his mouth. Snaps it closed.

"Oh, come now. That wasn't long enough. I hardly had time to notice you were cooperating."

"This is absurd." But he opens his mouth again, lets her lean in and look.

The color is nothing out of the ordinary. Pink to red. Similar to her own. Maybe a slightly deeper red. His tongue lays flat and relaxed, spreading like a thigh on a chair. The roof of his mouth is ridged and purplish, corrugated like a can. But how does it differ from any other mouth? He closes his mouth. Swallows. His Adam's apple bobs.

"That's more than enough, I'm sure," he says.

"I guess," she says. "But maybe you can give me another look later. Your mouth and I were just getting acquainted."

He settles back in his chair, starts to raise the paper, then stops. He takes Frances' hand in his own. He raises it to his mouth and kisses it firmly.

FROM THE NOTEBOOKS OF DR. CLIFFORD BELL:
Florida, 1930

CASE STUDY: ISOLATED AND MODERN SEMINOLES

The Seminoles in and near the city of Fort Lauderdale exhibit rampant caries, while those living deep in the Everglades have perfect dental arches and *not a single carious tooth*. The evidence in support of my hypothesis is staggering.[1]

The Seminoles exist in varying degrees of assimilation. They have spent the last half century at war with our U.S. government, and some of them have moved ever deeper into the swamps to maintain their

---

1. Frances and I stayed for a week with Mrs. Ivy Stranahan, the widow of Frank Stranahan, a man who is widely considered one of the founders of the city of Fort Lauderdale. Mrs. Stranahan is a committed Seventh Day Adventist, a member of the Christian Women's Temperance Union, and a teacher. Many of her pupils are young Seminoles, and she says that it has been through teaching that she has come to know and love them as family.

The Stranahan home was originally built as a trading post, but some years ago the late Mr. Stranahan built a new trading post closer to the railroad and the couple remodeled the original post as their home. Mr. Stranahan built the large porch on the original trading post so the Indian traders could sleep there when they came to do business. The upstairs of the trading post has served as a community center and has been the site of many dances, dinners, and gatherings over the years.

way of life. Still, the state of Florida continues to grow, and the land available to the Indians continues to shrink. Even the swamplands are being developed and farmed. I am glad to have had the opportunity to visit these primitive tribes before they are forced to entirely surrender their way of life.[2]

Some Seminoles spend part of the year living in villages of traditional "Chickee Huts," that serve as tourist attractions. In these villages, the people do basket weaving, wood carving, beading, and doll carving, and allow tourists to observe them and buy the things they make.[3] As you might expect, the diet in these villages is a blend of traditional with modernized foods and their teeth and facial structures demonstrate this in-between status.

The children at the tourist village wore excessive strands of beads around their necks. Not a sliver of skin was visible beneath the inches of beads that were coiled in layers upon layers. These children, who were relatively friendly and cooperative, demonstrate the narrow nostrils, jaw, and cheekbones typical of all of the Modernized Indians I have thus far studied. Likewise, their dental arches are narrow and their teeth are crowded, often growing on top of each other, overlapping all through their mouths. Together, they suffer dental decay in 40% of their teeth.

---

2. Some of the Indians spoke of their desire for designated, private tribal lands where they can hunt and fish and exist in the ways of their ancestors. Still others would like to resume the more agricultural lifestyle that they had before the Seminole Wars. In their current state, they are continuously pushed further into the swamp and their lives are nomadic. I believe that designated lands are the only way they will be able to preserve their culture and their health. *We white men are a plague upon them.*

3. At the Miccosukee village, we also witnessed a most alarming evening of alligator wrestling and alligator hypnosis. The Seminole and Miccosukee include alligator tail in their diet, and there is a growing market for alligator skins in the trading posts. (It is apparently a popular material for boots and belts.) The men of the tribe learn to wrestle the gators as children. They flip them on their backs, wedge their jaws open, even hold them high in the air above their heads. It was quite remarkable the way the young man held the alligator in his arms. He did not exhibit even an ounce of fear.

Conversely, in the isolated groups, I did not find a single carious tooth. *The evidence that modernized foods are destroying our teeth and facial structures is staggering.*

These Seminoles—the ones who are living deep in The Everglades—are extremely mistrustful of Whites, and especially of government. I am exceedingly lucky to have made the acquaintance of Ivy Stranahan, as it is apparent that the Indians trust and respect her and her late husband Frank. Those Indians living deep in the swamp, instead of in the city or Chickee villages, would not have even showed me their faces, much less their teeth or their food, if I did not have the assistance of John Leahy, a dear friend of the Stranahans, who speaks the Seminole language and served as my guide when we canoed into the swamp in dugout canoes[4]. Even with Leahy as my ambassador, I was keenly aware of my status as an outsider who had not earned the trust of these people.[5]

Each time we arrived in a village, we found it abandoned. Had I been alone (which I would not have dared, the dangers coming in the form of snakes, alligators, and the Seminoles themselves), I am certain I would have thought the villages absolutely empty, so complete was the silence when we arrived. However, Leahy would set about poking into the houses and the trees, calling to the people, making it known that it was him, their friend, and that I was not a government man, and soon

---

4. The swamp is every bit as beautiful as it is terrifying. Many Floridians are anxious to drain it for farmland or to build new cities, but it is difficult to imagine they would be successful—the land is alive and voracious, teeming with vines and snakes and insects. Even with a million plows and machetes, it would be a challenge to restrain this wilderness, but then again, it is remarkable how much progress they have already made against it. They are determined to wrangle it into orderly orange groves and neat rows of sugar cane.

5. In this situation, Leahy was invaluable. However, for future travels I wish to keep Frances with me as well. She was extremely helpful at the Chickee village, and in Ft. Lauderdale proper, but I left her with Ivy Stranahan when I went into The Everglades, and I missed her assistance. She has always taken excellent dictation, but during these research expeditions, her most important job will be talking to people. She is gentler than I, and more attentive. She will occupy people in conversation so I can work.

enough people emerged from the sweltering shadows and, eventually, showed me their splendid teeth. They are, without a doubt, some of the healthiest and most structurally exquisite individuals I have ever met.

ALASKA

Frances

1930

To see me, the pilot has to crane his neck, turning most of the way around, but this doesn't stop him. It seems he needs eye contact when he speaks, but maybe it's for my benefit, so I can see his face, read his lips a little, fill in the blanks of what I can't hear over the considerable noise of the engine. I am crammed in the tiny backseat next to the camera and a couple of heavy parkas, hats, and fur-lined boots that Cliff and I are hoping we won't need. It is June, after all, but we are further north than I have ever been. Clifford sits in front, next to the pilot.

"Mount McKinley!" the pilot shouts. He gestures vaguely. "Over there! The Yup'ik call it Denali! Twenty-thousand-three-hundred feet! A real grand dame!"

The sky to the east is opaque with fog. Occasionally we fly through a thin patch of clouds, and I can make out layers, clouds upon clouds. Beards of the ancients, I think. God's beard tangled in the propeller. There is no mountain in sight, but I nod back at the pilot, hoping that my acknowledgment will encourage him to turn back around and keep his eyes on where we're headed. Even if he can't see much, it seems he should face the direction in which the airplane is aimed.

The pilot has been to Sleetmute only once before. "Not much of a town," he says. He is speaking to Clifford, now, but still shouting, so I can hear most of it. "Maybe fifteen families. At least half of them related, and maybe a few related twice, if you know what I mean. It's a limited gene pool."

Clifford laughs uncomfortably. "But I've heard there's at least one white man there. A mining engineer?" he says. "So outsiders must make it there now and then. And certainly, the young people must leave? To seek their fortunes and such?"

"If booze and sex are what you call fortunes!" says the pilot. I squint out the window, trying to see the mountain, which I have begun to think of as shy.

"It's hard to believe there's a mountain out there!" I shout. "Or land below us!"

"Oh, it's out there all right. Let's hope we don't get close enough to see her."

We have to fly 150 kilometers off route to find the next pass after the planned crossing is too foggy. There isn't much talking for the last hour or two of the flight. I can't tell if the silence is because the pilot needs to concentrate on flying the plane or because both the pilot and Clifford have decided conversation is something to avoid—the pilot bored, and my husband prude, although Cliff himself would call it *propriety*, would call the pilot *crass*. But out here, I expect crassness. I expect sex-starved men with tobacco stained mouths and beards and fingers. Even in our Anchorage hotel—one of the nicest in town—I saw women shuffling into the hotel lobby in dirty dresses and smeared makeup. Prostitutes, I'm fairly certain. And why not? They probably have children to feed, not to mention themselves. And the men were mostly unshaven, many of them surprisingly fat, wearing filthy parkas and boots. To be touched by those hands, those mouths—it would be like being caressed by a bear. Or maybe a man who was long ago turned into a bear by an enchanter, and the spell is just now, after many years of bearhood, slowly fading, and his human hands are emerging from the fur. Bright eyes glinting, surrounded by a ragged beard.

But these bear-men notice me. I have not felt so visible in years. 51 years old—I have no illusions. I am a soft, round, aging woman. But these men look at me. They turn their heads and stare. Maybe they are just marveling that a woman so old has managed to migrate this far north. Or maybe they are sizing me up as a housekeeper. But they don't look like the sort of men that care if their houses are kept. And I have seen the dwellings of such men in the first fishing village we visited. Squat shacks on the shore were black both inside and out, filthy with smoke from heating oil and cooking grease. Despite all the ice and snow, winter in Alaska is not a pristine season. Not in the least. But these men! They would bury me with their bear bodies, their filthy parkas and sealskins, and they would laugh about it. I have heard them laughing. Guffawing. To be buried by one of these laughing bears. I imagine the rough snag of their torn fingernails and calluses scraping my skin. I feel small beside them.

The clouds have thinned and I can see land beneath our airplane. There is a silver-gray river, black trees, and gray-green land dotted with pale rocks that look almost like sheep through the fog, and they are rapidly getting closer. Definitely rocks. Huge rocks. A cluster of houses emerges from the dark land, and I see lamplight or firelight, warm and orange and small, and then we are past the village, and then we are landing with a bump and taxiing unevenly down a gravel strip, the wings shaking and rattling as if they are barely attached.

Sleetmute: the perfect name for this place of clouds and dark silence. The clouds seem to dampen everything but the cold. A white man greets our plane, stepping close and waving up at us, the very mining engineer we have heard about. The infamous white man of Sleetmute, Alaska. He introduces himself only as Mike. It seems as if he's been waiting for us. Alongside the runway, there is a small clapboard shed with a shingled roof covered with blackish-green moss.

"Welcome to the Sleetmute Airport," Mike says. "As you can see, it's a bustling place." He laughs and shakes our hands as we climb down from the cockpit. "Rough flight?" The pilot begins handing down pieces of camera equipment and parkas, and Mike accepts them, stacking the luggage beside the plane. "My wife has some stew on for you. You like moose meat?" He directs the question at me.

"I can't say I've ever tried it," I say. "But I'll be glad to find out."
Mike hands me a parka that the pilot has handed down. "Put that on if
you're cold. We can load the rest of this up in the truck and I'll drive it
into town for you."

"Town" is a cluster of 14 round houses, with smaller round additions
on the back. The back rooms, Mike explains, are the bedrooms, while
the main domes are where the family cooks and eats and visits. Where
they sew sealskin parkas or, in the case of his wife, carve caribou bones
and the tusks of long-dead mammoths. Mike parks the truck in front of
one of the huts and makes sure the tarp is tight over our luggage before
leading us into the house.

His wife is a native woman with round, full cheeks and mouthful of
the tiny, seed-pearl teeth, perfectly aligned but for a single gap where one
is missing on the bottom. Her name is Mabel, and her house smells of
woodsmoke and fish and something else that I decide is probably moose fat.

It turns out that I like moose meat. Or at least I don't hate it. It is
not so different from beef, but is a bit tougher, with the distinct flavor
of liver. Mabel doesn't eat with us—she says she has already eaten—but
she sits with us while we eat.

Although Mike looks dirty and rugged, like all the men I have seen
in Alaska, he eats slowly, chewing each bite carefully, and he never speaks
with his mouth full. Even when Clifford or I ask him a question, he
chews his food for what seems like forever, then swallows and dabs the
corners of his mouth with a cloth napkin before he answers. The meal
is full of long pauses, since Clifford, who at home regularly speaks with
his mouth full, imitates Mike's manners.

Mabel sits in a dark corner beside a lantern and a small pile of tusks.
"Wooly mammoth," she says, when she sees me looking. Her English is
a little hesitant, but she goes on. Mike tells us she is one of the only villagers that speaks much English at all, besides him. "They used to live
here. A long time ago. The tusks are everywhere." She hands me a tusk
and I inspect it, turning it over in my hands, examining the carved lines
and leaf shapes.

"What's it for?"

"To look at," Mabel says. "To put on furniture. Sometimes I dig out the center. Make it hollow to fill with gunpowder or tea. Mike takes them downriver and trades them for better boots or berries or whatever food is available." She explains that she finds them scattered in the grass near the village. That they are sometimes woven into the grass. That you have to learn to recognize the feeling when your foot strikes one, how it differs from the feeling when your foot strikes a rock or a branch or a root.

"But if you go looking," she says, "You must be careful of bears. It is good to sing or talk or shout. Let the animals know you are coming. The bears do not often hurt us, but they are here. They are everywhere around the river, especially in this season because of the salmon. They would rather catch fish than bother with humans, but we must be careful of them."

I nod. Clifford, too, has warned me of bears. Earlier in the spring, the pilot reports, a man near the town of Bethel was mauled by a grizzly because he accidentally got between a mother and her cubs. As the story goes, he had no idea they were even there, no idea he had stepped between a mama and her babies, and no time to react when she came at him.

"They're surprisingly fast," Clifford says, as if he has seen one before. "Even though they're huge. You can just stay in town, though. If a bear wanders through, it will know it's in human territory. And anyway, there will be other people around if you stay in town, near the houses. That way you won't find yourself alone with one of them."

I have no interest in meeting a bear. I saw one in the museum in Anchorage. A taxidermy grizzly, upright forever, bearing its teeth, front paws raised and larger than my head, sharp, curved claws.

The men finish eating and dabbing at their mouths, and Mike says he'll take us next door, to his daughter's home, where we can sleep. The daughter and her husband will sleep at their other daughter's for the few nights we are here. I thank him and say goodnight to Mabel.

In the morning, the fog is gone, and I am surprised to see that, from here, Mount McKinley is a clumsy-looking mountain, blocky and without delicacy or spire. Although the day is gray, it is bright, and occasionally the sun sets everything glowing. The Kuskokwim River runs in a gleaming oxbow alongside the village, wide and swift, any rocks and obstacles submerged in snowmelt. The green of the Alaskan fauna is dark and dense—nothing like the green of Ohio. Ohio green is dappled, the forests bright on sunny days, at least in the morning, before thunderstorms have time to build. In Alaska, the green is heavy and impenetrable. It isn't raining, but the world feels soggy, as if the whole village could be lifted and wrung like a dishrag, and out we would fall—dentist and wife, natives in their sealskins, tiny people, like toys with haphazard arms and legs, and from the river would fall the red and silver salmon, like sequins.

The pilot, who slept on the floor in the front room of the hut while we slept in the bedroom, stumbles out to the street—a pair of muddy tire ruts—stretching and yawning with exaggerated sighs and groans. He stands beside me, stretching his back, switching his hips back and forth. "Well now, there she is," he says. "Mount McKinley, our furtive giantess."

"Have you ever been up it?" I ask, to make conversation.

"Oh, no. I only climb in an airplane. But I've been up and over her who knows how many times now. I've got no interest in seeing her at the ant's eye view. Much prefer the bird's eye myself." He scratches at his beard. His cheeks are bright pink above it. His is the face of a man who drinks hard and spends far too much time out in the cold. "What do you say we get some coffee going? I'm sure your husband will be wanting to get to work. Where is the old codger, anyway?"

Cliff is older than the pilot, but also more youthful, and certainly more clearheaded. "He went to introduce himself to people in town. Or at least look around a bit."

"Well, he doesn't waste a minute now, does he?" The pilot pulls a flask out of his back pocket, unscrews the cap, and takes a deep swallow. A few drops glisten in his beard below his lip. He wipes them away with the back of his hand and takes another drink, a quick one. "Got to get this day started right," he says. He holds the flask out to me and I wave it off.

After breakfast, Clifford photographs Mabel smiling broadly, show-ing the gap where her tooth is missing. I ask her about her children, and she lists the names of 22, but when I ask where they are, she lists six or seven and gestures vaguely at the sky or the mountain, which I think means they are dead—wandering spirits. The others, it seems, from the way Mabel points to specific huts or in specific, singular directions, live either in the village, with her, or downriver. Clifford says he wants a good look at their teeth. 22 children from the same parents would provide an excellent control group.

"Probably no more than 15 or 16 are living," I point out. "And it sounds like most of them don't live in town." But Clifford says he can find the ones that live downriver, that those will be some of the most valuable subjects—born of the same genes but eating progressively more industrialized diets the closer they get to Bethel, at the mouth of the Kuskokwim, where there is an outpost and plenty of store food. Clif-ford looks a little frantic at the prospect, his eyes darting furtively as he rambles on. He is excited.

I want to tell Mabel that I was a mother too, but it seems compli-cated to explain it, to explain how we lost him, to see that flicker of confusion. When I used to tell people about Ben's death, in that first year, I began to recognize a pattern. First, their eyes would shine as they imagined our loss. Then, a crease would appear in their forehead—they wondered how I could forgive my husband, and how he could forgive himself. But Mabel has lost children, too.

There's no time for such a conversation, though. Mike has appar-ently put the word out that the dentist wants to discover the mysteries of the village teeth. A cluster of people has already gathered at the door of Mike and Mabel's home. Cliff talks while they open their mouths, and he inspects them, scanning for decay, making a couple of notes in his book, then dismissing each person with a nod. I stand beside him with a few dental instruments, a bottle of sterilizing liquid, and a cloth to wipe them clean, but Clifford mostly ignores the tools, only occasionally asking for a pick and pressing it against a molar, testing for decay. It never sticks, not even once. The people have strong teeth. He doesn't expect to find any caries since there are no stores nearby. People in Sleet Mute eat caribou and moose and salmon and berries. They eat well by necessity. There is nothing else available.

A healthy mouth is a sign of a healthy body; a healthy body a sign of a healthy mind. Cliff looks at the angles and spaces of their teeth: are they crowded? Translucent or rough? Stained or sour or loose? He counts caries and missing teeth, studies jaw structures and measures the spaces between nostrils, considers overbites and underbites, foreheads and chins. Later, he will collect samples of food—milk and meat or fish or berries or kelp or seal oil. He'll send these specimens home to the lab.

Few of the people speak to us. When it is their turn, they step toward Cliff and open their mouths and let him have a look. Or most of them do, while a few don't seem to understand his request, or pretend not to, despite the way he stands waiting, a half-smile on his face, or that everyone in line before them stepped up and opened wide. Some laugh and throw their heads back, so it is difficult to see their teeth. Sometimes Cliff asks them to laugh so that he can see the overlap of their bicuspids or incisors or a narrow dental arch, but these villagers have excellent arches.

A girl steps up to Clifford, smiles a little, teasingly it seems. She is maybe 14, with splotchy pink cheeks. Her eyes have an unusually high arch to them, repeating the arch of her eyebrows, so she appears joyful, about to break out into a wild grin. She is wearing a coat made of some sort of canvas, the hood pulled up but not cinched. Clifford asks her to take the hood down, pantomiming the request, but she just stands there, hands heavy at her sides.

"Let me have a look?" Clifford says, and opens his own mouth by way of demonstration. The girl looks at me and says something that seems like a greeting, so I say hello. She puts a hand out for a handshake, so I take it, and she pulls my hand in and inspects it, stroking the back of it like a pet mouse, tenderly. Startled, I pull my hand away, and she laughs in earnest before turning back to Clifford and opening her mouth wide.

She is a strange girl, young enough to be my grandchild, but she does not seem like a child, despite her small size and bright face. Her black hair is not braided, like most of the girls', but tucked loosely into her hood. When Clifford is done, she takes my hand again and shakes it vigorously.

"So nice to meet you, dear," she says, in perfect English, and I wonder if these are the only English words she knows, a perfectly memorized phrase. Her voice is high and lilting. For a moment, I think she is making fun of me, but she looks me in the eyes so intently. More likely she is imitating the tone of the person who taught her the words.

After lunch, Mike says he is headed upriver to where the men are catching spawning salmon. Easy fishing, he says. He welcomes us to tag along if we are curious, or want more mouths to consider. It seems there can't be many more people in the village than those we saw before lunch, unless the little homes house far more people than it appears, but we follow Mike upriver on a narrow, muddy trail, occasionally stopping to untangle or hack through the willows. We walk for about twenty minutes before reaching the fishermen, who have built wooden racks on which to dry the fish, and are hauling salmon onto the banks. Some of the men slice the fish open at the bellies and scoop out the roe. A few boys are busy heaving the giant creatures out of the river and onto the racks to dry.

The day is incredibly still, and Mike says that this is unusual. Most days, he says, the wind blows, coating the fish on the racks with sand, and this helps them dry, but is also the reason the people have such small teeth. He smiles for us, a regular Cheshire grin, showing off his worn-down teeth.

"We eat the dried fish, which would be tough enough as is," he says. "But the sand really permeates them, and it grinds our teeth down, bite after bite."

Cliff makes a note in his book. "But I've seen people chewing through leather a number of times today," he says. "I assumed that was the cause of the ground-down teeth—people using their teeth to bite through things?"

"Oh, you ain't seen nothing," says Mike. "Our teeth are one of our best tools around here. These men can carry a hundred pounds in each hand and a hundred more hanging from their teeth."

Cliff laughs skeptically.

"No, really," Mike insists. "They carry things in their mouths all the time, hanging from ropes, or leather straps. You wouldn't want one of these people to get ahold of your arm, much less your finger. They'd bite straight through the bone, given reason."

One of the boys sees me watching as he heaves a large fish up from the bank. He shoves a hand into each of its gills and lifts it high, straining a little. It is two-thirds his height, hanging from his head to his knees, and probably weighs a good 30 pounds. He shakes it so the tail sways back and forth, and he laughs, staggering under its weight, then drops it back beside the others. He looks at me again, checking his audience, then straightens the fish out and runs his hands over it, as if he is tucking a younger child into bed.

Everyone is busy catching or cutting or drying the salmon. Clifford sets up his camera and dental tools on a log, the tools resting on their chamois case. He waves the workers over one at a time and looks into their mouths, looking for caries, noting chips and discolorations, looking for exposed pulp. (There is none, despite that the villagers' teeth are remarkably worn, past the point that would expose pulp in most people.) I stand beside him, noting the subjects' names, ages, and dental details as Clifford reports them, but the progress is slow and tedious.

The river is red with fish, hundreds of them, pivoting their tails, swimming in place. How do they find their way to this spot? And why? "It's too amazing to believe," Mike says, standing next to me while Cliff works. After all those years in the ocean, swimming thousands of miles over bright coral, alongside fish of every color, at depths so deep no sunlight reaches them, one day they feel that it is time to turn around. They swim all the way back from the sea to the river, back upstream through fresh water, further and further upstream, leaping rocks, flinging their bodies up waterfalls. Mike says they use the sun to find their way. "Though some of the men say they use smell. That they have an ancient memory of the scent of their birthplace."

This is the place where they will leave their eggs, or fertilize and defend them, snapping at challengers with their strange hooked mouths. This is where they were born and where they will die.

"But if they die here, they're lucky ones," Mike explains. "Some of 'em swim almost all the way home only to be eaten by a wolf or a bear or an otter. Or we catch them. We're probably their biggest predator."

I wonder if it matters. They come here because the other fish around them come here, because something in their ancient minds says *swim*, says *spawn*. Salmon will continue to hatch and grow and swim out to the ocean and eat and swim back and spawn and die. How is it so different from us, from Cliff and me flying over the mountains in a rickety bush plane, canoeing downriver, so far from our home? What if we die here, in Alaska, or next month in Scotland? What difference does it make if I die in Ohio or Egypt?

My bladder is full. I can't wait any longer. I decide I'll just duck back behind the mess of willows and find a place to relieve myself, and I lean in and whisper this to Cliff, as if anyone would understand. As if they'd hold it against me, and anyway, they can likely guess where I'm going and probably don't care.

"We're just about done anyway," Cliff says. "I'll just make a few more notes while you're gone." But when I tunnel through the willows, I find more fishermen, more boys and men hauling fish over the bank. A crew of them is busy cutting the eggs from fish bellies. I keep walking, through marshy muck and puddles, sometimes hopping rock to rock in the direction of the woods that are not far off. It is darker back here, where the evergreens begin, and I will only need to take a couple of steps into the edge of the trees to be completely hidden. I remember the warning about bears and begin to sing to warn any lurking beasts of my approach.

In a cavern, in a canyon,
Excavating for a mine,
Lived a miner, forty-niner
And his daughter Clementine.
Oh my darling, Oh my darling,
Oh my darling Clementine.

I begin another round, singing a little more loudly. I only know that one verse.

Then I see the airplane, an old one, crashed and abandoned years ago. It is rusted and smashed, and there is some sort of canvas wrapped around the bent metal of the window frame and flapping loose from the wings, which are double-decker wings, the kind from which stuntmen dangle on ladders and wave to their audience. I think it is what they call a "Jenny," and it looks like it has been here for a long time, twenty years or more, but more likely it's the weather that makes it look so ancient. A heap of snow is piled on the wings, dirty and scattered with seeds and pine needles. Where there isn't snow, there is a layer of dark green moss. The nose of the plane is lodged in a snowbank. Some long-forgotten crash. The plane is missing one wheel and sits at a crooked angle, its nose toward the woods.

I want a good look inside the cockpit, which I can see is partially filled with snow, but suddenly I worry that the pilot is still in there, a skeleton in a threadbare coat, a pair of aviation goggles fixed to his decayed face. But if he *is* still in there, wouldn't someone want to know about it? His family, whom he had once upon a time kissed goodbye before he flew off, never to return? *Lost and gone forever.* I step closer.

Maybe there had been a hunt for him and his plane, dogs running out across the tundra, other planes flying low, filling the silence with their buzzing and groaning. Or maybe it happened in bad weather, a sudden blizzard, and days passed before anyone could even get out and look for him, and by then they had given him up for lost, which he most certainly was.

I hear an animal noise—a sort of grunting. I stand still, but the sounds continue, loud enough to be a bear, but I'm close enough to the plane that I'd be able to see such a large animal. I step closer. Maybe it's a wolf or a coyote, nosing around in the pilot's decaying rucksack, rooting out still sealed cans of beans or salmon. Not that I want to meet a wolf, exactly, but I am far less afraid of a wolf than a bear. But then the grunting is joined by moaning, a keening, human sound, and then I see them—a couple wedged in the cockpit, on the low side, pressed into the corner closest to me.

It is the girl from the morning. The one that had taken my hand, that had spoken to me. She is still wearing the dirty canvas jacket. The grunts are coming from our pilot. His eyes are closed. He is behind the girl, burying his dirty beard in her neck, and the girl is looking at me, her face turned and pressed against the shredded seat of the plane. She doesn't seem to care that I am there, that I am watching, though the keening has stopped. Her gaze is steady and she grips the edge of the plane tightly, the edge of the bent window frame. The pilot goes on grunting like a truffle hog. I can't make out the separate shapes of their bodies, only the different fabrics of their parkas—canvas and sealskin. The girl stares at me from beneath her hood, neither smiling nor grimacing. Her face is completely placid. Then she closes her eyes.

I turn and walk slowly away from the plane toward the edge of the woods. The plane is not my discovery after all. Maybe the whole town knows about it. Maybe it is a known spot for fornication. A destination for teenagers and filthy pilots. Whoever crashed it is either long dead, his clothing crumbled from his body, his bones dragged out and gnawed clean by animals, or he climbed out of the cockpit wiping his brow, proclaiming at his luck, at God's providence, whistling into the village, a grateful survivor. I have not discovered an unknown, abandoned plane crash, but something else. But what? What have I discovered? A man and a girl. Continuation of the species.

The sounds fade until they are replaced by new sounds—mosquitoes buzzing, the scrabbling of chipmunks or mice or birds in the branches. In the shadows of the trees, I stop and feel my heart thudding in my chest.

A girl who knows one sentence of English. A girl who spoke to me in a lilting voice. My breathing is ragged, as if I have been running. She is only a girl. I slow my breathing deliberately, holding a deep breath and letting it out slowly. She held my hand, that girl. She touched it tenderly, and looked into my eyes. I look at the trees, how the light grows dim and gray deeper into the forest. She is not asking for my help. There are no bears, no wolves, no fishermen here. I am completely alone. She is not asking for anything from me. I peel down my layers, squat, and watch as the stream of my urine melts a hole in the crusty snow.

TOOTH STORY:
POLAR BEAR

The night before Cliff and Frances were to depart by canoe for the next village between Sleetmute and the sea, Mabel sealed their boots and parkas with wax. The best boots, she said, were made of sealskin and sinew, but the waxed leather should work well enough for the week or so before they left Alaska.

In the morning, after they packed their things into the boat, Mabel held her hand out to Frances, a polar bear's molar resting on her palm, an inch and a half wide, with three jagged yellow-brown roots and a much whiter cap. The chewing surface was deeply grooved and stained. She apologized that it wasn't a canine. Indeed, the canine of a polar bear is an impressive thing, two inches long, sharp, and sickle-curved. Frances had seen them worn as necklaces, carved with patterns or combined with claws. But the molar was a solid thing, a jagged chunk, and she thanked Mabel for the gift.

In Frances' collection box, the tooth was in two pieces, sliced down the middle. Clifford had cut it in half to determine the age of the animal. A bear's tooth is like a tree, adding a layer of cementum each year the way a tree adds bark. Under a microscope, the layers showed as wide and narrow bands, each band separated by a dark line that marked hibernation and the beginning of a new year. Frances' tooth came from the mouth of a mother bear. She had been thirteen years old when she lost the tooth, and had birthed four litters. In the years that she nursed her cubs, the band of cementum was narrow; all her calcium had gone to production of milk for her cubs.

Mabel's family had eaten the bear during the winter of 1927, stewed and dried and roasted.

POSTCARDS FROM THE
OUTER HEBRIDES
1931

Dear Elizabeth,
We're in Scotland! The Hebrides Islands! A sketch of this new land-
scape: a wet, black road wanders between golden grasses. A fat plover
runs from the grass to the shore. Waves wash the sand slate gray and
cold. The clouds are like living creatures, building and billowing
and yawning. There are no trees. I suspect the thrashing wind scours
the soul into something better here than in other, stiller places, into
something cleaner.

Love,
Frances

Dearest Sister,
On these islands, the people live in black houses with half-round
roofs, peat smoke seeping from the doors and windows. Always the
peat smoke, even in summer! They say the smoke seasons the earth
so the oats will grow. And the peat itself grows thick and pure across
the land, preserving anything that falls into it: a fallen fork glistens,
untarnished. A cat that crawled off to die centuries ago maintains
the fur she wore in life. A perfect, soul-less body. The earth here is
an atmosphere opposite that of our mouths. In our mouths: bacte-

ria, oxygen, acid, and sugar, eating away at any crumb, any oat or
fish scale, even the enamel on our teeth. Our mouths teem, but the
bogs here are almost entirely without bacteria. How terrifying to
be a child here. The earth is a beckoning maw that you might fall
into and drown. Your mother might find you years later, perfectly
preserved, a doll in a fur-trimmed parka. But always the bog would
call to you, it seems. I can hear it now, if I try, a low rumbling voice.
But don't worry about me. I think children are the most susceptible.

Yours,
Frances

Eliza B,
Saturday in Stornoway. Boats bob in the harbor, but the fisherfolk
are not boisterous like you might expect. They mill about the streets,
singing and praying. They are churchgoers, every one. On Sunday
mornings, the men return to sea and the women trudge through
town with bins of cut and cleaned fish, wearing rubber boots and
oilskin suits, their heads wrapped in neat little turbans of fabric. I
keep my doubts to myself.

Faithful,
Frances

Dear Elizabeth,
     Sometimes, I am surprised at how ever-present my Benjamin is,
how he lingers, even after all these years. How have 12 years passed
without him? Perhaps I shouldn't be surprised. I didn't think I'd
ever recover from his death. In a way, that's true, but it is so different now. There were so many months when something as small as a
tomato could set me weeping. But now I welcome such flickers and
shreds of him.
     After tea, I offered to do the washing up for our hostess, a
woman whose children Cliff is including in the study. So there I
was, washing dishes in that tiny, unfamiliar kitchen on an island

way out in the north Atlantic, and suddenly he was there, perfect in my mind: my Ben, beaming at me, six months old, the age at which he discovered laughter.

Teaspoon, saucer, eggcup: I stacked the dishes next to the sink and watched the rinse water run down the drainboard back into the suds. I scrubbed crusted egg yolk from a plate. My hands softened and pruned. But for the briefest moment, each bowl become my baby's arm, each fork a little foot. I washed between his toes.

Do you remember how, as an infant, he had a double chin and dimpled elbows? Goodness, he was fat. When he was old enough to wash himself, he was no good at it. I was surprised, for some reason, to learn that bathing is not an inherent skill—that it must be taught. Ben would towel himself dry and forget to wash behind his ears. I found fine lines of dirt in the creases behind his knees. And if I did not clean his ears for a few days, a crust of yellow wax would form around his ear canal. If, at the dinner table, I leaned toward him with a damp napkin, he would push my hand away, wipe his mouth roughly, smearing whatever it was across his cheek—milk, or mashed potatoes, or toast crumbs. So often he had food stuck to his face.

There I was, standing at the sink. I pulled the plug from the drain and watched the water swirl down. He was not there. Not in a cup or spoon. Not the dripping dishcloth. But for just a moment, he had been. For a moment, I had him again—my soft, fat child was there in the dishwater, taking a bath. I wonder if this happens to every mother, not just those of us whose children have died, but to those who have lost their babies to time, to adulthood?

Love,
Frances

TOOTH STORY:
MUIRNA MACLEOD

In her collection, Frances had a tooth from the mouth of Muirna MacLeod, a girl from the Hebrides Islands. Muirna was fifteen when she died of tuberculosis—what they called the white plague, maybe because those sick with it grew so pale. Muirna had been gone three years before Clifford and Frances met her father, Martin, who gave Frances the tooth, a carious molar pulled when Muirna was fourteen. She had lost all her teeth by the time she died. Or most of them, anyway, and a dentist pulled the rest so she could wear a set of artificial teeth. It wasn't uncommon in Stornoway. Plenty of people wore dentures.

Martin himself was a rugged man with bright eyes and a wide, square jaw. Clifford declared he possessed a "high type of manhood." Even among the rugged people of the Isle of Lewis, Martin stood out. He and his wife lived with their two remaining daughters in a "black house," a stone foundation with a thatched roof. The house had no chimney and the smoke from the peat burning on the hearth oozed through the thatch so it looked as if the house were smoldering, but if you went inside, you found that the place was immaculate, with smooth, floral patterned wallpaper and a gilt-edged tea set. Martin's wife had grown up in Stornoway, but Martin was from St. Kilda, a lonely slab of rock and turf way out in the Atlantic.

"It was a rough life on St. Kilda," Martin said. His youngest daughter poured tea and brought more oatcakes from the stove. "The tweeds are the finest in the world, but it was difficult to trade them, being so far out. Soon, there won't be a soul left on the island." He sipped his tea. "My mother sent me to Stornoway for school and I lived with my uncle. A lucky thing since that's how I met my Alva." He patted his wife's hand.

Cliff and Martin reached for the same oatcake. "That one's for you, my man," Martin said, drawing his hand away, then taking another. He passed the marmalade to Cliff, but Cliff declined, blushing.

"On St. Kilda, we fished birds right out their nests," Martin said. "Puffins. Guga. We had the finest cragsmen—and women, too." He described how a young man would be lowered down over a cliff with a pole and a line. He'd noose the birds, pull them from their nests by the necks, wings flapping. The birds snapped their own necks in the struggle. "They're delicious," he said. "Salty things." His words conjured the island, wind-scoured and rocky, the blue of the sea sparkling below.

"That's how my father met his end," Martin went on. "He was a champion cragsman, my old man. I was but a lad when the rope broke on him. He didn't fall far, but he landed on a bit of turf so far down, yet so far above the sea, that no one could get to him. Not a soul. The poor fellow. He broke his leg. We could hear him calling to us, but we couldn't reach him. His brothers took a boat out on the sea below, calling up to him, and he dragged himself to the edge, but he couldn't climb down. On the third day, we heard him singing. A bit wild, his voice was, singing one of the old songs. And that was it for him. He sang himself on to the other side. His bones must still be there, resting on that bit of turf. The birds probably thought it served him right, the old pillager."

Frances wondered, but did not ask, why they had not simply lowered another man to him, why they could not haul him up, or lower him down on a fresh rope. Perhaps, she thought, there was only one rope on the island? Perhaps the story was inaccurate. She let it go, picturing the poor man wasting away, delirious and singing.

Martin gave Frances the tooth on their last day in Stornoway, after he'd taken Cliff fishing in his boat, after Cliff had examined Martin's daughters' mouths, finding the mouth of the youngest full of decay, but the older one in excellent shape. "She doesn't eat sweets," said her mother. "She just hasn't the taste for them." When the Bells left, Martin's girls were in the harbor, waving at their boat, their dark curls blowing in the wind, and Martin stood beside them, his hands his on hips, laughing as if he had never known sadness.

Muirna's tooth was a rotten black thing, but it recalled for Frances those girls with their ruddy cheeks, and Martin with his bright eyes, and the pubs in Stornoway, so full of singing on Saturdays. The streets were full of strong women hauling tubs of fish up from the harbor, and the wind blew endlessly over the sea.

POSTCARDS FROM THE OUTER HEBRIDES
1931

Schwester,

Despite their pure lives and the scouring wind, tuberculosis eats through the glands of the young. They call it the white plague, and it festers in their lungs, erupts through their necks. The city people blame it on the peat smoke. *Who can breathe in it and live*? But for centuries it has been this way. For centuries, the islanders have slept in the smoke, and eaten in the smoke, swallowed it in mouthfuls, drifted through it while they dreamed, and mixed the burnt peat into the soil to fertilize the oats they eat. Cliff might be the first person to pay serious attention to that. He trusts the knowledge of the people, centuries of knowledge. Cliff says it isn't smoke that feeds the tubercules, but rather the new foods they eat in town. Foods shipped from London, from the continent, from the industrial mills and conveyer belts. Angel food cake, canned marmalades, colorless tinned vegetables, and heaps of confections in crinkly wrappers. Stay away from them!

I send you sweet wishes, but please eat apples,
Frances

Dear E,

Sometimes I wonder if what we're doing is of any use. If, maybe, Cliff is wrong. But that isn't it. If he's wrong, he's wrong. We're still here, and the people are grand. Bright cheeked. Their laughter is hoarse. And many scientists have been wrong before they have been right.

Cliff packed a box of peat, oats, and dried fish with skins for the lab. When we return . . . (When will we return? It will not be for months yet, perhaps even a year.) When we return he plans to mix different densities of soil and sand to see how tall the oats grow, to test the islanders' knowledge and ideas about burned peat as fertilizer.

I received your letter dated April 6. You must be nearly ready for the May Day festivities by now. I hope everything goes (went?) swimmingly. I expect that it will (did?). Your dancers are always perfect.

I wonder, Dear Sister, if you would consider, after all this time, forgiving Cliff? And no, by using the word "forgive" I do not mean to imply that I agree with you that he has done something that requires forgiveness, but I know that this is how you feel, how you think of things. I do not read your letters to him, but I know that your anger pains him, and adds to the ever-lingering pain of losing our child. You and he were such wonderful friends when we were young. I know you haven't forgotten—you have always had the better memory! I remember how you called him Mollusk? You're the only one who could get away with it, you know. Wouldn't it be lovely if, when we return to Cleveland, we could spend an afternoon in the yard, just like the old days, working in the garden, and then hitting the birdie for a bit, though probably less fiercely than we used to. I'm sure the two of you have a lingering score to settle over the badminton net, and how I'd love for that to be the only score remaining between you. How he would love it, too, to have you back—his old friend, my dear sister. Think about it?

Have I mentioned that I miss you? I miss your visits to Cleveland, our morning walks up the hill, past the school where the children laugh, the swings creak on their chains, the occasional soggy mitten is abandoned on the side of the road, and you, telling me about some new potato dish, or how to grow better carrots. I do miss you.

Windblown,
Frances

Dearest E,

On the edge of town, the oat mill rests its wheels and stones and rusts its cranks. The ovens are cold. Boats bring smooth white breads, heavy bags of sugar. They leave laden with the catch: flat fish, oysters, lobster, cod. Off to London with them. Off to the canning plants.

How can bones grow strong on sweets and starches? How can blood stay pure? The children breathe sloppily through their mouths, the lower jaws always hanging loose, agape and (I am sorry to say it) stupid-looking. Sometimes I want to close their mouths for them. Just sidle up and nudge those jaws into place. But I refrain. I keep my hands to myself.

Love,
Frances

Dear Elizabeth,

You are so far away! We planned to visit the Isle of Skye, but Cliff has decided it is too far, and we do not have time. A shame, I think. Who wouldn't like to visit the sky? It must be rather lonely there, but distance protects it, too. It is too far for the shipments of sugar and canned foods. I suggested it would be useful for comparison, but Cliff is anxious to move on. Plenty of comparisons in the future, he says.

And so we're off to Switzerland! Do you remember how we loved *Heidi* as girls? How we braided our hair and wore kerchiefs on our heads. How we tried to yodel? I was so desperate to own a goat. Well, I will see what it's really like.

Yodelayheehoo,
Frances

TSCHAGATTA
Switzerland, 1931

And here we are, as promised, back in the Swiss Alps, where Clifford and Frances are happily hiking from village to village, peering into the mouths of children, measuring jaws and foreheads, scraping teeth and probing mouths and tallying caries, collecting bread and cheese and milk. They wear thick socks and boots. They admire the cows with their bells, the few brave spring flowers, the wooden masks carved by their host, Estelle. And Estelle—storyteller, mask carver—feeds them bowls of sheep stew and thick rye bread. She teaches them to milk cows. Cliff already knows how, of course, having grown up on a farm. He refuses to squat on the stool, waves her off. "Why doesn't Frances take a turn? She has never milked a cow, have you, dear?" He wanders to the next stall where Estelle's husband, Ludovic, is milking the other cow. Cliff stands with his notebook and pen, admiring Ludovic's jawline, and Ludovic looks over and smiles, and Cliff writes something in the notebook.

"You must squeeze as you pull," says Estelle, wrapping her hands over Frances', and together they fill the bucket with frothy milk. Together they carry the pail to the kitchen, swinging it gently between them, laughing like girls, which makes Frances miss her sister, but she likes Estelle, her new friend, one of the first on their travels. She considers if she will write to Estelle after they leave this village, and imagines the long journey her letters will complete if she writes to Estelle from Cleveland. Cliff walks behind the women with his notebook, noting the way Frances' kerchief has slipped back from her head, revealing her silver hair. When did it get so silver? How had he missed the change?

Estelle and Ludovic are generous hosts, although Ludovic speaks only a few words of English. Frances and Clifford are endlessly confused by the way his words begin in German, but slip into what sounds, to them, like gibberish, and so they speak to him mostly in smiles and nods and handshakes, which feel a little ridiculous after a while. But when they leave, they will hug him, each in turn, and kiss his cheeks, first the right and then the left, and thank him in German, and bow and nod smile once again.

It is their last night in Switzerland—the cheek kissing and luggage dragging are only hours away—and the sun is sinking, tucking itself behind the inky ridge of mountains, casting its pink glow across the crusty traces of snow. Standing in her kitchen, Estelle asks Cliff to fetch a bag of rye from the mill. She circles his bicep with two hands, although it is not a particularly well-developed muscle. "Strong man," Estelle says. Perhaps she is flirting, just a little, or perhaps she is flattering him so he'll help her. Maybe she is simply teasing. He cannot tell. "You're the one for the job. And if you go now, you'll catch the *alpenglow,* which means that by asking you to do this, I'm actually doing you a tremendous favor." She holds her hands wide to demonstrate the size of the favor—three feet.

And so Clifford pulls his boots on once again and trudges up the hill, feeling his heart rate increase. His breathing grows a little ragged. The altitude makes walking uphill more difficult, and while he is not unhealthy, neither is he young. He fetches the rye, a heavy sack that he slings over his shoulder like a slain animal, and turns back toward the village. At the horizon, the sky is lurid pink and orange, and the snow reflects it. He looks up as he walks, admiring the deepening shade of blue as it grows dark. Estelle was right—it's a gift to be here at this moment, breathing the cool mountain air, watching for the first star. He pats the sack of grain on his shoulder as if it is a child or a dog.

The Swiss villagers have impressed him with their bright eyes, unlined brows, wide-set nostrils. Their teeth are aligned in perfect arches, a little slimy, a little stained, because they do not brush them, yet even without brushing, and without a dentist, they are almost entirely without decay. In a week, he has examined the mouths of 75 villagers and found fewer than 25 caries, not a single incidence of tuberculosis. What was their secret? Plenty of cheese, thickly sliced. Rye bread from local grains. Meat once a week.

Lanterns begin to flicker in the windows, and Clifford hears a wave of laughter somewhere in the distance. A door slams. A cowbell clangs. It has been a lovely week with these rugged people. If possible, he and Frances will return next summer, in July or August, when the flowers fill the valleys, or maybe they'll come during Fasnacht, the holiday week they've heard so much about. He has set up an ongoing study, prescribing a diet for the children in this village, which isn't so different from the diet they already follow, but they've promised not to deviate, not to drink chocolate milk or eat the sweets that are sure to make their way to this village now that the train line comes so close. He'll compare their teeth with the teeth of the children in the next village, one notch closer to the train and to the cities, closer to the sugary jams and wrapped candies that will surely rot their teeth, poor kids.

The cowbell clangs again, suddenly very close behind him, and Cliff turns, expecting to see a child leading a cow down from the hills, but instead he sees a monster—a masked *tschagatta*—a man wearing long white furs over his back and shoulders. It is rushing toward him, running downhill, not even stumbling, but sort of falling toward him, running fast, shaking the bell in the air like a fist. It has antlers and yellow rings painted around the holes of its eyes. Its mouth is jagged with teeth and it shakes its walking stick and rattles the bell.

For a moment, Cliff stands perfectly still. It's ridiculous, he thinks, a furry man in a mask, *a grown man*, he tells himself. *It is a man.* But it's running right at him. It's charging! Coming for him! He drops the sack of rye and begins to run, his feet slipping in the half-frozen mud.

Estelle has been insistent that no one dresses as a tschagatta anytime but Fasnacht, which is in early spring, before Easter. She would not even show them a photograph of the procession. She swore there were no photographs in existence, that the creatures were fleeting and mystical, that they would not stand still for a camera. "You have to be here," she said. "You must see them in person. Only one week a year."

A grown man in a mask, but his heart is pounding and the bell is coming closer and his feet are scrambling, slipping in the mud, and the bell keeps coming closer and closer, and the stick and the teeth and the yellow eyes, the black holes of the eyes, and why does he keep looking back over his shoulder? The bell. The bell. And he slips, and he slips again, and the bell keeps clanging, and then he's down in the mud, fallen like a child, but still scrambling, his hands in the mud, the mud seeping through the knees of his trousers, there in the middle of a half-frozen street.

The tschagatta reaches him and crouches beside him, breathing raggedly through the black hole of its mask, and Cliff looks at it, at the human eyes within. *A grown man in a mask.* Side by side, they kneel in the mud, until the beast sits back on its haunches and growls a low, animal sound. It stands, and grabs Cliff's collar and hauls him upright, choking him a little, and Cliff coughs and leans his hands on his knees, breathing too hard, and the monster says something in Swiss German, his voice surprisingly quiet. Cliff looks up at him, up at the mask that is looking down at him. The monster cups his jaw in its furry mitten and pulls him upright. It is still six inches taller than him, and it raises its other mitten to Cliff's face. There are black claws affixed to the mittens, and it drags a single claw down Cliff's cheek, a single claw drawing a line slowly over his cheekbone, down to his jaw, a slow line rolling like a tear.

Cliff's heart thuds.

"Hallo, friend," it says, softly, in English. It pats him on the shoulder. It takes a small knife from a pocket somewhere within its fur and layers and opens the blade slowly, dramatically. "Come," it says. It cups Cliff's jaw in its hand. It tips his face toward its own as if to kiss him, but then turns his face to the side, its mitten over his ear, dampening the sounds of the world, just for a moment. It holds his head steady and pulls at what's left of Cliff's thin hair, the silver wisps around his ears and the back of his head. It laughs and raises the knife and slices carefully through a few strands of hair. It snaps the blade shut, and raises the little tuft high.

"Mine!" it shouts. It tucks both knife and hair into a pocket and turns away from Cliff.

A man can be a monster. But this one is not. It is a regular man that understands fear, that understands that all he needs to do is be there, that Clifford's mind will do the work, will make him into the most fearful thing imaginable.

The tschagatta shuffles slowly away, hunching beneath its fur cape, and it laughs to itself—a slow, dramatic laugh. It does not turn back, but trudges uphill toward the mill, where it disappears behind a ridge. Cliff stands there panting, hands on his hips, catching his breath, waiting for the thunder of his heart to slow.

And then Estelle is there, appearing in the narrow space between two houses, and Frances is following close behind. The two women step out from between the houses to meet him, smiling broad, insulting smiles.

"You made a new friend?" Estelle says. She is beaming, but Frances looks uncertain, like a puppy with its tail between its legs.

Cliff shakes his head. "What was that?" he says. "What was the purpose of that?"

"Oh, come now, Dr. Bell. It was all good fun. Your very own tschagatta! We should all be so lucky!" Her voice is bright. Cliff can't muster a laugh. He can barely speak. He turns away from her, looking back up the street toward the mill, toward the place where the tschagatta disappeared. The bag of rye he dropped is split and spilled across the dirt, wasted.

"Cliff?" Frances says, but he turns away from her and walks uphill to spilled grain. He looks down at it, feeling his heartbeat slowing now. He feels the beat in his throat. His breathing is slower now, too, and quieter, but his face is burning. He presses the back of his hand to his cheek.

"Dr. Bell!" Estelle calls. "Don't be so serious!"

Frances has followed him and puts a hand on his arm. "Dear, it was just for fun," she says. She takes his hand. "A game. Estelle has offered to give us the mask as a gift."

"It is true," Estelle says, joining them, but standing a few feet away. "Your very own tschagatta. The very one of your nightmares. It will live with you, which means you will have control of it. You have had a real Swiss experience. And it's not even Fasnacht."

"It's not the real thing, then," he says. "Not a real Swiss experience. It's not Fasnacht. It was just a mean joke."

The women look back at him wide-eyed and straight-faced, but laughter gets the better of Estelle. "You ran so fast, Dr. Bell! So fast!" she says between giggles. Even Frances is smiling a little, and she turns away to hide it.

He stands for a minute longer, looking at the place where the sun has disappeared behind the mountain. Soon it will be completely dark, only the stars lighting the sky.

He forgives them as much as he can. Over dinner, he fakes laughter and waves off their apologies, but in bed that night, he asks Frances why she did it. It was so unlike her. Such a cruel prank. He is laying on his back, his hand folded on his chest, staring at the ceiling.

"We didn't mean it to be cruel, dear." In her bed, on the other side of the nightstand, Frances turns toward him, but he keeps his eyes on the ceiling. "I thought you wanted to see a tschagatta," she says. "You kept asking to see photos. You seemed so irritated when Estelle insisted that they only came out that one week a year. As if someone couldn't just put on one of those outfits whenever they wanted. I honestly didn't think you'd be scared."

"I wasn't scared," he says. "Not exactly. But it was chasing me. I was just responding." His voice is quiet, too steady.

"I'm sorry, dear. I really am. It was meant to be fun." She props herself up on an elbow. "You know how everyone keeps telling us how unique Fasnacht is. How it's the best week of the year. How we should come back for it. But you know we won't. We'll probably be in the Pacific next year. And when Estelle suggested it, it seemed like an opportunity. It seemed fun."

"Estelle," he says.

"Why do you say it like that?"

"No reason," he says. "It's fine. It's all fine." He turns off the light on the nightstand between them. He waits for his eyes to adjust to the dark. Estelle reminds him of Elizabeth, who he hasn't spoken to in 12 years. Or it isn't that Estelle reminds him of Elizabeth so much as when Frances is with her, she behaves as she does when she's with her sister—girlish and exclusive. He becomes an outsider, an enemy, a little boy with cooties.

"Goodnight," he says. Tomorrow they'll be on their way to Egypt.

"Goodnight, dear."

He listens as she pulls the sheets up and he waits to hear her breathing fall into the rhythm of sleep. He turns onto his side, facing the wall, but lays awake, remembering the way he had paused before he ran, his feet rooted to the street, the bag of rye heavy over his shoulder. He knew then that it was a game, that it was a man in a costume, but his adrenaline had surged nonetheless. And then his legs had moved of their own accord. And now, in the dark room, Frances sighing in her sleep, he thinks it strange that Estelle never mentioned the importance of fear when she talked about the traditions of the Fasnacht. Fear, it seems to him, is at least as important as an indulgence. Or perhaps fear *is* an indulgence. When we fear for our lives but evade death, we are invigorated. His life had never been in danger, but it had felt real enough. It had felt as if he might have to fight for his safety. And after such fear, he feels stronger and more resolute. For a fleeting moment, he might be happy with simple things—with breath, with his steady heartbeat, with the particular blue of twilight.

For months, Cliff will dream of it. He had looked into the eyes of death. On the boat in Egypt, in a wattle and daub hut in Sudan, back home in Ohio, he will wake from a dream of the tschagatta: long white fur, mumbled Swiss-German, yellow-ringed eyes. And even as he wakes, he will hear the ragged breath from its carved mouth.

In the dream, when the monster touches his face, he won't resist. He won't cringe or pull away. He will look into the eyes behind the mask and see that they are human eyes, brown and blinking and looking back at him. Shining human eyes. In the dream, he will slip his hand beneath the monster's mask to feel its cheek. He will run his fingertips across the warm stubble of a shaved beard—the beard of man, a beard like his own—and he will touch the skin beneath the monster's eyes. And then he will wake, sweating in a dark room, the room full of his own ragged breath, and his fingertips will tingle, remembering the texture of the skin he had touched—the skin of the monster—human and smooth and tender as petals.

IV.

WELCOME ABOARD THE AIDA!

Kind Guests,

Let us be the first to welcome you to Egypt, the Cradle of Civilization! For thousands of years, people have lived and thrived in the Fertile Crescent and all along the Nile Valley, cultivating crops, building cities and timeless monuments, and developing the first known system of writing (hieroglyphs). You are sure to be amazed at all you will discover!

Let us also welcome you aboard our boat! The Aida is a dahabiya, an ancient Egyptian boat that is even depicted within the tombs of our ancestors! The word dahabiya means "golden one," and we think you will find The Aida is, indeed, golden. Rest assured that you can travel in ease and luxury aboard The Aida, your floating home upon the Nile.

When we dock each afternoon, and you venture into our cities, museums, and wondrous archeological sites, we advise you to keep the following information in mind to assure your continued safety.

1. **Scams, Scandals, and Pickpockets:** With the highest heights of civilization, also come lows of criminal
   behavior. Remain alert and aware of your surroundings
   at all times. It is, however, often said that Egypt's touts
   are the most charming in the world. They will offer to
   guide you through the thicket of trinkets and stalls in
   our beautiful souqs (marketplaces), draw your portrait
   in Egyptian charcoal, share a sweet hookah with you.
   You might even choose to accept one of these offers, as
   their services will be inexpensive, if unnecessary. Some
   say a charming tout is an essential part of the Egyptian
   experience. Allow that kindly "professor" to guide you
   to the "best bookshop in all of Alexandria," or to accom-
   pany you to his favorite restaurant. But beyond accept-
   ing entertaining (if somewhat dishonest) company, we
   recommend you keep your hands in your pockets and
   your elbows out. Learn the phrase "La shoukran" ("No,
   thank you"). Don't accept any gift a person thrusts into
   your waiting hands. Don't taste free samples. There is
   nothing free in Egypt, not even friendship or hospitality
   (though the price for these is not high).

2. **Dehydration, Sunburn, Heatstroke, and Extreme Tem-
   peratures:** While the Nile Delta is some of the most
   fertile land in the world, our wonderful country is pre-
   dominately desert. While you can hide in the shadows
   of the souqs, and in the cabins aboard our golden boat,
   you will inevitably become acquainted with the hot
   sun. Take care to keep your skin covered and to drink
   plentiful fluids. Dehydration occurs when you expend
   more fluid (via sweating, urination, or diarrhea) than
   you have replaced. Drink water whenever you have
   the opportunity. If purified water is not available, tea

can substitute because it is always boiled first. Signs of dehydration and heatstroke (both of which can be fatal!) include irritability and confusion, thirst, dry mouth, dry skin, swollen tongue, weakness, dizziness, heart palpitations, and fainting. Symptoms of heatstroke include red, hot, dry skin, throbbing headache, muscle weakness or cramps, staggering, rapid shallow breathing, vomiting, and unconscious collapse (fainting). Should you or your companions experience any of the above symptoms, immediately seek a cool place, water, and medical assistance. Conversely, the desert can be downright frigid at night, particularly in the winter months. Travel with layers! Even the most sweltering afternoon can segue to a freezing night.

3. **Crocodiles:** The Nile Crocodile is an aggressive and opportunistic predator, a generalist capable of taking almost any animal as prey, including full-grown human beings. They spend most of their days basking, and often do so in shallow water, with only their eyes apparent over the surface. They often sit motionless for hours, waiting for prey to approach, and then they attack, using their conical, sharp teeth, or holding an animal underwater until it drowns. Crocodiles were sacred to ancient Egyptians who both raised them and sacrificed them in temples. Thus, many crocodiles still dwell in the water near temple sites. Watch for posted warnings and always steer clear of the water's edge.

Once again, we welcome you aboard The Aida, your floating home upon the Nile. We wish you a most magical journey!

Signed,
The Captain and Crew of The Aida

A SINGLE GOLDEN THING
Frances
Egypt, 1931

The Nile River stretches for 4,258 miles, from Lake Victoria in Uganda north to Cairo. The White Nile meets the Blue Nile, and together they gather silt and push northward, winding between jungles and reeds and red desert rocks, ancient pyramids and bustling cities with narrow passageways, the sun slanting through the dust, and finally the river empties into the Mediterranean Sea. All my life I have read about this place, and so it has never seemed real to me. The Sphinx and the pyramids, the infant Moses floating in his basket, God's plague on the Egyptians turning the river red with blood. The Nile has always been like a fairytale, all myth and magic and ink on paper. But here I am, on this boat, this *dahabiya*, sitting alone on the sundeck, watching the shadows lengthen as the sun sinks toward the horizon. Above me is a bright blue sky, and on the riverbank, a pair of boys are washing a cow, running their hands swiftly over her flanks. Backlit, the boys and the cow are thin silhouettes, bending and standing so gracefully as we slip past them. When Cliff and I boarded the boat, large crocodiles were flanking the ramp, basking in the water below and lazing along the banks, their mouths open to catch the breeze or a morsel, and now, watching the boys, I cannot help but wonder how they ward off the crocodiles, how they can know there is not one waiting as they wash the cow, waiting for them to step just a little further into the reeds.

A fleet of sailboats with giant triangular sails glides past in a staggered line, pulling each other like puppets on strings, or like geese through the October sky back home in Ohio. Geese always remind me of Ben. When he was three or four, he loved to chase them in the park. They would hiss at him, but he chased them anyway, stretching his bright woolen mittens toward them, laughing at their strange tongues. Once, he tripped and a goose nipped him on the bottom, but he only laughed more loudly. He loved those awkward birds, and together we would watch how they became graceful when they flew. We watched as they moved across the sky in their V formation, calling out in their hoarse, musical voices. I told him that when the geese flew, winter was coming. That soon the sky would be dull and silent. I would teach him to crunch through the skin of ice that formed on the surface of the puddles. I knew little, then, of missing something, of missing someone. Each spring, the geese returned.

Our boat is a flat-bottomed riverboat with three levels of varnished woodwork and a white-painted body. The name, *Aida*, is painted in neat green and gold letters across the prow. It is late afternoon, and while Cliff naps in our cabin, I watch waiters in long silk tunics drift among passengers sipping tea and smoking cigarettes. The very second anyone finishes a smoke, a cabin boy or waiter arrives with a fresh ashtray and whisks the old one away, its ashes not yet cooled. Here, there are no children lining up, opening their mouths, waiting for Clifford to measure their skulls and jaws, to count their good teeth and their rotten ones. No food samples to collect. No tools to clean or film to load. No pictures to take or equipment to lug. No interpreter translating for me, leaving some words out, adding a few here and there, while I wonder at all I don't know.

"Tea, madam?" a waiter asks. His accent is lilting and British though he is dressed in the embroidered vest and loose blouse of the locals, his skin a warm shade of brown. I cannot tell if he is a Brit who looks Egyptian or an Egyptian who speaks perfectly accented English. He balances a tray with a ceramic teapot and a circle of cups. I nod, and he sets a cup on the table and fills it before drifting off again, leaving the tea steaming beside me.

With a tapping of leather soles, a man approaches with a cane and pauses at the chair beside mine. "Is this seat taken?" His is tall, sunburned, and boyish: an Englishman in cream colored linen. His mustache is tobacco-stained.

"You're welcome to it," I say, although there are plenty of empty chairs. There is no need for him to take the one right beside mine, though the boat is small—only 16 passengers. The welcome brochure promised we'd have the chance to mingle with our fellow travelers, and I suppose this is part of the experience. He sits.

His name is Curtis Wheeler. He's an Egyptologist, he says, currently studying the precinct of Mut. A private tomb. Not even open to the public yet. Lovely there, he says. Dark and cool and full of mysteries. "But this boat! Isn't it just splendid?" He waves down a waiter for some tea. He sighs into his cup, inhaling the steam. "I just love *saiidi*," he says. "So robust. I quite prefer it to the northern style, though that's lovely, too, with the fresh mint. Much more delicate." He sips the tea and dabs his mustache with a napkin. "Utterly delicious!" he says. "And the flavor is enhanced by this gorgeous evening, wouldn't you say? And by your company, of course."

I feel my face flush and turn to the book in my lap. It has been a long time since anyone has flirted with me. Perhaps he's only being polite.

"My absolute favorite way to take tea in Egypt is out in the desert," he says. He looks dreamily into the distance. "To pause after a long ride and spread a blanket in the camel's shadow."

"I haven't had such a pleasure," I say. "But my husband and I are planning to ride camels to see the temple at Karnak."

"Karnak...well." He sips the tea. "It's quite popular." He dabs his mustache again. The tips of it are waxed stiff. "Desert tea is nothing like high tea, but that is precisely what I love about it. Although one can find plenty of high teas around here, too, you know. Even on the boat, they serve the loveliest pastries. And I do like a good *mille-feuille* now and then. I simply *must* have my custards."

He takes a pipe and tobacco pouch from his breast pocket. The pipe is hand-carved, its bowl in the shape of a man's face with a long mustache and hair that appears to blow back along the stem. "The coffee here is also excellent," he says. "Strong and sweet. Just how I like it." He pinches some tobacco from the pouch and begins packing it into the bowl of his pipe. "You don't mind if I smoke." It is a statement, not a question, but I nod anyway. He flicks the lighter a few times, watching the flame, but doesn't light the pipe.

"Do you have a particular focus within Egyptology?" I ask. He seems like a man who enjoys holding forth, and if I'm going to listen, it seems best to choose a topic I know little about.

"Well, the mother goddess is the sole possessor of my heart." He presses a hand to his heart. "Mut. She's my lady. Now and forever." He laughs. "But lately, I've been reading a great deal about the sun god, Ra, who was both Mut's consort and her creator. Nice work when you can conjure your own consort, no?" He takes the pipe from between his teeth—he hasn't lit it. Ra, he explains, pulls the sun across the sky in a boat. And then there is Khepri, a scarab that rolls the sun along like a ball of dung. And Atum, the *actual* sun god, the first god. "Out of chaos, he created himself," he says. "And then, because he was lonely, he made Shu and Tefnut. Some say he created them by masturbating— that they came from his seed—but directly translated, they came from a sneeze...*Achoo!*" He snaps his fingers. "Voila! Company."

For the second time, I feel my face flush, but Curtis keeps talking. I study the book in my lap, turning it over, embarrassed to look at him.

"It's not so different from 'Let there be light' now, is it?" Wheeler says.

I cough. "Well, I suppose it's a little different."

He gestures to the book, which I now notice is upside down. "I've interrupted your reading," he says. "I'll leave you to your book."

He stands and steps to the rail. He seems more serious standing there, puffing on the pipe, which he has finally lit, cheeks drawn tight, the smoke trailing from his mouth like a sigh. His hair is blond, but turning white. He wears a silk scarf knotted about his throat, something like a boy scout.

I try to read a few pages, but my eyes are tired, as if I have been reading for hours, and even when I run my finger along the page, I keep losing my place. Curtis Wheeler leans his elbows on the railing of the boat, smoking his pipe and watching the world pass. He's a prattler, a man who rattles on about dead things, beetles and stick-legged gods, but I cannot help but think he seems lonely. He has square shoulders, a strong jaw. I have not really looked at a man in years. Not even Clifford, whose appearance I am so used to. Looking at Cliff is almost like looking at myself. There is a small mirror on the wall in our cabin, framed with silver and bits of lapis lazuli, and when I saw myself in it earlier, I was surprised at my face, which seems thinner these days, and as pale as ever. We have not had many mirrors on our travels, and I have not missed them.

I smooth back the loose hairs around my face, the irritating curls that always frizz in humidity. Baby hairs, Elizabeth always calls them. We inherited them from our father, I suppose. My mother had heavy, smooth hair that fell flat and against her back, and when she pulled it into a ponytail or a bun, her hairline was clean and precise. I touch the soft folds of skin at my throat, where the skin is papery and loose—the skin of an old woman with a double chin, a few odd whiskers sprouting here and there. Even without mirrors, I try to keep up with the whiskers, to pluck them as they sprout. Like many older people, I find I am drifting into some category between woman and man, although the people we meet almost always address Cliff first and rarely even shake my hand. Sometimes, it is my invisibility that makes me feel most like a woman.

I pull my hat down, tipping the brim to shade my eyes, and I smooth my blouse. I regret that I did not buy something nice to wear from the shops in Aswan. Something elegant for dinner on the boat, or to wear in the cities. But it seemed unnecessary. In five days we will be in Sudan, sleeping in a mud hut, and then we'll be off to the jungle to see the pygmies. I close my book.

"It was lovely to meet you, Mr. Wheeler," I say, standing.

"Call me Curtis," he says, turning and bowing. "Please. And the pleasure was entirely mine." He tips his hat and winks at me. For the third time, I feel myself blush. A slumping old woman with a hairy chin, and here I am, noticing the color of the man's eyes: blue.

In Egypt, it seems that Clifford is afraid of everything. In the souq, he keeps his hands in his pockets, guarding his wallet at all times. His eyes shift constantly from side to side, and if I linger too long in a stall, fingering the inkstones and pens, the bright silks or hand-bound leather books full of blank pages, or pause to look up at the chandeliers hanging from the ceiling, punched tin and sparkling glass, or remark on the ceiling itself—an arched stone cavern of light—Cliff takes my elbow and nudges me along.

"We have to keep moving," he whispers. "We don't want to look like tourists."

But the souq is full of tourists, and even if we keep moving, we look like them. No one will mistake us for locals, or even expats. Pale Americans and Brits in khaki, Italians and Turks and Germans in hats and scarves and sturdy shoes. The marketplace is full of languages, too: fricatives of Arabic, nasal French, snippets of English. I pause to listen. "It's like Babel!" I whisper, thrilled at the cacophony of tongues, but Cliff is worried about pickpockets and thieves in every doorway, watching for us, the most bumbling of the khaki-clad.

"You can't just stand here with your eyes closed!" He tows me along between stalls displaying heaps of orange and copper and red spices, tobacconists with jars of dried leaves, tall glimmering hookahs. He does not want to be seen gawking, nor asked for money. "And anyway," he says, "these things are just trinkets. Useless souvenirs. The only souvenirs I want are samples of the foods people eat. We can't be collecting junk. We have enough to carry as it is."

But even when I stop at a stall selling legumes—dried lentils of every color, dappled beans—he pulls me onward.

"We want the things people *actually* eat. We must get our samples from kitchens, from wives and mothers who cook them."

Never mind the local women handing money to the vendors in exchange for paper packets of dried beans, their heads and shoulders draped in scarves that frame their faces. Women who are surely wives and mothers and daughters. When I pause before a stall displaying dates and other dried fruits, he tells me there are plenty of dried fruits available on the boat. And so we walk too swiftly through the stacks of clocks and lanterns, the mirrors and frames, carved wooden doors, leaning bicycles, chattering monkeys, cats and dogs and donkeys, clothing, jewelry, ashtrays, instruments, suitcases, tapestries, and scarves. We pass by piles of pale garlic and varicolored onions, pomegranates and dates and tomatoes. We pause for nothing. Briefly, I think of Curtis Wheeler, how comfortable he seems in Egypt, how it seems he would be comfortable anywhere, lounging in his linen suits, stopping to talk to women and locals as he drifts across boat decks and through marketplaces alike. Like us, it is obvious he is not Egyptian, but he dines in these restaurants and lingers in tea stalls anyway.

I ask Clifford what is the point of visiting the souq if we're not going to look at anything, not going to talk to anyone. He sighs. "We're taking it in," he says. "The whole atmosphere. We don't have to buy things to experience this place. We need to stay safe." He checks his watch. "Are you hungry? Why don't we go back to the boat for lunch?"

And so we eat most of our meals on the boat, where the food is clean and British and the water is filtered, though it still tastes like rust to me, and the tables are draped in white linen, and the chairs are wicker with little cushions.

Once upon a time, months ago, or years, when the idea to conduct fieldwork took hold, Clifford said he that had always wanted to see the pyramids, but now that we are here, in Egypt, the days are so hot and bright, and there is the ever-growing stack of photographs, the pages of notes waiting to be turned into a book.

"I want to get organized," he says, stabbing a piece of beef with his fork. "I need to get some of this down while it's fresh." But I want to see the sites, the great pharaohs and their necropolises, to wander through souqs and teashops.

"We're on vacation, in a way," I argue. "No research until Sudan, right? And why spend the money for this beautiful boat if we aren't going to enjoy ourselves?"

"But I enjoy my work," Clifford says. "And I *don't* enjoy haggling with men over the price of a camel ride. Plus, research isn't just what happens in the field. You know that. The writing and analysis are always waiting. I have all the notes from Cairo to sort through."

I see Curtis Wheeler winding his way between tables, cane in hand, though the cane seems all ornament, entirely unnecessary. I stand and wave to him. "Curtis!" My voice comes out louder than I intend, and the other diners turn to look. "Curtis Wheeler!" I beckon to him, gesturing to the empty chair at our table. "Would you like to join us?"

Our plates are nearly empty, though the waiters haven't quite swooped them up yet, and Clifford is picking the smooth pit of date from his mouth. At the center of our table is an untouched plate of chocolate biscuits, and as he sits, Curtis Wheeler takes one and bites into it. The crumbs cling in his mustache. He chews the cookie and swallows, but the crumbs remain. Somewhat belatedly, he shakes Cliff's hand across the table.

"Your wife tells me you're a dentist," he says. Clifford nods. Curtis' suit is wrinkled as if he slept in it. It hangs too loosely on his shoulders, as if he has recently lost weight, but it seems at least as likely that he's a man that can't be bothered to have his clothes tailored.

"Do you know much about ancient Egyptian dentistry?" Curtis asks. He finally brushes the crumbs from his mustache.

"Not much," says Cliff. "I'm more interested in contemporary dentistry. Mrs. Bell explained my project?"

Curtis nods vaguely. "Nutrition and dental health. Primitive diets and such." He waves his hand, dismissing this strand of conversation as if he can't be bothered with the details, as if the project does not interest him in the least. He takes out a little notebook and pen. "The ancient Egyptians were incredibly advanced, you know. Would you let me tell you just a bit? I think you'll find it fascinating." He does not pause for approval. "They may have been some of the first dentists." He opens the notebook to a blank page and draws an eye over a curved tusk.

"The hieroglyph for dentist," Wheeler says. He is gleeful, as if Cliff has been waiting all his life for this information, this little drawing, a secret code.

"Ancient Egyptians actually cared a great deal for their teeth. This," He taps at the curved tooth with the tip of his pen, "*might* be the tooth of a crocodile, the king of the Nile. Or it *might* be the tusk of an elephant. It's yet to be determined! A great mystery in my field. Arguments in support of both." He closes the notebook and tucks it back into his pocket. Then he takes it out again, tears out the page, and hands it to Cliff. "I love the unsolved mysteries of hieroglyphics, although personally, I prefer to think that's the tooth of a croc. Elephant tusks hardly seem related to human mouths."

"Well, now, I don't know," Cliff says. He studies the drawing. "The curved end looks a good deal more like a tusk than a tooth to me." I take the paper and squint at it.

"Why would a crocodile tooth be any more closely related?" I ask.

"An excellent question," Curtis says. He sniffs. "And one to which I do not have an answer. But if it were a tusk, it would throw off the entire scale. Not that there's a consistent scale in hieroglyphs." As if to distract us from the nonsense he is spouting, he waves to the waiter and orders a glass of red wine, which the waiter pours for him immediately. He takes a hearty swig, then dabs at his mustache with a linen napkin. "You two *must* visit the museum in Alexandria. You really *must* make time for it. Even if it means putting off Khartoum for a day. Or leaving the boat a day early, though I should *hate* to think of you missing a single day on this gorgeous boat." He gestures broadly around the room and takes another swallow of wine. "The Ancient Egyptians thought that cavities were caused by a worm that lived inside the tooth," he says. "They dug it out with metal tools. But it was the root! The root of the tooth! Can you imagine? The incredible *pain*."

"A root canal?" Clifford says.

"Yes, yes. But they had no nitrous oxide, no ether, no chloroform! The pain must have been immense. Can you even imagine? I suppose they used birch bark or herbs of some sort as an anesthetic. Some sort of poultice. They used all sorts of herbs, of course. All sorts."

Cliff turns to me, interested at last. "Even the ancient Egyptians practiced root canals."

"Clifford has done a great deal of research into the practice of root canals," I say to Curtis. "It's one of his primary areas of expertise."

"Such a brutal practice," Curtis says. "I had one myself not too many years ago." He lifts his glass to his mouth, tips his head back and drains the final drops of wine. He sets the glass back on the table with finality. "I'd love to stay and chat, but I'm late to meet a friend in town. I've got to run. But it's been a pleasure, friends. A pleasure. Let us do it again." He pushes back his chair and stands, smoothing his hands over his rumpled suit. He leans to shake Clifford's hand, but when I put out my hand, he clasps it in both of his and bends to kiss it. "A pleasure, m'lady," he says. "A true pleasure." I feel myself blushing as we watch Curtis thread his way through the tables on his way to the door, cane leading the way as if he is blind.

"A strange fellow," I say.

"A bit of blowhard, I'd say. I bet he's kissed more ladies' hands than there are in the city of Cairo."

I push the plate of biscuits across the table to him and, to my surprise, he takes one.

Do the people pray before eating? Do they put their knife in their left or right hand? Do they skip the use of a knife altogether? Do they shake hands in greeting? Do they shake hands with women? Do they eat bread or some equivalent? Do they eat dairy products? Do they eat vegetables? Beef? Pork? Sheep? How do they dance? What is that instrument? And that one, with the shells? What is it called?

The entire time we've been traveling, I have been exhausted by questions. By the end of the day, all I need is a dark room and a blanket pulled to my chin and I'm instantly asleep. Never mind rushing rivers, shanty songs, babies crying, the drone of distant conversations. I close my eyes and am immediately asleep. But now, in our room aboard the Aida, it seems I am getting used to it—as if newness and disorientation are now a way of life. Or perhaps the luxury of the Aida has provided just enough complacency to allow for insomnia. I lay in the dark, eyes wide open, listening as

Cliff's breathing falls into the rhythm of sleep. Through the open curtains, I watch the blue-black night, squinting now and then to see the stars.

I close my eyes and drift, making my way toward the dark edge of sleep, my mind shuffling through images of crocodiles dozing in the hot sun, opening their wide mouths to cool themselves, revealing their jagged teeth. Crocodiles slithering through reeds on their scaly legs, sliding into the river, dragging their long tails behind them. Crocodiles disappearing into the green water. I know they are there, just beneath the surface, waiting for me, waiting to strike.

Do crocodiles live in this part of the country? Do they live along every part of the Nile? And what about hippos? I have heard that they can be even more vicious than crocs, and that they can run terribly fast. Both hippos and crocodiles can sit so still, half-submerged in water, so one doesn't even know they're there, their skin blending with the river and mud, only eyes and nostrils exposed. Curtis Wheeler called the crocodiles "glass eaters," and when I laughed, he went on. "The word crocodile means pebble worm, or pebble man. You know, for the texture of their skin."

Curtis Wheeler dabbing at his stained mustache. Blinking his blue eyes. Smoothing his rumpled suit. Drawing in his notebook with a silver pen.

At the Temple of Horus, I spot Curtis' head few inches above the rest of the crowd. He's wearing his straw sunhat and has a blue scarf knotted around his throat.

"Ahoy!" he shouts. He waves at us. "Top o' the morning!" Cliff waves and looks away, but I shout back.

"Hello, Mr. Wheeler!"

Curtis pushes through the crowd and shakes each of our hands vigorously. "Delightful to see you!" He acts as if it has been days or months since we have seen him, and even Cliff can't help but smile at his enthusiasm. I invite him to join us for the tour of Horus' tomb, but he declines.

"It's a wonderful tour," he says, "Just wonderful. I know you'll love it. But I need to pick up some supplies for my site."

Curtis is wearing a pair of ugly canvas shorts quite similar to the ones I bought for Cliff, necessary for the heat on this part of the journey, the part I have been calling our "Expedition Days," as if all of the last year and a half hasn't been an expedition. Clifford calls it "The Safari," but I think safaris are for shooting wild animals. It seems an impolite term if what you're looking at is people. Cliff hates the shorts. Or rather, he hates his legs, which have somehow gotten pale and shiny in the last year or two. (*Where in God's name did all the hair go?* He said the first time he put the shorts on. He leaned down to study his legs, ran his hand over his shins. *Bald as birch.*) He tried wearing trousers on our first day in Cairo, but he sweated like a pig. Ugly or not, he is stuck with the shorts. Curtis' legs are suntanned and gleaming with curly blond hair. His calf muscles are lean and defined, as if he has spent his life climbing mountains.

"I'll find you two later. We'll have tea!" He shakes Cliff's hand. He gives me a quick wave and leaves us, gently pushing his way through the crowd.

The tour guide begins walking, and we follow the group along the riverbank. The guide turns to face us, walking backward, gesturing to something on the river, but I can't quite hear him.

"What sort of fellow digs up mummies?" Cliff says. "It's rather morbid."

"Some might say the same of dentists," I say. "Not everyone is interested in other peoples' mouths. I think he's lonely. He probably misses conversation."

"But Egypt is full of Brits!" Cliff says. "It's like an appendage of London. London with sand. Brits more or less run the place. They build the dams. They claim the best mummies for their museums. They manage all the archeological digs."

"I suppose you're right."

"If anything, the war only made this place *more* British."

"Well, I kind of like him. Why are you so opposed to making friends?"

"I'm not," he says. "I don't know. I just don't trust the guy. He's like an overgrown boy. And he's too friendly. He doesn't even know us. Why should he be so happy to see us?"

My laugh comes out as a snort. Our guide stops in front of the temple and launches into a lecture. His voice barely makes it back to us, and the people behind us jostle forward, pushing past us. "I think he's interesting. You don't have to talk to him, but I'm not going to be rude. He's done nothing to us. I see no harm in making a friend when we have the chance."

Apparently, the tour's over because the crowd begins to disperse. Cliff checks his watch. "Did you hear when we're supposed to return to the boat?" When I say no, he leaves me, pushing toward the guide, and I stand there alone, finally looking up at the walls of the ancient temple that surround me, glowing brightly in the sun. The pillars are covered with carvings—hieroglyphs—which remind me of Bon Echo, although the rock there is granite, a much darker and harder stone than this.

There isn't a single person around us that looks Egyptian, not even our guide. The shadows on the figure looming above me are growing longer and bluer. It feels as if the sun is leaking out of the walls and pooling on the ground. I think of the mummies stored in the earth beneath me, in the walls and columns. We are probably walking over bones with each step.

Cliff returns. "We're on our own until 5 pm. Until dinner, really."

"Look at this place," I say. "It feels like there are ghosts everywhere. Like they're moving through us."

He sniffs. "Ghosts," he says. "But I suppose I know what you mean. There's such an abandoned feeling to this place. No one knows who even lived here anymore. All these lives, practically forgotten. All these people that lived here, and nothing now but mysterious symbols no one quite knows how to read. At least if there *were* ghosts, they might know each other. They might remember everyone who lived here. As it is, they're lost to us. Lost to time."

"But they left this place behind," I say. "It's a lot, really. They're hardly forgotten. People are still studying them. And here we are, all the way from Ohio to see it.

"I suppose." Cliff nods.

"For you, it will be your book," I say. "Your book will be your ghost, speaking to people in fifty years, a hundred maybe."

"If I ever finish it. I might disappear. Just fade away. Like most people."

If Ben had lived, he would remember us. He would visit our graves, and probably have children of his own. But without a child, we're more or less the end of the line. There are our nieces and nephews on Clifford's side, but Elizabeth is childless.

But for the moment, I just want to see this place. Karnak and the pyramids and the Sphinx. Does it even matter if I am forgotten? But for Cliff, the measure of his life is the legacy he leaves. I don't particularly care about the pages that need to be written, the photographs and notes, the lab samples, the millions of teeth around the world, the millions of malformed mouths, the perfect mouths. We'll die, and some new family will move into our house in Cleveland. Children will once again laugh in the now empty rooms. They won't think of us, the quiet old couple that once lived there. The boy whose teeth are buried in the garden. The whole world is a palimpsest of lives—of bones and teeth and houses slumping into to the dirt, while new homes are built, new babies are born. But standing here, in this ancient city, where so many others have stood, walking where people have walked for thousands of years—in some ways it seems like enough to honor those who built these things, to hold the torch and pass it on, though they will not know me, though I am only one witness in a parade of nameless souls.

After Ben died, I often wished to encounter his ghost. I wanted some sense of his presence, to know that he was with me in some way, in some form. I would have welcomed a haunting—slamming doors, flying books. But there was nothing. He was nowhere. And maybe that should be a comfort. That he rests in peace.

Cliff takes my hand. "Ready to head back?" he says. "I'd like to get some writing done this afternoon. And I might need a nap first. This heat!" He wipes his forehead with the back of his hand, and turns to go, pulling me along.

TOOTH STORY: CROCODILE

I suppose flowers would have been too obvious a gift for a married woman, and Curtis Wheeler wasn't the sort to give common gifts anyway. A crocodile tooth was both less conspicuously romantic and more personal than candy or jewelry—and she was married to a dentist, after all. He gave her the tooth of a crocodile wrapped in white tissue paper.

They sat side by side on the sun deck, sipping mint tea, my poor, ambitious father offstage somewhere, napping or writing or shuffling through his stacks of photographs, studying smiles and dental arches. Curtis took the wadded tissue from the pocket of his rumpled blazer and held it out to Frances.

"I thought you might like to have this."

She unwrapped the conical, yellowish tooth.

"From a crocodile," he said, beaming.

She blushed, which was becoming predictable when she was around Curtis Wheeler. "Thank you so much." She set the tooth upright on one palm and turned it on its tip, studying it. She thought it would make a strange and lovely necklace. A sort of amulet, although what it would protect her against, she had no idea.

"It's from an old croc, most likely," he said. "See how it's a bit worn down? They're usually much sharper. Crocs can grow new teeth, though. I've been told they can replace a single tooth fifty times." He told her it came from a tomb, that the tombs in the area were full of mummified crocodiles. "They're sacred, you know. Because of the god Sobek. He's known as 'pointed of teeth,' and 'he who loves robbery,' but he's considered *apotropaic*—magic, that is. He wards off evil, among other things."

"Other things?"

"Well, mostly he protects people from the dangers of the river, but he's a general protector. Crocs are fiercely protective of their young. In fact, many of the crocodile mummies are buried with dozens of baby crocs on their backs or in their mouths."

"Ugh," she said. "They killed the babies?"

Wheeler nodded and chewed on the stem of his pipe. "They probably bred them for such purposes. Hundreds of them guarded the tombs at El Fayum. They called it the Crocodilopolis."

She turned the tooth on her palm once again. "I collect teeth, you know. It's a strange hobby, I suppose."

"Not all that strange, no." He sucked on his pipe, though it wasn't lit. "This will be one of the more exotic teeth in my collection."

He nodded and lit the pipe. The smoke, when he exhaled, was thick and blue. It drifted over the boat railing and dissipated. She liked the smell of it, like sweet burning leaves in autumn with something else, something she couldn't quite name, something ancient, like dark libraries and tearooms.

He spent so many hours among the dead, thinking about the afterlife. It was a strange version of the afterlife to her, a world in which the dead traveled in boats and ate bread and drank beer and were protected by crocodiles. Spending so much time surrounded by death had to affect a person. Who had he lost? Who did he imagine was traveling in one of those boats, drifting on the endless rivers of the underworld? A brother who died in the war? A wife, maybe? Someone who had traveled with him as she traveled with Cliff? Or someone who had stayed home, and each time he returned to London she had welcomed him back with a warm supper, a soft bed? Maybe she had died while he was traveling, and now when he returned, the house was cold and silent. But it seemed unlikely. He didn't wear a wedding band, and he didn't seem like a married man. He seemed like he had always been a bachelor, though she wasn't sure what it was that gave the impression he was unattached.

The swift, smoothness of his walk? His boyish knees? Maybe it was his sloppiness—a wife would make sure he got his suits tailored. But maybe it was just the attention he gave her that made him seem single. The way he kissed her hand and brought her a gift.

She asked him to tell her about his work at the temple of Mut. Was it a new project? Or something he'd been working on for a long time?

"Not new, no," he said. "But the site is still closed to the public. I've been working on it since last February, and I have until the end of the year before I must share my findings with the university. But the whole project builds on a much longer project. Do you know about Mut? The mother goddess?"

She knew nothing about anything. Egypt was almost entirely new to her. The Bible was pretty much her only previous insight to Egypt.

He laughed. "It's not a bad beginning, really," he said. "Judaism and Christianity are much newer than the Egyptian texts that I study, but their stories do overlap with my work. The Egyptians wrote about Osiris, who was dismembered and resurrected. Some people think he could be a sort of precursor to Jesus. The Egyptian texts are so old, and there are so many versions and interpretations of them. One can't be too caught up in a single narrative. Much of my work comes in comparing versions, adding to the compilation of stories and knowledge."

She folded the tissue around the tooth and set it on the table between them. He kept talking.

"But Mut is the sole possessor of my heart. And my time." He laughed and took another draw from his pipe. "Mut is the mother of Amun Re," he went on. "But she is also the mother of all of Egypt. The mother of many gods. She was not born of a woman. She's motherless, you might say." He looked into the distance as he spoke, almost as if he were in a trance. "Mut is divine in all ways. Her symbol is the vulture, which the ancients considered a maternal creature."

"In America, we consider the vulture a scavenger," Frances said. "A garbage picker."

"Indeed. They scavenge. It's a valuable skill. But they also have very wide wings that they use to shield their babies. The vulture is a fierce mother. Not to be reckoned with." He paused and puffed out another blue cloud of smoke. "Do you have children? Perhaps you understand the vulture better than me. Perhaps you understand things about Mut that I will never truly understand."

"I was a mother," she said quietly. "But it was long ago."

"Your child is…" his voice trailed off.

"He died when he was twelve." And then her tongue simply went on speaking. She could have lied, or at least neglected to elaborate, but instead she told him the whole story. "It was my husband," she said. Traitorous tongue, clanging against her teeth, the story spilling out. Her mouth continued to speak, vocal cords vibrating along. "Or not exactly. It was an infection. But my husband…. He had a cavity, and Clifford gave him a root canal." Curtis gasped, but she kept talking. "We didn't know how bad it was until it was too late to save him."

Finally, she stopped speaking. She turned to look at him. He said nothing, but she saw that his eyes were shining, slightly teary. His pipe smoldered in his hand. He put his pipe down on the table between them, then reached across and took her hand.

"I'm so sorry, Frances," he said. "What an awful loss."

"It was many years ago," she said. She dropped her eyes. "But of course, I still miss him."

He shook his head, half in disbelief, half as if to shake off the awful thing.

"I don't mean to make you uncomfortable," she said.

He shook his head again, emphatically.

"I rarely tell anyone about him. To speak of him casually—I don't know, it seems…" She trailed off.

"I don't know what to say, Frances. I've never been a father." He shook his head again. "And your husband, he must—I simply don't know what to say."

She squeezed his hand, and for a full minute they sat like that, holding hands, watching the green water lapping at the shore. Finally, he spoke.

"Would you like to see the tomb?" he asked, turning to her. "My worksite? The precinct of Mut? I would very much like to take you there. I think you will find it quite interesting. The paintings are exquisite, and the location is not yet open to the public. It's a unique invitation, my dear. Would you like to come?"

Of course, she said yes. "And Cliff?" she added. She dropped his hand. "He'll want to come, too, I'm sure."

Curtis coughed and relit his pipe. "Of course," he said, coughing again. "Bring him along."

FROM THE NOTEBOOKS OF DR. CLIFFORD BELL: EGYPT, 1931

Summary of Cairo and Alexandria: In Cairo, we visited a boys' school where the students were accustomed to consuming plentiful sweets due to living in a large city. Their abandonment of traditional diets is nearly complete and the incidence of dental caries is approximately 12%. (High, but I am surprised it is not higher.) The boys had significantly narrow foreheads and close together eyebrows. Many had recessed chins.

We also met with a tribe of nomads, thanks to the director of the boys' school who was able to introduce us. The children and adults of the Arahs tribe consume copious amounts of camel milk and legumes. The dental arches of this group were notably fine, and the young women were particularly striking.

While I have promised Frances four days free of research, I have noticed (informally) that the young women in the city streets of Alexandria and Cairo are notably less beautiful, often exhibiting recessed lower mandibles and overlapping or widely spaced teeth. In Khartoum, we will visit an Arab boys' school which will provide an excellent comparison with the boys' school we visited in Cairo. I am anxious to get to the Belgian Congo, Ethiopia, The Sudan, Mombasa, etc., where the racial stocks are some of the most primitive in the world, promising to be largely untouched by modern, industrialized diets.

History of Root Canals—Tooth-worm[1]: In ancient Egypt, when a person got a cavity, it was believed the tooth had been invaded by the vicious tooth-worm, a blind, pale critter, something like a maggot. A surgeon would dig the worm out, sometimes also removing the tooth, so there were no longer lodgings for the worm. Egyptians claimed to have seen the worm, its soft head burrowed deep in the gums, down into the jawbone, its point of entry indicated by a black tunnel. The toothworm—*which was, in fact, the nerve of the tooth*—lived across cultures: Babylonia, Egypt, Germany, India. Some dentists (sorcerers? witches?) tried to smoke the worm out by burning henbane seeds. The source I found in the Cairo library included the following translation from a Babylonian tablet:

> After Anu's creation of heaven,
> Heaven created the earth,
> Earth created the rivers,
> Rivers created the canals,
> Canals created the swamp,
> Swamp created the worm.
> The worm went weeping in front of Shamash,
> His tears running in front of Ea.
> What food will you offer me?
> What will you give me to suckle?
> I will give you ripe fig and apricots.
> And what good is that to me, ripe fig and apricots?

1. I learned of the tooth worm through a man named Curtis Wheeler, a British Egyptologist we've met aboard The Aida. Apparently, like us, he is taking a few days of leisure *en route* to his work site. The man is very friendly and seems eager to befriend us, but I'm not sure why—what could a middle-aged dentist from Ohio and his middle-aged wife offer such a man? Frances says friendship, but it seems too simple. We'll only be on this boat for a few days. It's too fleeting to bother. Wheeler is self-centered and excessively talkative, but it was in a fit of rambling "conversation" that he insisted on telling me all about ancient Egyptian dentistry. My interest was piqued at the mention that his beloved ancient Egyptians practiced endodontic surgery.

Lift me, and between the teeth
And gums let me settle!
I will suck the blood of the tooth,
And from the gums I will bite its roots.

Ancient Egyptian recipe for filling a cavity:
   1 Nubian clay
   1 green eye lotion
   Crush together and apply to the tooth.

On taking teeth for granted: As both a dentist and a man who lost his teeth to illness, I cannot help but marvel at how many people take their teeth for granted! Teeth are essential to survival—not to mention that they communicate our well-being, our health, and our social class—yet people do not take care of them. They do not respect them, although they are one of our most powerful natural tools. I have seen mothers feeding their babies sweets and refusing them the breast. I have seen children gnawing on sticks and on their fingernails. They do not understand that respecting our teeth begins with what we eat.[2]

Tobacco Use and Oral Hygiene: While I currently don't have time to consider the effects of smoking tobacco on dental or systemic health, without close study I can claim with certainty that tobacco is detrimental to oral hygiene. The smoker's teeth, whether he delights in cigarettes, pipe, or hookah, are consistently stained. His gums exhibit evidence of periodontal disease including halitosis and staining (and likely decay, including loosening of the teeth within the gums).[3]

2. Sometimes I want to march around with a sign that reads: *Teeth are what you eat! They do not grow back!* Would that I could have the phrase translated into a dozen languages and pass out pamphlets everywhere we go.

3. Again, it is Curtis Wheeler who leads me to this observation. The man simply will not go away! He appears at every turn, flaunting his short pants and waxed moustache. (Which is horribly stained by tobacco. I'm surprised his teeth are not in *worse* shape. They're surprisingly straight, but when he grins the yellow stains are apparent.) At the Tomb of Horus, in the dining room each evening,

Chemical Analyses: I have collected 127 samples of food from our travels thus far. Foods collected include salmon, evaporated milk, peat grass (used to grow oats), soil (used to grow oats), oats, codfish, puffins and guga (birds from Scotland), cheese, rye bread, milk (from cows, camels, sheep, goats, human females). All of these will be analyzed in the lab in Cleveland.

---

everywhere we go, he's always waving at us and rushing to our sides. Frances seems charmed by him. She doesn't see that he must be like this with everyone, that he's a cad. She insists that because he and I are both scientists we should be friends. Quite honestly, I don't know if digging up old mummies and guessing at how people lived is science.

THE WOODLOUSE

At this point in their journey, Frances, my dear mother, is 52 years old. More than anything, she resembles a scoop of vanilla ice cream, with every angle melted and licked smooth. The truth is, Frances was never particularly beautiful. We tend to want our heroines with long hair and smooth skin, full breasts, straight white teeth, and a ferociously beating heart, but my mother was none of that. Her teeth were a little yellow and a little crooked. She was short, and her hair was slightly frizzy. Not curly enough to be called curly, but not perfectly straight, either. A color somewhere between dishwater and mouse. Even when she was young, it was not her bright eyes or hourglass figure that caught my father's eye—although truthfully, she had both. What drew Clifford to her was her attentiveness, her questions, the way she sized him up. She was a good listener. She made him feel good about himself.

People are vain, Ben, she used to say. *You won't go wrong with flattery, with questions, with a keen ear for the story they want to tell.* And for the most part, she was right. But what she never mentioned, what she overlooked, is that people are also keen to *hear* a good tale. They like to be entertained once in a while. They like to have interesting friends, who convince them that they, by proxy, must also be interesting. Frances' stories often remained untold, tucked somewhere beneath her tongue, waiting like woodlice under a brick. And lest you think I'm cruel in my assessment of my own beloved mother—our Frances—I assure you, I am not. Beauty is a brief and fleeting thing. I loved my mother for her stories best of all. She taught me that perceptive people—the patient ones, the ones who bother to ask—are rewarded. One needed only to lift that brick the slightest bit and those bugs would scurry every which way, racing from the darkness into the light, bustling and rolling, tiny feet jittering along the tender skin of the forearm, up and over the collarbone, along the neck, directly into the whorls of the ear.

My father was often too busy talking. Too busy thinking, though her questions often helped him think. And it wasn't stories that captured Curtis Wheeler, either, our chatty dandy with his waxed mustache. (Forgive me, but despite my father's shortcomings, I'm a loyalist. Clifford is my father, after all, and to put it bluntly, Curtis Wheeler was a cheeseball. That my mother was smitten by his blue eyes and his knees—*His knees!* —it is beyond me. Death has revealed much to me, but it has not revealed the mysteries of lust, which apparently preyed even upon my mother.) Like my father, Curtis Wheeler learned that Frances was an excellent listener. She made him feel good about himself, and he was lonely.

When Frances told Clifford about Curtis' invitation, he coughed lightly. He mentioned his notes on Switzerland, and on the boys' school they had visited in Cairo. There wouldn't be much time after they arrived in Khartoum for writing, for organizing his thoughts, for sorting the photos and the samples. And he didn't much like Wheeler anyway. And somehow Frances found herself confessing: she had told Curtis Wheeler about me, about my death, and that it was my father that had performed the fatal surgery. The orange silk curtains fluttered lightly over the open window. Clifford stood silently, staring at her, not even defending himself, and Frances mumbled something unintelligible. And then she said it again, more loudly.

"Maybe you *were* negligent." Words she'd never believed, but here she was speaking them.

They stood there, silent, and then he turned and left the room. He slammed the tiny cabin door—a flimsy bang, more of a snap—and she sat on the bed and watched the blades of the fan circle. Twelve years and she had never said it. She had refused even to think it. When I died, Elizabeth told her to leave him. *How could they stay married?* Elizabeth had asked.

Even if it wasn't his fault, even if he'd done everything he could, even if it was an accident, a tragedy, how could she even look at him without thinking about how it was his hands that drilled into her son's mouth? His hands that didn't clean the tooth out well enough. His hands that were *negligent*. And if she couldn't look at him, how would she be able to kiss him? How would she be able to love him?

Back then, in the dining room of their Cleveland house, Elizabeth had stood up and looked down on Frances, her eyes full of irritating sympathy, and Frances had looked away. She looked out the window at the trees losing their leaves. She said nothing.

How little Elizabeth understood of love. How little Elizabeth understood of this loss, the loss of her son. Frances couldn't bear to lose another person she loved. How utterly alone she would be if she lost her husband, too. And Clifford shared her loss. Clifford was the only other person who came even close to understanding the gray emptiness in which she stood. The changed world around her. Together, they had been swallowed by it. Infected by it. Whatever it was that killed their child— the bacteria—would fester in her the rest of her life. It was immortal.

But now she had said it.

Maybe you were negligent.

Words she hadn't even believed when I first died and didn't believe now. But *by God*, it felt good to say it. To imagine it was true. To absolve herself of guilt. To blame *someone*. She lay down on the bed and stared at the ceiling. There was no way she was going after him. Then she got up again and pushed the curtains aside and looked out the window and thought of crocodiles. In this moment, she felt like one of them. Not like their prey, but like their friend, strong and sharp-of-tooth. It would be a long, silent night.

In the morning—the day they were to visit the Temple of Mut— Clifford professed a blinding headache. He had eaten something that didn't agree with him—hardly an uncommon occurrence on their travels. He felt woozy. Frances pressed her hand to his forehead, but he brushed it away. "Go," he said. "I'm better off here, resting." She leaned down to kiss him, but he held up a hand as a shield between them. "In case it's catching," he said. She kissed her fingers and pressed them to his forehead.

And she was off! To the camels! The tombs! The dust spinning through a shaft of sunlight, filtering down from the earth above, dust particles that may have been the skin cells of the dead. The raided tomb! The empty sarcophagus! The canopic jars tipped on their sides! The mummified bones of crocodiles torn from their wrappings! What did they find there, Frances and Curtis Wheeler, together in that empty cavern, the Temple of Mut?

That quiet humming? Something like bees? It is her shame, steady and frantic. She has been married to my father for such a long time. She blamed it on the heat—the sun was so blindingly hot. Or perhaps it was the ancient magic she had heard so much about. How it swirls through ancient Egypt, all those spells and souls adrift. Perhaps it was the sphinxes.

But Curtis' attention flummoxed her. *His knees!* She said to no one. *His knees!* Wheeler tells his shameful stories with pride.

Press your ear to the rock at Lake Mazinaw and deep within you will hear voices singing, shouting, murmuring. Brags and laments, pride and shame. Frances tells her part quietly, but deep within the buzzing hive, there is also honey.

THE TEMPLE OF MUT
Curtis Wheeler

And here we are, Frances, my lovely lady, here we are. The entrance to the tomb. The Temple of Mut, the great mother goddess. Indeed, the gate is flimsy, hardly a deterrent to thieves or curious tourists, though few of them pass here. They stick to the main drag. I suppose they're like your husband—a little afraid to walk alone in the kingdom of the dead.

Oh hush, I'm only teasing. A little teasing never hurt anyone. And you did say the necropolis made him uncomfortable, did you not? Well, it's a perfectly normal response. I suppose it's far more abnormal to be comfortable with it all, as I am. I am absurdly comfortable. I'm at home here. The dead are my family. My people. They're such good listeners, haha. Anyway, there is a sturdier gate a little way down the passage. Come, come. I have the key.

You know, tomb robbing has been an important force in shaping the design of the tombs. So much jewelry has gone missing over the years. Over the centuries. Canopic jars tipped over and shattered. Sometimes even the mummies were stolen. A fellow like myself would finally reach the center of a tomb and discover that the mummy was gone from the sarcophagus! Even before fellows like myself were rooting around in the tombs, there were robberies. Way back when the tombs were built. There have always, always been tomb raiders, my dear. The people began disguising the location of the tombs by setting the temples further away. They even built false burial chambers to confuse people who didn't belong there. Somewhere within a maze of distractions and dead ends, rested the body of a dead pharaoh, protected by distance and red herrings in the form of cheaper treasures.

My dear, you're holding your breath. It's quite hot in here, you know. You must keep breathing. Let's have a rest. A sip of water? Let me get that pack for you. You're quite a sloppy drinker, my dear. And terribly sweaty. Look at how your shirt is stuck to you! Oh, well I suppose it's difficult for you to see your own back, but you'll have to take my word for it. You're utterly drenched. Come now. Switch on your torch. There are things to see here. Plenty to see on our walk to the tomb.

The mummification process? It's quite elaborate. The organs are removed and stored in canopic jars. A canopic jar? Well, funny you should ask. The name's based on an error. They're named for Canopus, a young Greek who came to Egypt as the captain of a ship. A priestess fell in love with him, but he did not answer her pleas. And then, as the story goes, he was bitten by a serpent, and died in Egypt, far, far from his home. The jars are named for him, although he may not have even existed. History is loaded with such mistakes, just loaded with them. Chock full.

What's interesting is that the brain wasn't stored in the jars. It wasn't even salvaged. They prodded and poked at it with a special metal spoon. They just jabbed and jabbed at it until it turned into a sort of slurry that drained out through the nose. They thought it was nothing but mucus! Old good for nothing brain, ha ha.

It was the heart that mattered to them. The heart was thought to be the seat of the soul and the intellect. But it didn't go in the jars, either. They thought it was too good for that. They dried it, then returned it to the body before wrapping the entire corpse up in linen strips, although I'm skimping on details here. What matters is that the heart remained in its place. It had to be weighed against a feather, you see. If it was heavier than the feather, well, it went right into the jaws of Ammut, the crocodile-hippo-lion goddess. Chomp-chomp and too-da-loo! A tough racket indeed! No heart is lighter than a feather! But there's magic, you know. We must assume there's magic if anyone is to succeed on their journey to the underworld. Magic lightens the heavy heart, I like to say.

Here, here with your torch. Shine it on this wall here. It's utterly covered with drawings. Instructions and such. How to get to the afterlife. A kind of pictogram map. Shine your torch here.

The first time I was in here, I felt like Quixote in the Cave of Montesino. You've read it, of course? Well, it was like I dreamed it the whole thing. This perfect cave of wonders! When I returned to the city, I could hardly believe it was real. But I came back, and it was still here! It was real! Much to my delight!

Shine your light up here. We're in the burial chamber now. Did you feel how the air shifted? A little less dense. And you can smell it, perhaps? A trace of the oils they used?

That's Nut there, the Goddess of the Sky.

Oh, I don't know why I'm whispering. I suppose I just hold her in the highest respect. She utterly takes my breath away. See the stars on her flank? She forms a sort of canopy over the earth god, Geb—she's the sky. With her body. And each night she lowers herself down upon him in divine coitus. And each day, she carries the sun through her body, a red disc that travels among the stars. Her arms have to be long like that so she can touch the earth. Magic again, you know. So much magic. Keeping the heart light!

Sometimes I think of the burial chamber as an ear, and I am a single hair within it, trembling on the taut membrane of the eardrum. But pshaw! You must think me all too strange. Come, have another sip of water. Let me take your pack. Are you tired?

That's just a rat or a mouse there. Nothing to worry about. There are houses above us, you know. No one lives in them anymore. At least not legally. The government made the people move into the city. They used to build their homes up there as a way of protecting the dead. They painted their houses brightly, and from a distance, when the sun falls upon them, it looks like a village of painted scales and butterfly wings. It's utterly splendid! I have always wondered what it is like to live above the tombs. Over the bones of crocodiles, and the robbers that dare. The magic dust of the dead rising, the dust of crumbled papyrus, all rising like ash in a flue and drifting through the dreams of the people living above.

Their greasy hair pressed into the pillow, the greasy pillow pressed into their mouths. But pshaw. I'm rambling. I'm talking nonsense. The magic you know. It must be the magic getting to me, haha.

Some more water? It is rather stuffy in here, I know.

Goodness, my dear, you look beautiful, resting beneath Nut. You look utterly striking. You have the loveliest eyes. Even in this light, I can see them. You look like a girl. Like a bride. A hungry bride. A starving, beautiful bride.

Oh! Careful now! I'm so sorry! I couldn't help it. I couldn't help myself. You looked so lovely. I'm terribly sorry, my dear, terribly sorry. Come now. I won't do it again. I'll keep my hands and my lips to myself. You must think me quite daft. Utterly daft. Indeed, you're quite right. I don't know what got into me. Please. Forgive me now. It's just me. Old Curtis Wheeler, the daft Egyptologist with my socks slumping down my shins here. Just daft old Curtis. I got a bit carried away. I just love it here so much, and I love having you here. I'm terribly sorry. Terribly sorry. Forgive me now.

Yes. That's an excellent idea. Let's just pretend it never happened.

Yes, yes, we should go. Come now. There's still the lake. You really don't want to miss it. I promise you won't regret it.

A GRAND PASSION
Frances

Egypt, 1931

But we don't go to the lake. We don't even leave the Temple. Not yet. On the ceiling over our heads arches the blue body of Mut, and the sunlight cuts through the darkness of the tomb, falling from an opening above. The band of light falls on Curtis' shoulders, lighting his eyes while most of him remains in shadow. He shines the torch at the ceiling, and whispers something that's not science, not reason, not even faith. Something about magic and dust, something about feathers on butterflies. He calls me beautiful. He takes the rucksack from my shoulders, and when he touches me, it ripples through my body.

The kiss startles me. I step back, fall into something, stumble and blush. And he is ashamed and apologetic. But I take the hand he offers. I don't hear his apologies. Or I don't listen. Instead, I pull him close. I'm the one that does the kissing the second time, and I don't apologize, and he puts his hands around my waist, around my hips, and pulls me closer, and I do not resist.

I have forgotten about the lake, the waiting camels, the lunch to be eaten above ground, in the sunlight, in the land of the living. I have forgotten about Clifford back at the boat. There is only Curtis Wheeler. His hands pressing into my back, his fingers untucking my shirt and finding my bare, sweating skin beneath. There is only his mouth against mine and my mouth on his neck and my hands in his sweaty hair and the fumbling with clothes.

I have never before fumbled with clothes. There has never been any man but Clifford, who unbuttons his own shirt while I unbutton mine. Clifford always sets his shoes next to the bed, side-by-side, toes aligned. He folds his pants. Turns back the bedclothes and pats the spot next to him on the bed.

But now there is Curtis. His chest is covered with blond curls, bright as the hair on his head, and I like the way the hair feels when it rubs against my breasts and then his hands are on my breasts, his mouth is on my nipple. His skin under my hands, my fingers reading his body, the curves of his biceps, his butt.

Afterward, on the ground, we curl toward each other, half-covered by our clothes, and by a blanket that Curtis pulls from his pack. "For tea," he says as he shakes it out, but I don't care why he has it—if it is for tea or seduction. I touch his knees, the knees I have admired. Boyish knees. I sit up to kiss each one.

Even years later, when I am a very old woman, I will blush when I think of this. With shame. But also with pleasure.

"I thought these things only happened in books," I say. He pulls me back down and kisses me.

"What would our book be titled?" he asks.

"Love Among the Tombs," I offer, laughing.

"The Goddess' Consort," he says.

"Once Upon the Nile."

"A Grand Passion," he says. He runs a finger upward along my sternum, my neck, my chin, pauses at my lips. When his eyes meet mine, it is too much. I look away.

My life could have been so different. Could I have had this? Something like this? My body against another's body. The warmth of it. The heat. But then I would not have had my son, my Benjamin. And I would not give him up. Not even for this.

Curtis' hair is coarse and tangled between my fingers. I think of Cliff's smooth, bald scalp. Cliff always cringes when I touch his hair, the fine fringe around his ears, and so I rarely do it, but now I bury my nose in Curtis' hair, inhaling a scent of dust and sunshine. His hair is unwashed, but I like the smell of it. I take it in my mouth, tasting it, feeling the strands against my tongue. He tangles his fingers with mine.

The light has moved and we are entirely in shadow, watching the dust drift in the beam to our left.

"Asaad will wonder," Curtis says, and for moment I can't remember who Asaad is—our guide, the owner of the camels that brought us here.

But I don't want to leave.

There will be no grand passion in my life. This is it. This afternoon is the whole of it. This hour. This minute. I close my eyes, and for just a moment, I imagine that I could stay here. That I could have an all-consuming love.

But even in books, such passion burns out. It ignites and incinerates and leaves the lovers with nothing. Or at least it's never simple.

I imagine telling Cliff I won't go with him to Sudan, that I won't go with him anywhere, that I'm staying in Egypt with Curtis Wheeler (who has not asked me to stay). I think of the house in Cleveland, where the dust is by now thick over every surface: the fireplace mantle, the candlesticks, the tea cups. The clock, unwound for many months, is silent, waiting for our return, waiting for Cliff to turn the key, to wind it, and bring it back to life. Until then, the house sleeps, outside of time.

But if I stayed in Egypt, I would have nothing. My traveling clothes. My tooth collection. Curtis Wheeler. Perhaps not even him. Or not for long.

In the twelve years since Ben's death, I have never blamed Cliff for what happened. Why now? Maybe I should have blamed him at the very beginning. If I had blamed him, I could have forgiven him, and forgiveness means the beginning of something new. But no matter what I said yesterday, I know it wasn't his fault. He was not negligent. He is not a careless person. He has never been negligent. And if he was, I don't think I could forgive him.

I close my eyes and feel Curtis' chest rising and falling beneath my hand.

Does belief in accidents cancel belief in God? Is chaos evidence that
God does not exist? And if it was God's plan to take Ben, what kind of
a God is that? These are not new questions. How is it that, after twelve
years, these questions remain? But if I have learned anything in our travels it is that I understand very little about God. I understand almost
nothing about the world.

Faith and accidents. Accidents and faith. Chaos and love and
unfathomable grief.

Curtis traces the veins along the inside of my arm, his fingers light
as the feet of flies. On the boat, Cliff is probably pacing the cabin, or
sitting at his desk, writing. Flipping through the stacks of photos. All
those children we have met and measured and counted. Years and years
of work. But it is Cliff's work. It has always been Cliff's work.

It would be no different with Curtis. He has his tombs. His parch-
ments and translations. What do I have? What belongs to me? With
Curtis, I would have my body, languid in his arms. And I would have his
body. His coarse hair. His knees. His hands pressing and tracing me. His
mouth. And I would have other people, friends. Curtis is nothing if not
friendly. He talks to people. To everyone. Even Asaad, the camel guide
that brought us here, knew him and obviously liked him. *Mr. Curtis.* He
is not afraid of people. With him, I would not be afraid either.

But with Cliff, I had a child. I have the memory of our child. I have
Florida and Alaska and The Hebrides and Switzerland. Our friends in
Cleveland. James and St. Stanislaus School. The watermelon eating con-
tests and the haying parties. Our house. Bon Echo, and the cabin there,
quiet now, boarded up, but still ours. Still mine. We fit the logs together
with our hands. And the echo that rings across the lake. But is any of
it really mine? There is little in my life that I don't share with Clifford.
Memories and work and travel and children cannot be parceled out,
untangled, cut into equal pieces along perfect lines.

It is as if I am clutching two corners of a quilt, and Cliff grips the
other two. And like that, the two of us have walked through life, the
quilt stretched taut, slacking a little when we draw close to each other,

then snapping tight when we argue or drift, but no matter how much we tug, the quilt remains between us, connecting us to each other, each piece a piece of our life together. The quilt is exquisite, shot through with threads of grief. But I will not let go. I don't even think I can. I won't leave him.

But neither do I feel particularly guilty. I search for it—the guilt—pressing at my diaphragm, clouding my vision—but it is not here. This is mine. For these minutes, this hour, this is mine.

I breathe in the scent of Curtis' hair and then push him away so I can look at him. He looks back. Unblinking blue eyes. Neither of us speaks. He unfolds our arms and reaches our hands into the column of light falling from the opening high above. Our hands are illuminated, tangled together. He sighs twice, once with contentment, once with exhaustion.

"Dear Frances," he says. He kisses me. "Will I ever see you again?" He strokes my hair and touches my eyelids, one at a time, closing them, and for a minute I keep them closed. I don't answer, and he touches my lips with one finger, acknowledging the silence, and after some minutes we untangle ourselves and we stand and we begin to dress.

THE OPENING OF THE MOUTH

A Funeral Dialog, translated and adapted from fragments of The Pyramid Texts by Curtis S. Wheeler.

June 17, 1931

Dark body with your splendid heart,
Let me go among the dead.

> Take with you these jars of beer, these loaves
> of bread.
> The dead, too, must eat.

My mouth is given to me
With that small chisel of metal.

> The air is the song
> moving through your opened mouth,
> The song is a kicked stone, tumbling.

Let me

        Go, with the sun in the prow.
        Go, in this boat, with your open eyes
        Go, in this boat, with your open mouth
        Go forth, day and night, night and day.

With the leg of the calf,
with honey on my lips,
with cool water,
let me.

        As a star traveling through the body of night,
        With blue fish, with crocodiles,
        Over reeds, over mud,
                Go.

With your little finger,
Open my mouth.

        With the tip of my little finger,
        I have opened your mouth.

V.

TOOTH STORY: ELEPHANT

In Sudan, their guide and interpreter was John Rec Puk, a Nuer man, well over six feet tall, with extremely dark, satiny skin. Rec's forehead was marked with six parallel scars that dipped slightly in the space above his eyebrows. He told Frances that the lines had been cut into his forehead when he reached the end of his boyhood. They served as evidence that he was a man and a Nuer, and the evenness of the lines bore testament to his bravery: he had not flinched when the elder drew the blade across his skin that day so many years ago. Rec spoke five languages fluently. He had learned English from missionaries when he was a child. His people had worked for the British during the war—they had been forced into it, but Rec said he considered himself lucky to have been singled out for his proficiency with the English language. His work had been mostly as an interpreter, which he did now for pay. Frances wondered aloud to Cliff about whether Rec truly liked his job. He was friendly enough, but it meant so much time away from home, and he hadn't ever exactly *wanted* to learn English, but Cliff dismissed her question. They were paying him good money, he said, as if that were all there were to it.

Rec traveled with them from Sudan to the Congo, to Tanganyika and Mombasa, introducing them to village chiefs and missionaries, captaining canoes, instructing them on the appropriate gifts to give the people they met, interpreting languages and behaviors. He often narrated events in song, inventing lyrics about the river on which they paddled, about teeth, about whatever they encountered.

The Nuer were singers, Rec said. They sang about birth and death, about hunting and fishing and cattle. They had songs for when a young man came of age or when a couple married. Each person had his own song, too—one that told the story of his life, a song that slowly gathered new verses as the singer gathered years. Rec was unusual, though, in that he practiced his songs in front of Frances and Clifford before he had refined them. The Nuer usually practiced their songs in private, singing as they walked to the river for water or as they pounded grain for a meal. They were always singing, but most people did not sing a song publicly until they had perfected the verses. "But you, Dr. Bell and Mrs. Frances, you do not understand my words, and my work is to be with you. To guide you. So I practice my songs while I work, like any man."

Occasionally Frances asked Rec what he was singing about. "The way the fish swim beneath our canoe," he said. Or, "How the dentist wears his hat."

When they were in Rec's village, she heard people singing everywhere. When she stepped out of their borrowed hut, a woman's voice cut through the morning, bright and piercing, and from the other side of the village, a lower voice pulsed its song. A boy sang as he shuffled along a trail, walking beside his cow, patting it on the rump.

But on the day Frances found the elephant tooth, she was walking alone, a little behind Cliff and Rec, listening to the birds and the wind in the grass. She was surprised at the beauty of eastern Africa. She had expected it to be a desert, a wasteland of dust, but even in the plains, where there was indeed plenty of dust and flat open land, the sky was remarkable—so wide—and when the sun set in the haze, it blazed ancient and rosy, pinker than she had ever seen. The grasses, too, were beautiful, and the people seemed to balance the wide band of the horizon with their willowy height.

That day, walking to the lake, where Rec had promised they would find plenty of wildlife, Frances had devised a game in which she would stop walking and look around, slowly rotating a full 360 degrees, making an effort to open her eyes as widely as she could, as if by opening them more widely, she could take in more of what she saw. She took deep breaths, inflating her lungs to their fullest, trying to absorb the expansive sky, the land around her, trying to capture it in her mind so she would always be able to find it there.

She would have passed up the tooth, taken it for a stone, but in one of her slow rotations, she kicked it, and her toe felt the density of something more porous than rock. *Bone,* she thought at first, remembering Mabel and her wooly mammoth tusks back in Alaska—that dark, wet place. She bent to study the bone, touched it gingerly, afraid it might be hiding gore or insects, but it was dry and clean. It seemed it had been lying there for months, maybe even years.

She learned later, from Rec, who seemed to know everything about everything, that if an elephant lives into its sixties, evading lions and crocodiles and human hunters for a full lifespan, it goes through six sets of teeth, each set consisting of four gigantic molars. New sets grow in at the back of the mouth, creeping forward—caterpillar teeth—nudging out the older set, which is, by then, worn down from chewing. The teeth are huge and flat, with a pattern of looped ridges that grind and mash grasses and leaves in tremendous quantities. When an elephant loses its sixth set of teeth, it can no longer eat, and so it starves to death, a toothless old creature.

Frances didn't know which set her elephant tooth was from—the first set, that falls out when the beast is only two or three years old, or that final set, the loss of which is an indication that the end of life is near. Perhaps her tooth was one of those unremarkable middle-aged teeth that meant nothing but the passing of time. She picked up the tooth and tucked it under her arm.

Ahead of her, Rec and Cliff neared the lake, and Rec held up his hand, telling them to wait. They were fifty yards from the shore, but Frances could see a group of elephants bathing in the green water.

"A female group," Rec whispered. "The males are more solitary once they're grown." A mother elephant sprayed water over a calf that stood patiently at her side, the water running over its ears. Frances, Cliff, and Rec settled there, in the grass alongside the trail, and ate their lunch, watching the elephants splash and drink.

Rec said that elephants grieved like humans, that they wailed like old women over the bones of other elephants. Frances asked if they also celebrated—births maybe? Or the arrival of a new set of teeth? Rec laughed. "I have not seen such a celebration, but I don't know that I would recognize it. Perhaps they do."

Cliff wanted Frances to leave the tooth behind. It wasn't part of their research, and it wasn't a good enough specimen to sell to a museum. It would just take up space, he said. In the end, it would just collect dust on a shelf in Ohio. What would she do with it? It would end up like a rock in the garden. What was the point?

But it wasn't a rock, Frances said. And the elephants—they were marvelously spirited! She longed to go closer. To touch their baggy skin. To see the clumsy baby. But Rec said that they were protective creatures, and occasionally attacked humans if they felt threatened. Still, Frances felt some kinship with them, as she had with the camel she had ridden back in Egypt—Nefret, which meant beautiful, although the camel was anything but. They had met so many people in so many places, but sometimes it was in the animals that she glimpsed what it meant to be human, to be part of a community, or to be outside of one. To be a mother. To mourn.

It was only part of a tooth, maybe half, but it weighed nearly four pounds. Still, there was no way she was leaving it behind. It wasn't much larger than a box of food samples, and Cliff collected those in each place they visited, shipping them back to his lab in Ohio, though half of them didn't survive the journey. The tooth wouldn't fit in her collection box— it was as big as the box itself—but she wrapped it in a flowered kerchief she had been wearing on her head and carried it back to the village by the knot of fabric.

TYPES OF PARASITES WE WERE
WARNED ABOUT

Frances

East Central Africa, 1931

NOTE: Travelers to East African countries are at high risk of infection, disease, or serious illness due to insect bites (mosquitoes, flies, fleas, ticks, and lice). Diseases caused by insects include malaria (mosquito), dengue fever (mosquito), yellow fever (mosquito), filariasis and chikungunya (mosquito), leishmaniasis (sandfly), Congo-Crimean hemorrhagic fever (tick), typhus (lice), and plague (fleas). This is an incomplete list.

Parasites and their larvae can be found in abundance in stagnant water, and in moving water. Take no shortcuts in boiling or purifying your water. Insects also live in soil (wear shoes!) and in undercooked meats (cook meats thoroughly!).

Additionally, due to possible rabies exposure, travelers should avoid wild dogs and other aggressive or bizarrely behaving animals.

Everywhere we go, we sleep beneath a mosquito net. We never let our bare feet touch the ground for fear of jiggers that will burrow into the soles of our feet to breed. We pull our socks high and keep our boots tightly laced. Mosquitoes hover beneath the tables in the eating huts, seeking tender spots on the backs of our knees, an exposed ankle, a hand resting on a lap, so we take meals in our tent, the lamp burning bright, emitting the foul smell of castor oil. We keep the lamp lit even while we sleep.

Our first night with the Maasai, we lie awake, listening to lions attacking a herd of zebras. More than the snarling of the lions, who don't roar—they don't have to—it is the zebras that keep us from sleep. Zebras screaming. Shapeless, chaotic sounds that seem forced out of them. Twisting wails and groans and gurgles that fade too quickly, but echo endlessly.

In the morning, I step out of our tent into sunlight that falls flat and golden across the mud houses, the packed dirt and cooking pots. I watch four men leave the village before the cows, the boys, or the women who will walk for water. The men hold their spears at the ready, checking for ambush, but completely unafraid. The spears continue the long lines of their bodies, extending them into the sky. They do not find the lions, but rather the remains of the zebras. Hyenas will be next, they tell us. They are probably already there. Listen, they say, and you'll hear them laughing.

At lunchtime, I watch three men bleed a cow by plunging a lance-tipped arrow into its neck. The cow is on the ground, its back and front legs bound, a band cinched around its throat. One man holds the cow's horns to steady its head. Another presses a hand across the beast's neck as if to calm it, while a third draws an arrow back against the bow, just slightly, and shoots the beast at close range. They collect the blood in a gourd, mix it with milk and drink it, passing the gourd along, one to the next. When it comes to me, I look to Rec, our guide, who is from another tribe—the Nuer—but knows a little of the Maasai language, and certainly knows more about all this than I do. He nods at me, and it does not occur to me that he could be wrong, that it may not be okay for me—the only woman in the circle—to drink, until I have already tipped my head back and sipped, and then it is too late. I pass the vessel to Rec, who also drinks. The cow is still hobbled in the dirt at our feet. No one says a word to me.

Cliff is writing furiously in his notebook, trying to get it all down, but he is so busy taking notes he barely has time to watch the procedures, his head bent, notebook braced against his thigh as he squats near the men, listening to Rec's murmured explanations. I want to be closer to the action, and try nudging my way into the circle, but the others are still waiting for the gourd to come around, and I make no progress.

I watch between shoulders as the men staunch the wound in the beast's neck with ash, and the blood stops immediately. They untie the cow's legs, and she lifts her head and stands. The crowd parts for her as if she is royalty. A few people slap her lightly on the rear, or briefly grasp her horns, the way you might grip a child's face in greeting if you have not seen him for a long time, and he has grown. The cow nuzzles past the people and begins to graze in a patch of scrub grass. She is completely unperturbed as if she has just awoken from a nap.

Cliff missed the staunching, but I will tell him about it later. He is the photographer, but by now I am the better observer. I am the eyes and ears. Maybe he relies too much on his camera, or he is too busy analyzing, asking questions about what something might mean. I think our travels have taught me how to pay attention, how to see. I am a collector—a watcher and listener—while he is a scientist. He can do what he wants with what I report. I'll just keep collecting tastes and scents and songs and teeth.

Dinner is fried beef, brown beans, and unleavened bread. Clifford chases the beans around his plate with his fork. I understand why the people here use their bread to scoop up the food, instead of forks and knives. It's practical, and I want to put down my fork. I want to scoop the beans up with the sour, spongy bread, as I have seen the locals do, but I do not do it. I stab a tough piece of beef and begin to chew.

Parasite /perə sīt/

noun: parasite; plural noun: parasites
>   an organism that lives in or on another organism (its host) and benefits by deriving nutrients at the host's expense.

>   Derogatory: a person who habitually relies on or exploits others and gives nothing in return. (syn. cadger, leech, passenger)

Origin: *mid 16th century: via Latin from Greek parasitos '(person) eating at another's table,' from para- 'alongside' + sitos 'food.'*

We eat at their tables: sometimes with them, sometimes alone. We eat their food, and we collect it: dried fish, berries, biscuits, cod, bread, cheese, butter, lentils, beef, milk. We gather soil and thatch and grass seed. We document what they eat, how they grow it or catch it, how they prepare it. (*Mashed with a pestle in a gourd, dried and stretched, mixed with milk.*) We take photos of food and teeth. What do we give them in return?

Sometimes we give them photographs. They squint at them, turn them over, press their thumbprints into the faces on the paper. We give them salt or rice or flour. Clifford pulls their rotten teeth, disinfects their wounds, doses them with quinine if they are feverish. Sometimes we hire them. We pay them as interpreters or guides. Sometimes we give them money. But is it enough? What do we give them?

I watch mothers feeding infants who latch to their breasts. Greedy little things. And the mothers, crouching in the dust or sitting in a circle with other mothers, go on talking or preparing food, letting the babies tug and bat and them. I remember my own child's toothless gums around my nipple. Those first days of pain when we were both still learning how to nurse. And then, how soothing it became, his wet mouth, his sweet soft head. How he often fell asleep, warm and grunting, and we would doze together.

But a baby is a sort of a parasite, too. How it latches inside the womb, drawing nutrients through the umbilical cord, and even after birth, he gives only intangible things—strange soft comfort, gentle heat. He takes so much: sleep, milk, clarity, time. But I would give all of these again to hold that little flea that was mine.

Anopheles Mosquito: *From the Greek for "good for nothing." Bearer of malaria. Stick figure with wings and a long, tender proboscis—barely a hair—but it punctures skin. Saliva goes out, blood goes in: swelling, itching, fever, delirium. Her belly fills with blood like a lamp with oil, a transparent jewel. The angle of her resting body is steeper than that of other mosquitoes. The angle of her biting body is that of a broken plank.*

Note: *Other types of mosquitoes carry yellow fever, dengue fever, elephantiasis.*

Prevention/Treatment: *Daily dose of quinine. Smoke from campfires and cooking. Castor oil in the lamp. Eucalyptus oil. Birch and tar oil. Citronella. Pyrethrum powder, incense, long sleeves, basil oil, and bed nets.*

We run our fingers through our hair, through each other's hair. We check each other for the fat, crawling bodies of ticks. We shake our clothes, shake the bedding, smash anything that moves.

By the time we reach Kenya, I have put my fingers in the mouths of countless children. All over the world, I have pulled their lips back to reveal their teeth for my husband's camera. Sometimes, their teeth are slimy, even tinged with green, as if covered with a thin layer of algae. In every village or city, I pull their lips back at the corners and put my fingers in, four at a time. Sometimes they smile for the camera. Sometimes I feel their bodies against my own and I breathe with them as they hold still, as they smile. By the time we reach the Wakamba, the Jalou, the Muhima, I know beyond doubt that mouths, and children, are strong.

In the photographs, the children often appear to be jeering. Sometimes their heads are tilted upwards, their eyes closed, as if they are praying. They look transcendent. They look like the sculpture of St. Teresa I saw in Rome, where we were tourists for three days before we traveled north to Switzerland.

In Rome, we did not look in a single mouth. We ate pastries with custard and pear, sipped wine on a tiny veranda. Cliff was bored and restless, but I loved it—the ancient stone city, the Italian men in their wool suits. And St. Teresa in her white marble robes, eyes closed, mouth open. An angel held an arrow at her heart, but it seemed the angel had already stabbed her and was laughing about it. It seemed that some magical poison coursed through her veins. *The Ecstasy of St. Teresa*. In Cliff's photographs, some of the children look like that, frozen in ecstasy.

In other photos, they look complicit and proud, their dark eyes glinting. I put my fingers in their hot, slick mouths and feel their heads press against me, their narrow shoulders against my hips. I stretch their lips wide and wait until I see the shutter open and close—a black eye, a flower unfolding and refolding. Only my hands are ever included in the photo. Sometimes a scrap of my dress makes a faded floral backdrop, but Cliff always excludes me from the frame. Only my hands are visible, holding open the child's mouth, stretching their lips wide.

I wash my hands while Clifford sets up his camera. The interpreter translates for the child's father. *Go ahead*, the father says. He nods. *Do what you wish.* He says something to the child, who has sleepy eyes. He is the same height as me. Ten years old, the father says.

I stand behind the child while Clifford pulls the dark cloth over his head, scoots the tripod a little closer and focuses the lens. I touch the boy's shoulder. "Okay?" He turns toward me, then back to the camera, but says nothing and does not smile. I reach around the boy, my arms resting lightly on his shoulders, and place my fingers at the corners of his mouth, but he does not help me by smiling to reveal his teeth.

"Please ask him to smile," I say to the interpreter. I pull the boy's lips with my thumbs and forefingers, feel his slick gums, the hard teeth beneath them, and I wait for him to grin, but instead, he snaps at me. The swiftest bite. He catches the tip of my thumb between his teeth, biting thumbnail and flesh.

I yell and jump back. It is my left thumb, and I shake it as if to fling the pain away. I study the thumb, turning it over to see the place where his teeth broke my skin. The smallest trickle of blood, almost nothing. The child blinks at me calmly.

"Why did you do that?" I ask. My voice is high and desperate. I squeeze at my thumb with the other hand, trying to make it bleed more, trying to make the pain stop. The interpreter steps back. He says nothing. No one speaks. Even as the pain fades, I want to slap the boy, but the father hooks his neck in the crook of his arm and pulls him away, back toward the huts. Over his shoulder, the father says, "Please excuse us. Please excuse my son. We must go."

The boy's mouth must be filled the metallic flavor of my blood. The boy hurt me—the white woman who does not know how to speak to them, who cannot understand a word they say. I never know what they think of me—not here, not in any of the places we visit. In each place, I watch the people, and they watch back.

I am sure the biting boy does not have rabies, but in our tent that night, Clifford suggests that we leave, that we fly to Paris, or at least return to Khartoum, where there is a medical research laboratory. They might have the vaccine there, he says, and our time is limited if I am to have the vaccine in time to prevent an infection. The vaccine is a series of more than twenty shots, injected directly into the stomach, notorious for the pain they cause, though I suppose that pain is less than the pain that comes with death from rabies. "A precaution," Cliff says, but I tell him it seems an excessive precaution, that the boy seemed perfectly healthy. I remember his clear gaze, the quiet blinking, how calm he seemed.

"There have been cases in which the disease manifested years after a bite," Cliff says.

I laugh to brush it off, though I imagine it for a moment, what it would be like, if, two years from now, I find I cannot swallow my food, cannot take a sip of water. I would know the madness that was coming for me. Still, leaving, flying all the way to Paris or London just to get a miserable vaccine that I probably don't even need—it seems paranoid. I suggest we ask Rec to talk to the boy's father, to find out if he is healthy, and for the time being, Clifford agrees.

I lay in our tent in the half-light, thinking of teeth and ghosts and children, thinking of green summer, of Ohio, and Bon Echo Lake with its cold northern waters, the rock where echoes live.

When Ben was teething, he went through a biting phase. He wanted something in his mouth at all times. He chewed on everything, and he bit me and bit me. The strange thing was that he didn't bite Cliff. He didn't bite other children or Elizabeth when she visited. Only me. When he was nursing, he bit at my nipple. He bit my cheek once. He bit my fingers. If I held him upright, with his body facing mine and his face looking over my shoulder, he bit at my neck and shoulder. My skin was marked by his teeth. There were scabs made by two or four teeth around my breasts and shoulders, little arcs, red and bruised. He drooled constantly, smearing his wet mouth against me, then pressing his face into my sweater, so my clothes were always damp in patches. His cheeks were pink and chapped from rubbing against my wet clothing. He looked terrible in those days, pale and unkempt and blotchy.

When he bit, I would shout from the pain, and by reflex, I shoved him away. He would cry, but the pain made me angry. It was the strangest thing. I have always been a calm person, but in those moments, I had to stop myself from shaking or slapping him. I would hand him to his father or put him in his playpen and leave the room—breathing, breathing—telling myself to stay calm. He was only a baby. He had no idea. But as soon as he was out of my arms, as soon as he saw me walking away, which I had to do to calm myself, and to protect myself from his teeth, he would begin to scream. I would walk away anyway. I had to. But for the briefest moment, I was pleased at his cries. Because he had hurt me, however small the wound, I was pleased at his suffering. And then I was ashamed of myself.

I step into the river and stand ankle-deep in the ancient, endless river, this river I read about as a child, the very river where Moses was once found in his basket. Here I am, standing in the Nile with my finger wrapped in a bandage. An almost-old woman. No longer a mother. But my body once knew the teeth of my own child.

Clifford got a photo at the moment the child bit me. He pressed the shutter exactly as the boy's teeth clamped down on my thumb, and when he develops the negative, I study the concentration on the boy's face. How careful he was. How deliberate and swift. Do I imagine a look of hatred on his face? Maybe he thought of the bite as research. *Blood of the white woman: Red. Tastes like metal. Same as mine. Same as the cattle. Same as a goat.*

For a time, Clifford has the children use their own fingers to pull back their lips, but the kids are clumsy, often only pulling their lips back partway, or lopsidedly, or they let them go before he has taken the photograph and the whole process has to be repeated. He examines every mouth in every village or town or school that we visit. He only photographs exemplary specimens—good or bad—but there is no room for wasted plates. I ask to resume my duties.

Tsetse Fly: *(Also called "Tik-tik.") At rest, their wings are folded and stacked atop each other. They are not themselves parasitic, but they are vectors that carry single-celled trypanosomes from person to person, horse to crocodile, person to horse, cow to person. Metronome tails swish them away, but still they land. A half-full tsetse, her meal interrupted by a swinging tail or slapping hand, seeks the other half of her meal. She inserts her proboscis mechanically, like a syringe, but regurgitates a little of her last meal into the new host. And the single-cells grow again inside their new host—human, horse, cow, crocodile, lizard, camel, pig, or antelope. Trypanosomes live within the fly and move from creature to creature, canny without thinking. They swim from the tissue to the lymphatic system. The swollen nodes are called Winterbottom's sign, augury of nothing good, omen of death, lumps swelling on the back of the neck. Then onward to the bloodstream! And onward to the brain!*

Sleeping Sickness: *1. Fevers, itching, headaches, joint pains 2. Confusion, numbness, lack of coordination 3. Trouble sleeping through the night, but often sleeping through the day.*

Prevention: *Wear long sleeves. Avoid rural places, especially those with outbreaks and livestock. Slaughter infected beasts. I have read that in Togo, clear on the other side of the African continent, mothers sprinkle dead tsetse on sliced melon and feed it to their babies as a form of ceremonial prevention.*

By the time we reach Ethiopia, Clifford has gathered ever-growing stacks of photographs of people from the many places we have been. Children and adults, smiling or grimacing or jeering or laughing or glaring. Pulling back their lips to show their teeth, perfect or imperfect, or my fingers stretching their lips wide. The boys from the school in Ohio stare out from beneath the brims of dirty caps. Alaskan children hold fish nearly as tall as themselves. Hebrides Islanders stand windblown in front of thatched huts. Swiss children smile with their shining hair, the hillsides behind them dotted with flowers. Egyptians pose beside camels or in a market stall. Maasai men tower over Clifford.

When Clifford studies the photos, he remarks on the symmetry or asymmetry of jaws, on the spacing of nostrils, the broadness of foreheads. But when I look at them, I am often surprised: a pale girl with a gap between her front teeth strikes me as lovely. Clifford remarks on the genetic deviation evidenced by the heterochromatic eyes of a boy from the Ohio school, but I think the child is enchanting. Cliff says that beauty is health, symmetry, and harmony with nature. But I think beauty is a ghost that flickers through the young despite their underbites, pinched nostrils, pallor or pigment.

It was once considered beautiful to be pale and fat. A fat woman was the pinnacle of beauty for the French, before the Revolution. I imagine her with smooth hands, eating cake and cream off a silver tray, her tea garnished with a sugar cube and an orange blossom. She smells of flowers—not of alkaline fields or salt, not of sweat or sulfur, not the smells of one in harmony with nature.

But even the orange blossom withers. On the ground, the soggy blossoms rot. Unplucked, the orange itself falls and is devoured by ants, or it is pushed along the dirt by rats. It grows a beard of mildew, and beneath it, the soil writhes with ants and maggots. The rotting orange feeds them, becomes them.

Clifford says that if Americans and Canadians—*civilized* people— do not learn how to eat properly, the future will be full of degenerates. All around us will be the misshapen faces of malnutrition, rotten teeth, hearts that don't beat a proper rhythm, blood that doesn't clot. The future will be full of pickpockets and racketeers. There will be no standard from which to measure their little chins and crowded teeth. People won't even be able to complete a simple math problem.

But in the stack of photos from Ohio, there among the crooked teeth and lopsided jaws and squashed nostrils, there is one of James laughing. When he laughed, he became something entirely new. In motion, he became strangely beautiful. Like a turtle pushing off the riverbank, slow and awkward on land, but when it slides into the water, it becomes a blade of sun, a graceful swimmer. In one context, James was unlovely, ungainly, but he was also somehow perfect.

Guinea Worm: *Dracunculiasis, little dragons. Water fleas eat the larvae of the worm, and if you drink the water, the fleas swim within you. The worms grow and mate in your intestines. The male worm dies, but the female, pregnant, navigates the length of your bones, following the tug of gravity, plotting a course through your hips, your femur, your shin bone, until she forces her way out through your skin, erupting through your calf, your ankle, your foot. She can be as thick as a strand of spaghetti.*

Prevention/Treatment: *Don't drink stagnant water. Filter every drop. If a worm inhabits you, you will feel her twisting her way down the course of your body. When she burrows her way outward (the end of a yearlong journey), don't plunge your burning foot into a river or lake to extinguish the fire. (In water, she will spray the eggs that will be eaten by the water flea and begin the cycle anew.) Instead, coax her onto a small stick. Wind her slowly, day after day, into a little skein; the stick is your turnkey. Keep her out of the water. Wait out the misery until your body, again, belongs to you.*

Cliff is beneath the dark cloth, ready to take a photograph of a man and his son, when red ants begin crawling up his leg. He is wearing boots and tall socks, so by the time he feels them, they are on his knees and biting. Fire ants. He brushes at them wildly, flinging them off, doing a mad little dance, the pain distorting his face. He makes a strange yowling sound.

The man waiting to have his picture taken is suddenly angry. Instead of helping Cliff to escape the ants, he flies at him, shouting and grabbing at his hands, holding his arms down, twisting his wrists while the ants continue to bite.

"What are you doing?" I shout. "Let him go!"

The man spits a stream of words, incomprehensible but for his anger. Rec holds up his hand, telling me to pause.

"Ants are the man's totem," he says. "He cannot allow you to abuse them."

"But they're biting him!"

Cliff twists, trying to free his hands, but the man is stronger. Cliff groans. His face is red with anger and pain.

"Please!"

The man's son, a boy slender as grass, crouches beside the struggling men and plucks the ants from Cliff's legs with careful deliberation, one at a time, setting them on the ground as if they are precious cargo. Cliff is still flinching with every bite, but he has given up fighting.

"You are okay, Dr. Bell?" Rec asks. Cliff nods. "I am sorry not to help you, but it is best to let things be. You must respect the totem. They will not forgive you if you kill the ants. No one will let you take their picture after that."

The boy continues transferring the ants from Cliff's legs to the ground. Cliff stands, wincing occasionally. The man releases his hands and nods to Cliff. Cliff nods back, but I can see he clenches his jaw—he's angry, probably still in pain. Rec says something to the boy, and then suggests everyone move downriver, leave the ants alone, but Cliff says he needs a break. He is done for the day.

"Forgive me," he says to the man. Rec translates and Cliff bows his head.

On our way back to our tent, Rec explains that the totems of different tribes and clans are sometimes the vehicles through which their ancestors made it to earth. They swam or crawled as tortoises, serpents, puff adders, red ants, cobras, waterbucks, fish. They grew as fig trees. They flowed as rivers and streams. They drifted from heaven with only a tree frond as a wing. They waded slowly out of a big lagoon. They emerged, minuscule, from the heart of a gourd.

Tapeworms look like long, flat white ribbons. They can live their entire lifecycle—egg, larvae, worm—within a single host. They can grow to be up to eight meters long. Each segment of the tapeworm body contains a complete reproductive system, hermaphroditic and complete unto itself. Many hosts are asymptomatic, but when tapeworms travel to the brain, they can cause regular seizures.

Prevention: Drink only purified water. Cook meat thoroughly. Wash hands regularly, especially before eating.

Rec's people, the Nuer, live almost entirely without trees on a broad plain of red dirt. Their houses are round with thatched roofs. The people are incredibly tall and thin. For dances and ceremonies they oil their skin, and it gleams like the deepest pools in the Nile. They have lovely teeth, which Cliff attributes to their diet—rich in milk and meat from their cattle, though they also eat wild rice, sorghum, and fish. Their most prized possessions are their long-horned, hump-backed cattle. They even take for themselves the names of their favorite cattle.

In the morning and in the evening, the sun burns round and pink through the dust at the horizon. I watch the men scrub their skin with dirt—they coat themselves with it—and brush their teeth with ash from dung fires, tucking a bit of charcoal between their finger and their gums and rubbing. I watch the boys and men walking with their herds, silhouetted by the pink glow, and listen to the shuffling hooves and the bells the cattle wear around their necks. I have seen Cliff dwarfed by the towering Maasai, and by Rec, but I am startled anew at how small he looks beside the Nuer men, who, for all their willowy height, look perfectly normal, perfectly proportioned, while Clifford looks pudgy and soft.

The first day in the village, I tell a mother her baby is lovely. He is a boy with bright eyes and long lashes, a taut, round belly. But Rec will not pass on my compliment. He grasps my forearm and pulls me back a step, as if I might hurt the boy.

"We call him *gaikame*," he says, quietly. "It is *this bad thing*. Not lovely. Or you can spit on him, if you want. You can curse him. It is the only way. *Gaikame*."

"*Gaikame*," I say, stepping toward the child again, speaking only that word. The mother turns the boy toward me, but I cannot bring myself to spit on him. Rec speaks a string of words—curses, I suppose, and the mother nods to him.

Later, Rec explains that God is liable to take that which we praise, that he will balance the tallies, distribute the good and the bad evenly to all. To praise a child is the worst thing a person can do, inviting God's attention and retribution. To spit on a child, however, is a blessing. When a man returns from a journey, he spits on his children, and if a woman fails to conceive a child, Rec explains, her father's family spits into a gourd and rubs the collected saliva on her belly. "It is life-giving," Rec says. "A child born after a such a blessing is named Ruei—Spittle—or Nyaruea, Daughter of Spittle."

I am, for once, grateful that I cannot speak the Nuer language, that the mother could not understand my praise. In the following days, I see others spit on babies, but I am never quite able to do it myself.

On the afternoon of our third day in the village, a storm blows in, dark and wild, and everyone runs for their huts. The old men, those who are not out with the cattle, fling tobacco at the sky from their doorways, speaking prayers. Rec crouches beside us in our borrowed hut, murmuring. *Come to earth gently.* Rain slaps the roof and a small puddle forms in the center of the hut. It is a swift storm, and afterward, the sky looks scrubbed and pale.

When Rec goes out to check on his family and inspect the damage, he returns with news that a boy returning from the cattle camp was struck by lightning and killed, just at the edge of the village. Or rather, he corrects himself, a man has died. He was twelve years old, but had received his marks last month—his *gaar*—the six lines cut into his forehead by an elder with a triangular blade. The scars indicate he was a man. Usually, Rec continues, when someone dies, they are buried quickly, with very little ceremony. No one wails or weeps. No one talks about it. Those selected to bury the person must wash themselves in the river after doing their work, before they are allowed to eat anything or touch anyone. Death is dangerous. But when the death comes from lightning, the ceremony is different.

"Lightning," Rec explains, "is *Kwoth's* fire, God's fire. If God wants you, no amount of tobacco will make a difference. Kwoth sends his fire straight to you, wherever you are. He sends the lightning through you. The spirit of a person struck by lightning joins God in the sky immediately."

Rec invites me to join him for the ceremony, which will begin that afternoon. I follow him to the edge of the village where the boy is stretched out with his arms folded across his chest. He is slender, his skin perfectly smooth and a little shiny. His eyes are closed and his forehead bears the six parallel scars—they are perfectly straight. He did not flinch. Despite the scars, I cannot think of him as a man. He is the same age Ben was when he died. The boy's mother kneels next to him. As the men begin to heap the boy with brush cut from the field, I study his bony arms, bent at the elbows and folded lightly over his narrow chest. There is little wailing or crying, and I remark on the matter-of-factness of the ceremony.

"Lightning is not a mistake," Rec says. "It is not a chance encounter. It is God's decisive action. To wail will only offend God."

The people build a mound over the brush and the body. In the center of it, two men plant a sapling, a spindly river tree—*nyuot,* Rec calls it—and from its branches they hang some of the boy's belongings—a horn spoon and ox tassels. At its base, they set a ring of pots full of boiled beer. They spread tobacco leaves over the mound. The boy's father brings a black ox to the shrine and they butcher it swiftly, killing it with a spear. The father distributes pieces of meat to various people around the shrine, but the hide is hung from the tree with the boy's belongings. The shrine is a plea that the boy will leave his family unmolested, a plea for protection. They are afraid of animated ghosts, of *jook.*

"He is *colwic* now," Rec explains. "A mobile spirit of the air, united with other *colwic,* and with God." He translates the words of the man standing nearest the mound, who is speaking out to the distant horizon, out into the bush. "Turn yourself away from us, friend. This beast is yours. We are separate from God, but you now have kinship with him. Where are you? Are you now in the great cattle-camp of the dead? You have joined God. God has given us death. God created death. Do not blame us. Do not molest us. And you, God, have you given us this badness, or is it simply the lot of creation?" Rec says the sacrifices will go on for a couple of days, that they might kill up to twenty animals on behalf of the various family members. The spindly sapling juts into the sky from its mound like a record of the lightning itself. As if it is burned on our retinas, an afterimage of God's furious landing.

In the end, all of us will be stripped bare. Teeth scattered in a garden. Death seems like a living creature sometimes, an animate being that lurks in a certain, swift movement of air. A nighttime hailstorm that comes and goes before you have time to wake fully, before you have time to realize that the sound is only hailstones on the roof. Here is Death, raining stars upon you, or shattering you in a bolt of lightning.

I filed Ben's fingernails before he was taken to the mortuary. Slim, white crescents like clippings of paper dolls. Clifford told me that they were still growing, that our hair and nails grow for a little while after we die, as if they are the last part of us to live.

We buried Ben in Cleveland, though he would have preferred a grave at Bon Echo. We buried him under a pear tree in the Methodist cemetery, near one of Clifford's uncles, and marked the grave with a stone lamb. It has been a decade since I have been to his grave.

Our house in Cleveland always smells of lemon furniture oil. The windows slump in their frames, thick and warped. The day after Ben died, I stood in the living room, looking out a blurry window, watching the neighbor's child push a toy over the cracks of the sidewalk. I often looked out that window, drying my hands, straightening my hair, leaning against the doorframe, while Ben played on the rug, his curly head bent over some project or other. I would never see him there again.

After Ben died, Clifford put all his tools in the soup pot and boiled them until the water was gone and the house smelled of vinegar. Toothbrushes, scrapers and picks, drill tips, scalpels. But then he flung the lot of them into the fire anyway.

"They won't burn," I said, uselessly.

Cliff left the house without his coat. He let the door slam, stayed gone for hours.

The next day, I cleaned the fireplace, raking up the blackened tools with the ashes and coals. I held a set of sooty pliers in my hands, opened

The Good Echo

the grips as wide as I could, pulling them apart, trying to snap them, or at least bend them, but they were solid and unbreakable. I took each tool from the ashes and laid them all in a row. Then I pushed them off the counter into the rubbish bin.

I grew to hate that house with its shining, creaking floors and empty rug. And Bon Echo was worse—the echo seemed, at last, to have fallen silent. There was nowhere we could go that was not haunted, but no place was haunted in the way I would have expected. In the way I wanted. There were no animated ghosts. A ghost would have been a comfort, the glimmering presence of my child, some light or warmth. A slammed door would have been a balm. But every place was empty.

Chigoe flea (Jigger): *Not to be confused with chiggers, these are the smallest of all fleas, tiny black pinpricks. The males, like other fleas, gorge themselves on a blood meal, then let go, fortified. But the females burrow into the skin, into the soft spots between toes. They embed themselves mouth first, leaving their back feet dangling in the air behind them, a tiny hole in their abdomens exposed. She attaches herself to the blood vessels and feeds continuously—swelling until a callus forms around her. She is a blister, pregnant with eggs. A caldera with her own volcano. The host itches and burns, but still the jigger clings. Finally, when she is full, she drops her eggs out of the abdominal hole and dies, sloughed from her host's body, discarded with dead skin cells.*

Prevention/Treatment: *Lace your boots up tight. Pull your socks high.*

Despite my efforts to prevent it, jiggers have tunneled into my left foot. The weal is two inches around, puffy and pink and I cannot stop scratching. Sitting on the edge of the bed, I smother my foot with calamine and wrap it tightly in gauze, so I cannot scratch it. I trim my fingernails to the quick, file the edges smooth. I am so tired of always paying attention, of seeing and hearing and absorbing so much, but almost never understanding. I am tired of boots and hats and mosquito netting. I am tired of sleeping with the lamp lit.

How I want to put out the lamp for once! It somehow seems that my foot would itch less in the dark. I want to lay in the dark and put my hand on Cliff's chest and feel his lungs filling and emptying. But when I suggest that we extinguish the lamp, just for a few minutes, Cliff says no.

"You know we can't." He wrinkles his forehead. "The mosquitoes." His skin seems shinier than usual, his face a little swollen. He looks old.

"I don't care," I say. "I just don't care. We'll be under the net. It's been so long since I've seen plain darkness. I'm tired of sleeping next to the lamp. My eyes burn even when I'm sleeping. I dream my eyes are on fire."

"Okay," he says. "But only for a minute." He turns the wick down, and the room is dark, and I put my hand on his chest and feel him breathing. I stare into the darkness. It washes my eyes, and I feel the quiet of it. I am ready to go home. I want to sleep night after night in cool, quiet darkness. To take darkness for granted. In Ohio, the only harm caused by a mosquito is the itchy little bite that quickly disappears.

Clifford coughs and I feel it rattle in his chest.

"Have I ever told you about Jasper?" he asks. "My childhood dog?"

It seems impossible that he has not, that we could have stories between us that we have not shared, but the moment I think this, I think of Curtis. How many other stories could we hold secret? It is my only one, and one I will not tell. But I have no memory of a dog named Jasper.

"He was a mutt," Cliff says. "Mostly shepherd. Very smart. I trained him to do all sorts of tricks. My mother hated it. She thought I spent too much time with him and not enough on my chores. But that dog was my indulgence. I really loved him."

I picture Cliff as a child, long before we met, back when he was a skinny little boy in overalls. Now, beneath my hand, beneath his skin, tucked neatly into his ribcage, his heart is beating its steady beat.

"I always took Jasper a scrap after dinner—some gristle or crust or whatever was left on the table—and I would toss it for him, and he would jump and catch it in mid-air, and gulp it down without even chewing. I could throw him a scrap from ten meters away, as high as I could toss it, and he would catch it every time. I don't know where I got the idea to throw him a pickle. I guess I thought it would be funny. But I threw a pickle for him, and he caught it, of course, and he swallowed it right down, and then he started coughing and pawing at the ground and rolling around. It was awful. But the next day he was ready to catch whatever scrap I'd brought for him. He just stood there, wagging his tail." He pats my hand. "I don't know why I did it. Maybe I wanted to see how far I could take his trust. Or maybe I thought that he was ultimately stupid, that he was just a dog. I don't know."

"What happened to him?" I say.

"Nothing much, I suppose," Clifford says. "I never did it again. I went on loving him. He went on catching whatever I threw. Eventually, he died, like all our farm dogs." He pauses. "We should light the lamp." But he doesn't move. Through the darkness, I can see the wardrobe across the room from our bed, something left behind by missionaries, other travelers, a darker shape on the dark.

"What made you think of him now?" I ask. "Of Jasper?"

But he has fallen asleep, his chest rising and falling peacefully beneath my hand, his breath falling into a rhythm of sighs. Was it just a memory, or was it a lesson? A story about betraying trust. A story about loving dumbly, always returning to the hand that feeds you no matter how cruel that hand may be. All of us betraying each other, whether we mean to or not. All of us returning again, turning our face to the sky, ready to catch whatever morsel comes our way—vinegar or wine. All of us seeking love, seeking inspiration, seeking connection with each other, seeking answers.

What are we doing here—Cliff and I? On one hand, it's a miracle that we're here, an incredible adventure, so much I never imagined I would see. And maybe Cliff's research will change the way people eat, will change the way they grow. But on the other hand, these people don't know us. They don't care about us. And we don't know them. Not even Rec, our interpreter, who has been with us for almost a month now. I will never be able to keep the tribes or traditions straight, to read the marks on their skin, to understand their languages. We will look at each other and smile, or we will look away, never understanding.

I have a sister still. My sister who knows me, and whom I love. And we have the cabin at the lake. We have seen so much. I have seen the ways that people live in eight different countries and so many villages. I have seen them through their windows at night, watched them reading and cooking and talking with each other. I have walked down crumbling alleyways and dirt footpaths between trees. I have been bitten by hundreds of insects. I have been bitten by a child. I have watched a family plant a tree for a boy struck by lightning and bleed an ox over his grave.

Cliff is snoring lightly, his breath falling into a rhythm, a little congested. Outside there is that constant shuffling of hooves, a baby crying somewhere. I push at the mosquito net with my fingers, simply to know it is there, then let fall back into place. I will not turn the lamp on tonight. I turn onto my side and feel for Cliff's heart beating in the dark.

Maybe in death, when my eyes are pressed closed, I might finally see everything. But I will not feel the hands that will wash my dead body, wiping the sour sweat away. Not the sponge dipped in the basin and squeezed, nor the clipping of my fingernails, the combing of my hair. No horsehair brush across my cheeks, adding artificial rosiness to my gray skin. But I want to feel that tender touch.

It has been sixteen years since we built the inn at Bon Echo. We have not been there since the summer after Ben died, since we sold the inn, although we kept a small cabin for ourselves. I have not seen the lake for eleven years, and I want to see it again. To sit by the fireplace on a long, black night while the snow swirls and stacks in the window frames. Firelight flickering on the walls. A braided rug in the middle of the room. A sealskin parka hanging on its hook by the door. Woodsmoke permeating my skin and hair. In the tiny kitchen, I will make tea, the steam and whistle filling the house. I will unscrew the top on a jar of blueberries picked in the summer and stored for just this night in the middle of winter.

FROM THE NOTEBOOKS OF DR. CLIFFORD BELL:
THE SUDAN, SEPTEMBER, 1931

Sugar Maple (*Acer saccharum*)**:** In the front yard of our Cleveland house, there is a tree that I love. An old sugar maple, each fall its leaves turn bright yellow, and as the fall continues, they deepen to orange, and then to the brightest shades of red. Each year I think that the leaves are more brilliant than ever before. And then it rains, and something about the gray weather or the moisture makes the leaves seem to glow with even greater intensity. When, after that first cold drizzle of fall, the sun returns—and it always returns—the leaves take on a brightness that makes it seem as if they are shining from within. It happens like this every year: the initial color change, the rain, the deepening brilliance, and then the darkening and falling, one at a time, delicate and curling, so different from the leaves of the black maple, which are also beautiful, but thick and tough in comparison.

These past few days, I have been thinking of that tree, and how, each year, as I watch it lose its leaves, I think of death. It is strange, perhaps, that fall has always been my favorite season, steeped as it is in dying and death, in lengthening nights and the dreadful approach of winter. But fall is so splendid, and I think the dread only adds poignancy.

I remember standing before that tree with Benjamin, both of us admiring it. He must have been nine or ten, only a couple of years before his death. I recited the beginning of Shakespeare's 73rd Sonnet:

That time of year thou may'st in me behold
When yellow leaves, or none, or few, do hang
Upon those boughs which shake against the cold,
Bare ruined choirs, where late the sweet birds sang.

I doubt I made it to the end of the poem. I don't remember how it goes after those lines, now, although I knew the entire sonnet once. I don't think Benjamin really understood it, but he stood there quietly. And then he took my hand.

And now I am nearly the old man Shakespeare wrote about, with winter creeping closer every day, and hardly a "leaf" clinging to my head. But my son has been gone for many years, and in terms of trees, he was only a sapling.

One fall, a few years after he died, I determined that I would be like that tree: my brightest days, the most splendid time of my life would come near its end. Just when it seemed I could do nothing more with my life but wait it out, reading books and doing crosswords, I would, instead, suddenly shine even brighter. Before I died, I would dazzle. It seemed a worthy goal, a good way to go. Should my aging body allow it, I would go out brilliantly.

After the debacle with the NDA, when I began working at St. Stanislaus School for Backward Boys, I thought I was beginning my final blaze, that I was in my yellow leaves. My research into the nutrition of young criminals and would-be criminals would be my crowning glory. My growing knowledge of the link between nutrition and health, both physical and mental, was groundbreaking. I was sure of it even then. But now I see that St. Stan's was barely the first brightness. I forgot about the second flare of color, the one that comes after the rain.

James might have been the rain. The work with James was a digression. It was my hope that if I could help James, I might be able to help other Mongoloid children. I could change everything for them. But after the maxillary surgery, when James' mouth collapsed back upon itself, he seemed more or less ruined. He was always a clumsy, vulgar child, but for a few weeks, it had seemed like I was getting somewhere, like he was getting somewhere. After that, which can only be called a failure, I could see that St. Stan's was not even the beginning. I reminded myself that the sugar maple always surprises me, getting even more vivid than I imagined it could.

Then Frances said yes, let's go to Florida. She said yes to Alaska and Switzerland and Egypt and Africa. So we would blaze together, two small trees with twisted limbs, glowing our brightest before the snow.

I have sent hundreds of samples of food and soil and saliva back to the lab in Ohio. I have taken hundreds of photographs and measurements. Even when we return home, I will have years of work ahead of me. Never as a young man could I have foreseen such a project for myself. Never could I have dreamed of this place—this ancient river, these dusty villages—nor of Switzerland, nor the Hebrides, not even Alaska.

But Frances is tired, and it occurs to me, after all these years, that she and I could be different types of trees, trees with different seasons, different lifespans, different colored leaves that fall at different rates. I have so much more work to do, but I have no interest in training a new assistant, some whippersnapper young scientist. I have no interest in leaving Frances at home, in our empty house in Cleveland. What would she do there, alone in Cleveland?

Everything is so easy with Frances. She knows me and my research methods. She understands my project, my need for sleep, the things I will and will not eat. She is good at speaking with the children when I am busy setting up the camera, even when she does not speak their languages. She asks them how to say things, pointing at her elbow or a button on her shirt, and speaking the word in English. The children always seem to understand her, at least well enough. She keeps a running list in her notebook of how to say the word tooth in various languages. Gaelic: *fiacail*. Italian: *il dente*. German: *Zahn*. And sometimes, when she takes dictation for me, she records things I have not even spoken aloud. Sometimes, when I see what she has penned, I see that she has written my *thoughts*—questions and connections that have not yet escaped my mouth, or even made it through the twists of my brain. I don't know if I could do this work without her.

We will return to Ohio. We have been so many places. I would willingly continue—to Spain, to France, to small villages in England or Ireland—there are many other places I wish to go. I have heard that on the Torres Strait Islands people live on fish and coconuts. And although I went to Peru briefly, alone, I want to return to South America. I knew so little back then. I collected skulls for analysis, but I did not look into the mouths of living people. Brazil, too, could be useful, as well as the native people of Guatemala and Mexico.

But in truth, I am a little tired, too. I am fifty-two years old. My father died at fifty-six. But the thought of Ohio—a summer evening on our porch, swing creaking, tomatoes and sweet corn on my tongue—things I love, but so dull! Ohio bores me! I am not ready to go. I have a book to write. A reputation to make or remake. My leaves haven't yet blazed brightly enough. I think I am still in that first flush. Maybe I haven't even reached the rain.

A BEDTIME STORY
(for Ben)

I called you Soap because your existence seemed magical, like a soap bubble, and so separate from my own. I have always thought of people as self-contained, isolated even, and although they sometimes cluster together, they sometimes collide and destroy each other. But you—my child, my perfect boy—you complicated this. With you it was different. You had grown within me, a bubble within a bubble, although even then your body was separate from mine, even if, for a time, you were dependent on me.

Soap bubble. Drifter.

Light is how we know that a bubble exists, rainbows swirling across its surface. And a bubble is so fragile, lifted and batted by air currents. A bubble is easily broken.

That night, like every night, I sat beside your bed, while you pulled the sheets to your chin. Sheets that smelled of wind and sap—it was laundry day. In the living room, your father was reading the paper, and we heard the crackle and fold of newsprint, the creaking of his chair, his wet cough. From outside came the groans of frogs, the rasp of crickets, leaves whispering at the sky. You asked for an Ojibwe story, as you often did that summer. You were eleven, and at the Lake, Ojibwe stories were all around us. The lake had been theirs, and in many ways, it still is.

I began with Nanabozho and the Wild Geese. Nana was hungry, swimming beneath the resting flock to tie the goose feet together with a willow rope. But the task took too long, and he was holding his breath. His lungs began to burn, and he let his breath out in a rush. He burst to the surface, gasping, and the startled geese lifted their wings and flew, scattering into the sky, shaking the water from their feathers. Nana held so tightly to his end of the rope that the geese lifted him right out of the water, and he trailed behind their formation, flying across the sky, heavy as a drowned sheep. Nana began to sing. He hadn't meant to go flying, but rather to roast the birds for supper, but now they were dragging him through the sky. But soon they wiggled their legs free of his knots and dropped him. He fell through tree branches and landed in a mulberry bush, laughing.

You knew this story well, and you wanted to try the trick for yourself. You asked how many geese would it take to lift you from the water. You had been practicing holding your breath underwater in the cold lake. How long would it take to tie the feet together? Could you hold your breath for two minutes? You practiced tying knots for speed. "Are geese ticklish?" you asked. A goose foot was as big as your hand.

But that night you stopped me. "Not that story," you said.

I was embroidering a tablecloth, and as I pulled red thread through white cotton, my stitches looked like a line of drops, like holly berries in snow. A red flower in winter marks the spot where someone has died.

"The one about the warrior in the spirit world," you said. "That one."

It wasn't a story from your book, but one I had been inventing for you based on what we had learned from the book.

The warrior came home triumphant from battling the wind. He was still wearing porcupine quills and fur. The red paint on the warrior's face was flaking. He had mixed it himself: iron oxide scraped from the rocks and mixed with the yolk of an egg. The warrior carried a small sack stuffed with willow tobacco and the long red tail feathers of a woodpecker.

Woodpeckers are such flashy little buggers. The way they flaunt their bright heads and tails. The way they go around knock-knocking, their taps echoing through the summer woods. They dart from tree to tree like a flame, like sparks igniting branch after branch. Such showoffs! Someone had to take them down a notch, so the warrior killed one and roasted it and kept its brightest feathers.

But now he gave the feathers and the tobacco to Keezheekoni's father as an offering, for the warrior wanted to marry Keezheekoni.

Even as a young girl, Keezheekoni had been known for her speed. She had beaten all the boys in footraces, and now, as a grown woman, she was still known for her quickness and her love of running. She would set down a basket of berries and take off through the forest, returning an hour later, panting and flushed and sweaty, her hair blown back and a few damp scraggles stuck to her temples. Keezheekoni had freckles across her nose, and the warrior liked to find shapes in her freckles, constellations of tobacco flowers.

Why did the warrior love her? Well, she was beautiful, I suppose, but she was also fast and strong. Let's say she was also smart, and that she knew how to be quiet when it mattered. She knew the languages of birds and neighboring tribes. She was friends with raccoons, and they brought her fish in winter. Who wouldn't love a girl that befriended raccoons? Like a raccoon, Keezheekoni was a bit of a trickster. She once stirred salt into the warrior's tea when he wasn't looking, and once, she told him they were going to a costume party so he would show up in a bear suit, complete with claws and crazed glass eyes, but he found he was the only one dressed up.

Why do we love anyone? I love your father because he is kind and brilliant and because he works so hard. And I love him because he loves me. Because he is restless, and because he (and God) have given you to me. But none of this explains anything about love. Why do I love you, dear? I love you because I have known you every minute of your life. Because you are part of me, although you are not me. Because you are full of surprises. Because you shout at the cliff to hear the echo. Because you rush ahead to hold the door open for other people. I love you even for the way you cried after you burned the nutcracker in the fireplace. And because you're a whirlwind. I love you for the way you cut that frog open to see what it contained, your hand so steady. You pinned its skin to the board so you could get a better look. For how you polish the magnifying glass on your shirttails (so like your father with his glasses). I love you for your concentration, for your curiosity, for the way your forehead wrinkles, for the set of your mouth, but also because you're so quick to smile. I saw when you stole that candy from Mrs. Olsen's kitchen. She saw it, too, and she looked the other way. She was probably embarrassed for me. That I had raised such a rude and selfish son, a little thief. But shhh...it was only a piece of candy. And I love you for daring, my little thief.

Who knows why we love? Who can explain it?

Five days before she was to be married to the warrior, Keezheekoni went berry picking with her sister. Keezheekoni sat down for a minute, taking a quick break. She stretched her long neck this way and that. She flexed her fingers. She was so tired. Her sister got up to get another basket, turning away from Keezheekoni for only a moment, still talking about their foolish cousin who had gotten lost walking back from the lake, a distance of only a half kilometer, and when she turned back around, Keezheekoni was fast asleep in the dirt.

Keezheekoni dreamed of endless water. She stood on the shore of a wide gray lake and knew the water was the harbinger of a journey.

A harbinger? It's like a sign. An omen. You remember how your Aunt Elizabeth cried when the bird flew in through the window last spring? How desperately she shooed it out? Elizabeth says a bird in the house is a harbinger of death. If a bird flies into your house, it predicts that someone will soon die. In this story, water is a harbinger of Keezheekoni's journey into death, which some people think of as another land. Your father laughs at Elizabeth for believing such things. He calls her superstitious. But harbingers make good stories. They add suspense or drama or fear. We hope the hero will triumph over whatever misery is foretold: maybe he will escape the burning trees, maybe she will not get lost on the wide gray lake, maybe no one will die if we shoo the bird out fast enough.

Some people think water is feminine, but I'm not sure why. Water takes the shape of the container that holds it. It is ephemeral and malleable and mysterious. Why are these considered feminine traits? It is true that a woman's mind is unfathomable, but so is your mind, and your father's. You, my love, are infinite and mysterious. Every mind is unknowable. Even our own. But part of the thrill of life is trying to understand each other, trying to understand ourselves.

Maybe water is considered feminine because of the womb, a private ocean in which a child grows. An unborn baby breathes like a fish. Even in the womb, it can hear, and it begins to sense its mother's moods. Does that private ocean ripple with anger? Slosh with fear? None of us remember those underwater sounds after we are born. We forget the echo of our mother's heartbeat. But before a baby is born, it learns the sound of its own heart and the sound of its mother's heart as they beat in chorus at the bottom of the sea.

But yes, yes, let's get back to the story.

Keezheekoni's dream brought with it a terrible fever. Across the lake, she saw a fire burning in a thicket and the heat burned toward her, but she found she could not run. On the third day of her illness, only two days before she was to marry the warrior, she died.

The warrior was heartbroken. The people brought smudge sticks and the blue smoke swirled around Keezheekoni's body, but he barely noticed their fragrance. There were drums for her, and singing, and a fire burned for four days as a vigil for her soul.

Back then, the Ojibwe didn't bury their dead right away. They wrapped the body in birch bark and for four days, they waited. That was the time it took for the spirit to find its way to the afterlife. But the four days passed, and still, the warrior lay with his head at Keezheekoni's feet, listening for the movement of her spirit, trying to hear the rhythm of the earth. He listened and listened. He relit the fire. He refused to eat.

But he could have anyone, the people whispered. *Does he think she will come back?*

He heard them whispering, and finally, finally, he stood up. He could not hear her heartbeat, he said. And he could not hear the beat of the earth.

Does anyone hear it? He asked. Has anyone ever *heard it? The earth is a mother without a heart.*

But the Earth lives, said the people. *See how she lives? See the sap of the trees? It is her blood. And if there is blood, there must be a heart.*

It is buried too deeply, then, he said. *It is a cold heart, hidden so far below the dirt. It is a feeble heart, too distant and weak.*

He brushed the dirt from his cheek and knees. He sat down and stitched himself a new pair of moccasins.

You could have another, the people said. *Look at this one—her hair is the shiniest of all. And this one—she can run almost as fast as the one you lost.*

But instead of looking for a new love, the warrior began to go on long hunts. He went to battle against the West Wind, against the Sioux, against the wolves. He was always gone, always returning triumphant, sprinkling some tobacco around the place where the body of his bride had rested, and then leaving again.

One day, the warrior tracked a bear into the darkest part of the forest. He shot it with an arrow and the tip burrowed deep into the bear's fur, deep into its flesh. A bear's fur, you know, is a thicket where anything might get lost: the tip of an arrow, a colony of fleas, a set of jacks or playing cards, maybe even a mouse. When you lose something, it is a good idea to check with the bears. See if they have hidden your key or your toothbrush or your shoes deep within their fur. But this bear was injured, or maybe just very old. It ambled along very slowly. The warrior ran after the bear until it fell to the ground.

The warrior leapt on the bear and their two bodies rolled this way and that, each fighting for his life. The warrior tried to cover his head, to protect himself from the bear's giant paws, but he also tried to choke the animal. The bear was like the shadow of a man, and the warrior began to fear that he was fighting his own shadow. What would he do without a shadow—if he won? It was his only true companion since his bride had gone to the spirit world. But the bear snarled and drooled and swatted at the warrior, so the warrior had to fight. And what would happen if he lost a fight with his own shadow? The bear lunged at him with its teeth and the warrior kicked hard. Then, quite abruptly, the bear stopped fighting, and the warrior felt its hot, fishy breath on his cheek. The soft heat of its leathery paws pressed against his own palms, and the bear spoke.

Listen, said the bear. *You can go to her. You can follow her to the spirit world.* The bear told the warrior he had only to walk all the way through the forest, and on the other side he would find an old magician living on the shore of a lake. The magician would tell him how to find his dead bride. Anyone could go to the spirit world, the bear said. He had never understood why more people did not make the journey, if only to satisfy their curiosity.

Have you been there? The warrior asked.

Very tenderly, the bear touched the warrior's cheek, and then, without answering, he laid his head in the matted grass and died.

For a moment, the warrior rested. The bear's arms were heavy upon him. He was a real bear, not a shadow. The warrior untangled himself from the bear's embrace and pried open the animal's mouth. He wrenched out a tooth and tied it around his neck. With his knife, he skinned the creature and hung its coat from a branch. He cut the meat from the bones and ate as much as he could. An entire bear was far too much food for one man. The warrior had planned to bring the meat back to his village, but now he wanted only to eat his fill and continue his walk through the forest. He prayed that the wolves would come, and they did, and they growled deep rumbling growls while they ate. They tore the fatty flesh from the bones and licked their chops. The warrior watched them until sleep settled on him.

No, my dear, I have never tasted bear meat. But yes, people do eat it. Would you like to? I imagine that we could find some. You can help me prepare it.

In the morning, the warrior continued his walk through the woods. Would it take a day? Days? Weeks? There were no landmarks, no birds, no meadows, and no cliffs. There were only trees. What if the bear had lied? He used the bear tooth to scratch into the endless trunks, drawing tiny triangles, like the tooth itself, marking his way so he could find his way back. And then he saw the lake, and the magician's tent was right there in front of him, as if he had followed a perfect trail from the bear to the magician.

The magician stepped out of the tent.

You are so slow, he said. *But lucky for you, your bride is rather weak with a paddle. She hasn't even made it across the lake yet, the poky thing.* The magician gestured at the water and the warrior saw a fleet of boats fading into fog. They did not appear to be moving at all. The warrior felt untethered for a moment, as if he were floating, his feet no longer on the earth.

Yes, it was like vertigo. Exactly like that. But it lasted only a moment, like a wave washing over him. He swayed and squinted across the lake. He looked down and found that his feet were still there, resting on the dirt, a stitch unraveling from the top of one moccasin. He bent down to retie it. He touched the earth, steadying himself. He pressed his palms flat to the dirt.

No, said the magician, taking the warrior's hand and helping him up. *If you want to follow her you have to surrender to the floating feeling. You must leave your body behind. You must paddle across the lake. Do not count your strokes. You will find your way, but first you must take off your skin. You must float away from your body.*

(You should try it sometime, darling. You just unzip it, just like pajamas. Step right out of it!)

So the warrior slipped out of his skin, surprised at its softness as it slid down his shoulders and fell in a heap around his ankles. Better than silk or merino or leather.

(That's true, dear, leather is often made of cow skin, but it is much tougher than human skin. Human skin, at least at first, is almost gossamer, almost translucent, but it dries out very quickly.)

The warrior's skin lay at his feet. He stepped away from it.

One step.

Two.

He was drifting. He felt himself growing lighter.

Once, he turned back and saw the magician bending to gather his skin, folding it neatly, like fresh laundry. The magician sold skins at the market on Saturdays. A high-quality skin could fetch some a pretty penny. What made a high-quality skin? Well, I imagine it had to be supple and unwrinkled, but with one or two well-placed scars. One wants to appear as if one has character, after all, and scars are stories, darling.

I touched the scar on your forehead, the tiny crater where you had split your head against the pier earlier that summer. You closed your eyes, and I combed your hair with my fingers.

The sale of a good skin could feed the magician, house him, and keep him warm for a month. There is always someone looking to change himself—to be younger or pinker or less wrinkly. There's always a market for a good, smooth skin. But the truth is, a new skin won't disguise you entirely. It falls over the same contours you've always had—your wide or narrow shoulders, the bump on your nose in the place you once broke it, the concavity where your ribs meet at your sternum. The new skin covers these like any garment. It's a new color, a new texture. Perhaps you get some new freckles. Some additional pigment. New lines across your palms. But in the end, you're the same person. We get so sick of ourselves sometimes, but there's no escaping ourselves.

You were in and out of sleep, and I was telling the story mostly to myself. Your eyelashes were bright against your suntanned face. Once or twice, you opened your eyes, and you focused on me, slowly, blurrily.

"But the bride?" you mumbled. "Keezheekoni?" You were tired of my digressions, and now I was guiding your first dream of the night. You were the warrior now, floating, freed from your body, drifting in a canoe across the wide gray lake. Hoping to catch up with your lost love. Hoping to see the spirit world.

The last thing the magician said as you pushed away from shore was that you should not speak. *Keep silent,* he said. *Say nothing until you reach the spirit world, and when you find your bride, do not touch her until you are on dry land. If you do, you will not reach the spirit world, nor will you ever be able to reenter your skin. You will float on the lake forever. Forever, you will remain a vagabond spirit.*

You saw Keezheekoni paddling so slowly in front of you. The set of her shoulders was familiar. You saw her as you had always seen her, in her beautiful skin with her long hair and long limbs. You bit your tongue and paddled faster, but the distance between your boats did not seem to close. You could not call out to her, and she never looked back. She never looked anywhere but ahead. It was completely silent. There was not even the sound of the water lapping against your boat. There were no birds. Even your paddle sliced through the water without a splash. Your lungs felt full, as if you could not exhale, as if you were made entirely of lungs, stuffed full with air. You paddled and paddled and paddled.

Ahead of you, Keezheekoni arrived on the opposite shore. Her canoe nudged the bank, but she made no effort to secure it or get out of the boat. She just sat there, defeated or tired, or simply not caring. What's the rush, anyway, once one has left the temporal world? The spirit does not age.

But you, my warrior, were not dead. Even free of your body, you felt the anxiety of time. Your canoe butted roughly against the bank, and as much as you could, being without legs or feet, or your legs and feet being in such an unfamiliar state, you leaped from your canoe and sloshed silently to shore, the splashes from your ephemeral body scattered around you like fog. But there it was: *dry land.* You could speak! You could touch her!

Keezheekoni looked at you, but her eyes were blank. Could she see you, floating as you were? Did she know you? She looked down at her own reflection on the surface of the water, and you spoke her name. She jumped a little, as if startled, the way she had that day when you had hidden behind a tree and jumped out at her—a cruel game, but you both loved it for the moment after the fear, the moment when you recognized the face of your beloved, when you realized it was only a game, the moment the laughter came. Keezheekoni leaped from her canoe and ran to you, and you said her name again, aloud.

Benjamin.

How does a spirit hold a spirit? The boundaries between the two dissolved and dissolving? I admit, my dear, my imagination fails. I have never been to the spirit world. I do not know its laws.

Benjamin.

You, sleeping warrior: it was not time for you dwell in the spirit world. You were sent back. Just as you lifted your hand to Keezheekoni's cheek, there was a whoosh, like the gust of a wing flapping, and you were blown back across the lake, and found yourself standing in the marketplace looking at your skin which was hanging on a wooden hanger in a stall, displayed like a set of long johns.

And that was it. Keezheekoni was gone. And on top of that, you had to buy back your skin, which was particularly difficult because the magician could not see you, or at least he pretended not to. You spun your skin on its hook and the customer offering a trade—four pounds of tobacco, four pounds of dried blueberries—was scared off by the sudden twirling. "I guess it's spoken for," said the Magician with a shrug.

Benjamin.

My Ben. You were asleep and dreaming, breathing so quietly. I heard your father in the other room, rocking his chair, shuffling pages of newsprint. For a moment, I sat there and watched you sleep.

And now you are gone. Your body is gone. I do not know where you are. I do not know the afterlife in which you drift. It is the body that separates souls, but without it, without flesh and bones, the soul seems unrecognizable. How will I know you, my love? How will I ever find you?

With my bare feet in summer grass.

When I swim in the lake.

When a fish leaps and its scales catch the sun.

How will I know you when I, too, lose my body? And how will you recognize me, your mother?

For now, I am bound here, in my body, in my skin, in my skull. Here, with the grass and the lake and the scales of fish. But waiting is a little easier because I love being a body. And there is so much to see here. So much you didn't get to see.

I listened to your easy breath as you slept. I touched your cheek, your eyelids, your forehead.

I said goodnight.

EPILOGUE

Endings, like beginnings, are thresholds built by storytellers. *But death*—you protest—*death is most certainly an ending.* Death is not pliable. It is not a storyteller's tool, but a fated, irrevocable ending.

But here I am, ongoing! Ear, voice, storyteller.

Death marks a change, then. Like a bookend separating letters of the alphabet. A transfer to a new train. A boat pulling away from the pier in a busy port. The sun sets, but it rises again. The moon wanes, but then waxes again.

Frances and Clifford return to Ohio. One morning, they get into a canoe, and Frances remembers the first canoe they paddled together, so many years ago, on their honeymoon at Lake Mazinaw, before I was born. Clifford was in the stern, and she was in the prow, and the boat continually drifted off-course. This time, leaving the Nuer village, they paddle in perfect tandem. Clifford corrects every little swerve of the craft with a perfect J- or C-stroke, keeping time with Frances. Their guide, Rec, is in a second boat, one with a motor, one full of cameras and glass slides, masks and beads and pelts and handmade clay figures of cattle, dental tools, pill bottles, and samples of dried fish and grains, yams and legumes, and a carved wooden box filled with teeth.

They push away from the bank and paddle through the reeds to the place where the current is swift and smooth, and from the shore the people wave. Rec sings, inventing the words of his song and singing in time with the putter of his boat's motor. He sings in Nuer first, for the people on shore, but then he sings in English for Frances and Clifford, and Frances wonders if his verses are different depending on the language, or if he translates straight across, but she doesn't ask. She doesn't want to interrupt his song.

> *On this day, the tooth doctor leaves us.*
> *The river is swift. Crocodiles sleep.*
> *Puff adders swim. Will we see him again?*
> *The tooth doctor and his woman,*
> *on this day, they leave us.*

He sings them halfway to Malakal, and then sings again as they paddle to the banks and pull the boats out of the water. He helps them carry their luggage to the Jeep that will take them to the airfield, and then he shakes their hands. Frances says she'll write from Ohio. She hugs him, and he lets her, her head barely reaching his chest. He pats her hair.

The plane lifts off, and it is as she imagined it would be on the nights when she could not sleep, when she was homesick for Ohio, for Bon Echo: the huts below, the imperfectly round roofs growing smaller, flattened by perspective, the Nile like a gleaming artery in the wide-open body of the earth, and then all around her is sky. They are their way to a place where there are locking doors and featherbeds and electricity and markets full of fruit. But she is not the same as she was when she left those things behind.

Once upon a time, in 1919, a dentist in Ohio performed a root canal on his young son, and the boy's mouth grew infected, and he died. It was sepsis, but for the sake of the story, we will call it poison. The boy fell into eternal sleep. The man blamed himself. He sought an antidote, but his search led him away from his guilt. He took in lungs full of air. He touched the soft pelts of rabbits. Sometimes he found answers, but he always found more questions, until, one day, he recognized that the questions were endless, and that he loved them as much as he had loved his son, that by following them, he would go on.

Once upon a time, in 1931, somewhere in East Africa, a woman, far from home, in a place where the people did not look like her, mused about beauty and love. Symmetry and strong jawlines were lovely, she thought, but they did not guarantee beauty. She had met many beautiful people: a strange girl in Alaska, a Swiss woman that lived between glaciers and carved terrifying masks, Scottish children with rotten teeth. John Rec Puk, a Nuer man who was so tall and dark and thin, who sang and spoke so many languages. And James, with his soft body and sloping face. When James laughed, when he extended his hands to the bees, when he rested his head against Frances' shoulder, he was beautiful. Beauty was entirely unpredictable. And so was love.

James sometimes lay his tired head on her lap. *Mrs. Frances, would you touch my hair? Mrs. Frances, would you tell me a story?* He pointed at the pictures. He laughed so coarsely. *Mrs. Frances, I love you.* James taught her that love is much more than beauty or intelligence, that there is another form of perfection. But James was never really hers. He would be entirely grown now. Too large for himself. Clumsy and overgrown and breathing through that open mouth, spittle collecting at the corners. But she loved him still. She loved the boy he had been. Pulling her across the garden by the hand, talking to the bees.

And then it is a morning in Cleveland, and Frances steps onto the front porch and opens her eyes wide to absorb the dawn. She closes her eyes and remembers an elephant bathing its pup in green water. Beautiful ghosts all around her.

January of 1932 is cold, but winter is always cold in northern Ohio. With dry, cold lips Frances kisses Clifford who is standing in the door-way behind her. She picks up her suitcase. *Don't forget to eat,* she says, because he often does if she isn't there to cook for him, to set the table, to call him to sit with her, to eat. She licks her lips and kisses him again, more warmly. She leaves him, my father, to his lab with his oat grass and pots of Scottish peat and lab slides. She leaves him with his manuscript. His book is halfway written.

She takes the train north to Ontario, north again to the Kaladar Station. In Kaladar, Ontario, Frances asks the stationmaster for a ride to the lake. No one goes there in the winter, but he drives her down the familiar road anyway, the car skidding a little in the frozen mud. They drive between spindly trees, trees not good enough for the mill, to the edge of the lake, the place where the echoes live. Frances is an aging woman, but she is still strong, and in Ontario, there is only the cold to battle—no tapeworms or lions, no grizzly bears or fungus. Cold is a familiar old nemesis. Night falls early and swiftly.

The lake sleeps beneath ice. Snow whirls over its surface. Down below, in the dark, sluggish fish move through the freezing water. She could catch them, and maybe she will, tomorrow or the next day. She'll drill a hole with the augur, the way her father once taught her, and stand at the end of the pier, cast her line into the hole, dangling a ball of dough.

She tears the boards off some of the windows of the cabin to let in a little light and builds a fire in the fireplace. She wraps herself in a blanket and rests her feet on the braided rug. Outside, Orion cartwheels slowly across the sky. Ursa Major points her nose at the Lynx. A trickle of smoke rises from the chimney into the dark above the cabin, and in the flickering light, Frances falls asleep.

She dreams of summer, and of me, her lost boy. I put my hand out and she takes it, and I lead her through the summer forest, sun luffing through leaves, and we walk along the edge of the rock together, looking down at the dark blue surface of the lake. Together, we prepare to jump. We prepare to bellow for strength as we fall toward the water. We'll punch through it. We'll kick back to the surface and rise, gasping with laughter. We crouch, prepared to leap.

Frances' toe nudges a small stone from the edge, and she watches it plummet, watches it hit the water, the ripples swelling outward from the tiny drop, colliding with the other ripples. And then, right before we jump, it is daybreak, and she wakes, alone in her bed in the cabin.

And she ventures into the morning of another day, a solitary woman, her breath steaming forth in the January sun. Standing on the porch, she shouts: *Good morning!* And her voice travels across the lake to the rock and then returns to her.

Good morning! Good morning!

Excellent company, she thinks.

She stomps her heavy boots—*one, two*—and that sound, too, travels and returns.

One. Two.

AUTHOR'S NOTE

The Good Echo is inspired by the life and work of Weston and Florence Price, who lost their young son in 1914, and traveled the world in the 1930s, seeking evidence for Price's theories about nutrition.

With Deepest Gratitude and Sense of Indebtedness
For the Devoted and Loving Cooperation and Cheerful Sacrifices of
My Wife and of Our Deceased Son, Donald,
Who, at Sixteen, Paid with his life
The price of humanity's delayed knowledge
Regarding these heart and rheumatic involvements
This volume is lovingly dedicated.

So reads the dedication of Dr. Weston Price's 1923 book *Dental Infections, Oral and Systemic,* one of the texts to which this novel is indebted. *The Good Echo* here and there incorporates lines and ideas from Price's book on root canals and focal infection theory, especially in the chapter "Different Kinds of Lightning," and in Clifford Bell's notebooks. I also owe a debt to Price's later book, *Nutrition and Physical Degeneration* (1939), in which he published the findings and anecdotes of the ethnographic nutritional research he conducted during the 1930s in the U.S., Canada, and remote villages around the world. Many of the spellings and names of tribes in *The Good Echo* are replicated from Price's book. It was also from Price's book that I learned of his research at a Cleveland boys' school: the character of James, and the experiment conducted on him, is drawn from Price's work with a sixteen-year-old boy with Down syndrome, then called mongolism, whose story particularly moved and disturbed me.

Price's wife, Florence Anthony Price, served as her husband's research assistant. In his book, she occasionally appears in photographs as a small woman standing beside a towering Maasai man, or as an interloper among a group of Bedouins and their camels. It is sometimes the floral pattern of Florence Price's dress that serves as the backdrop in photographs taken to demonstrate the facial structures and teeth of children; it must be her hands that hold open their mouths. It was, in part, Florence Price's quiet presence and imagined grief that called me to write this work of fiction.

In the writing of this novel I also relied on the books of E.E. Evans Pritchard, specifically *The Nuer* (1940), *Kinship and Marriage Among the Nuer* (1951), and *Nuer Religion* (1956). Although Evans Pritchard's books were published in decades following my characters' travels, his writing was vital to how I imagined a couple from Ohio might have experienced and understood Nuer life in the first half of the twentieth century.

The songs sung by the character of John Rec Puk, the Bells' guide in Sudan, were inspired by the book *Cleaned the Crocodile's Teeth: Nuer Song,* translated by Terese Svoboda (1985). Although the songs I have invented for Rec fall short of the magic and lyricism of the Nuer songs as Svoboda translated them, I am grateful to her for making the songs available in some form. Svoboda's book also includes her observations and explanations based on the time she spent with the Nuer in the 1970s, when she recorded the songs and translated them with the help of the people she met there. Her book was an invaluable window into Nuer culture.

These notes are, of course, incomplete: over the years I took to write this book, I have consumed countless folktales, traditional stories, and histories of people from Ohio, Florida, Alaska, Minnesota and south-central Canada, Switzerland, the Outer Hebrides, Egypt, Sudan, and South Sudan. These stories have been tumbled and collaged in my mind and on these pages. I am grateful for these stories, shared in various and delightful forms. It is my aim to celebrate the ways stories grow and change through times and cultures, how they guide and connect us, and how they endure.

ACKNOWLEDGMENTS

Excerpts of this book appeared previously, some in different form, in *Memorious, Gulf Coast,* and *North American Review.* Thank you to the editors. Thanks to my agent, Julie Stevenson, and to Diane Goettel, Angela Leroux-Lindsey, and everyone else at Black Lawrence Press, for seeing something captivating in this story, and making it the book that it is. Thank you to Cornell College for awarding me the R.P. Dana Emerging Writer Fellowship, which gave me time and a supportive community at a crucial stage in writing this book, and especially to Glenn Freeman and Rebecca Entel, who I am now lucky enough to call friends. To so many people at Earlham College, including my kind and generous students: thank you for pushing me, encouraging me, and employing me while I completed this novel. To my fellow writers at the University of Utah: thank you for the ideas and encouragement you offered when you saw the first stirrings of this book in classes, and even more for your companionship and your words. Scott Black, Gretchen Case, Matt Potolsky, and Lance Olsen: thank you for introducing me to so many new ideas, for asking interesting questions, and helping me shape my own. Endless gratitude to Melanie Rae Thon: you have taught me so much about writing, life, patience, attention, and compassion. Catie Crabtree, Robert Glick, Rachel Marston, Anton DiSclafani, and TaraShea Nesbit—you are my best readers, my dear ones. Thank you to my sisters, Brigid and Caitlin, and to my parents, Ed and Patty McAuliffe, who have always encouraged my curiosity and sense of adventure. And to Jesse, who is present in every word I write, always.

Photo: Brigid McAuliffe

Shena McAuliffe grew up in Wisconsin and Colorado. She has published stories and essays in *Conjunctions*, *Gulf Coast*, *Black Warrior Review*, *Alaska Quarterly Review*, and elsewhere. She holds an MFA from Washington University in St. Louis, and a PhD in Literature and Creative Writing from the University of Utah. She lives in Schenectady, New York, where she is an Assistant Professor of Fiction at Union College. *The Good Echo* is her first novel.